DEATH PLUNGE

Jake Hunter knew he had made a mistake. The crooked trail cut through increasingly steep cliffs and narrowed considerably. Now it was barely the width of the small wagon. The solid wall of red sandstone rose on one side, and there was nothing but a sheer drop-off on the other.

Hunter began to sweat despite the chilly drizzle as he fought to keep the gray and the wagon on the track. He had edged the wagon over another in the endless series of rock piles when a stone rolled under one of the vehicle's iron-bound wheels. He felt the wagon wheel bounce once, and when it came down there was nothing under it.

"Damn!" he roared as he felt the wagon begin to topple over the lip of the cliff. As Hunter slapped the reins on the animal's rump, the gray fought for footing. But it was too late. Seconds later, Hunter, the wagon and the squealing horse pulling it tumbled down into the nothingness.

TROUBLE IN TALL PINE

JOHN LEGG

ZEBRA BOOKS
KENSINGTON PUBLISHING CORP.

ZEBRA BOOKS

are published by

Kensington Publishing Corp.
475 Park Avenue South
New York, NY 10016

First printing: June, 1990

Printed in the United States of America

For Jo and Rick Ingram:
Good friends are hard to find,
and harder to keep.
Thanks for being there.

Chapter 1

Jake Hunter awoke in strange—to him, very strange—surroundings. He was lying in a soft bed in a well-kept home; that much was obvious. But it was a house unlike any he had ever encountered before.

Hunter shifted position, and the world flickered before his eyes as agony seared through every muscle. There was pain all over his body, and at the moment he had no inclination to assess what was damaged and how badly. He was alive; he knew that much from the incredible pain. That was all he needed—and wanted—to know about it right now.

He let the burning ache dribble away until he was resting in mere discomfort. The room was dim. There were odd vases sitting on what looked to be lacquered furniture. As a carpenter, he could appreciate the quality of the workmanship that had gone into the furniture, even though he could see it only from a distance and at an angle. Still, it was obvious the furniture was first-class. Stranger paintings—haunting, almost—hung on two walls, but he could not make out much of the artwork in the low light. The light was provided by two coal-oil lanterns on each of the walls with the art.

Where in hell am I? he wondered, the question almost panicking him.

He had been on his way to Prescott to meet his old friend Kevin McSween; that much he knew. He remembered that he had wanted to go there to forget some of his past, hoping to find a new future in the great untamed lands he had heard so much about.

The last thing Hunter remembered was a crazily spinning quilt of gray sky; tall, dark-green pines; brown earth and red stone. Then there was blackness.

Hunter moved his right arm very cautiously. There was just a lingering, dull throb in the shoulder joint. It was with an overwhelming sense of relief that he scratched his fleshy nose. It was only that ample—though not overly so—proboscis that kept Hunter from being a handsome man. He was rather self-conscious about it at times. He felt his face. His cheeks and chin were stubbly, and he estimated it had been nearly two weeks since he had shaved. Since he had not shaved since Cartersville, he must have been lying here unconscious for more than a week.

Hunter remembered leaving Elk Grove, Iowa, leaving behind a witch of a wife who did not want him, and the dead body of a man he had hardly known. Thoughts and flashes of the journey toward Prescott flickered randomly through his mind.

So, where the hell am I? Hunter wondered again, feeling the panic well up in his throat.

The bed was warm and comfortable, with a softness that was alien to him after so long in the army during the war and then all the traveling recently. Fighting back fear, he decided it was time to try to inventory his injuries. Perhaps he would be able to get up and move about if they were not too bad. That would go a long way toward helping him find out where he was.

His head throbbed, and even the dim light of the room, with the sunlight just edging past the pulled drapes, hurt his eyes. He closed them. His right arm was all right, he knew already, but when he tried to move the left, pain lanced through it.

He lay still a few moments, sucking in air to allow the

8

flames of agony to burn down to embers.

Calmed, he explored some more. He knew he had a few broken—or at least cracked—ribs, and his chest was securely bound. One leg was wrapped tightly in bandages, and he figured it, too, was broken. There were numerous cuts and bruises and scrapes all over his body.

With his right hand, he carefully pulled up the blankets and looked down at himself. He realized he was naked, but decided there was little he could—or wanted to—do about it right now. He let the blankets gently settle back down on him. He would not be going anywhere for a while.

He forced himself to put it all out of his mind. There was nothing he could do to change his situation at the moment. He was warm, comfortable, and, apparently, safe. His questions would be answered sooner or later, he figured. He sank back gratefully into the soothing embrace of sleep.

The room had not changed when he awoke again. He had no idea whether he had slept a minute or a week. There were the same strange furnishings, the same oddly painted vases, the same foreign smells emanating from another room.

But there were familiar things, too—the sounds of an active town—children screeching in their playful games, carriages and wagons rattling past, the clop of hooves, from far off the rhythmic clang of a blacksmith's hammer. Some smells were recognizable, too: the tanginess of horse manure, sweet, pine wood smoke, moist earth, his own stale sweat, the sourness of urine. He assumed the latter also was his own.

He tried moving once again to shift positions, but the pain had not lessened at all except that his head was no longer pounding—merely thumping. He almost smiled as his stomach grumbled, and he realized he was hungry. It brought to mind another question—how long had he been here?

Once again he tried to push himself up, but the agony ripped through him like a hot poker. He gasped and moaned, sinking back onto the fluffy down pillows. When the pain had lessened to barely bearable, he realized that he had wet himself, sometime recently. Shame clutched at him, and Hunter cursed at himself.

God, how could I do such a thing? he wondered. He was disgusted with himself. How would he be able to explain his being in such a condition to whoever was caring for him? he wondered.

And that brought back to the forefront all his questions. Where was he? Who was caring for him? How long had he been here? He was frantic for answers. He had to know!

Hunter determined that he would get up and find some answers, no matter how much pain there was. He had been wounded several times in the war and had always managed to get through life after a few days. He should be able to do this now.

He took several deep breaths, preparing himself for the agony he knew was coming. He forced his mind not to think about the pain, or to worry about what might happen to him when he made his move. Such thoughts would only defeat him before he could do anything, he knew.

Holding in one last big breath, Hunter shoved his elbows back and flattened his palms on the bed. Closing his eyes, he pushed up with all his might, swinging his legs to the side at the same time.

He felt as if he had a thousand burning sticks stabbed deep into his muscles and blazing hungrily on his skin. His eyes popped open, and he screamed involuntarily. The sound seemed to come to him from far away.

The room swayed in front of him, and night seemed to fall suddenly. As the blackness swept over him, Hunter heard another faraway scream. And then he saw the floor moving up toward him very rapidly.

Hunter opened his eyes again, slowly and carefully. He was back in the bed, and there were fresh sheets on it. His mind was foggy from the unconsciousness, and his head throbbed lightly. Once again he did not know whether he had been out a minute or a week.

He reached up hesitantly and felt his jaw and cheeks. Another two days, he figured. He decided to test himself again, to see just how bad off he still was. He delayed a moment, though, as fear brought by the remembrance of the last time froze him.

"Yellow-belly," he mumbled. Without delay, he tried moving his left arm. The shoulder ached dully, but he could move it. He tried the other, and that worked, as it had before. He actually smiled. He tried to sit up, but the pain seared through his chest. He fell back against the pillows, deciding it was not in his best interest to try too much too soon.

He could wait, he figured. The pain was not nearly as bad as it had been. Within a few more days he ought to be able to do some things. Once he had decided that, his mind leaped back to the questions that had been plaguing him.

His stomach rumbled, and it hurt. He felt weak, and knew that was not only from his injuries. He was starving. It had to be at least a week and a half, maybe more, since he had had any food at all.

The last time he had eaten, he remembered, had been in a miserable camp. Where was that? he wondered. And Reb. Where was his horse, Reb? He sank back, sweating. That was just another question that needed answering.

Hunter remembered a narrow trail, clogged with chunks of rocks, glistening from the steady rain. And he remembered the bouncing movement of the wagon. He remembered the wagon skidding off toward the side, and then the darkness. He shuddered, and pulled the quilt a little closer up over his chest.

But what had come before? His mind was aflame with

11

the questions, and he closed his eyes against the pain of it. *Think! he ordered himself. Think! What happened to you between Elk Grove and that treacherous trail.*

Suddenly he heard the door handle turn. He became more alert, trying to focus all his faculties. The door opened, and a figure stepped through it and into the room.

Hunter thought he must be in heaven. Then he discarded that notion. A person could not be in heaven and still have this much pain.

So he must still be unconscious. Yes, he thought, that was it. *I'm still out cold, and dreaming.* He must be, he reasoned, since this could not be real.

For through the door had walked a vision. A woman far too beautiful, far too ethereal, to be real.

"My name is Xiang Li-Sung," the vision said in a voice as smooth as freshly churned sweet butter.

Hunter stared as the vision moved closer to the bed and stopped next to it. Li-Sung reached out a hand and laid it gently on Hunter's forehead. The soft, feathery touch sent a tingle straight from his hairline to his toes.

"Fever's gone," she said in that wonderful voice. "I think you will be all right now."

Hunter could not speak; he just stared. Xiang Li-Sung was short and slightly built, with delicate wrists and a slim, graceful neck. Her cheekbones rode high under soft, almond eyes that appeared to slant upward at the outside edges. Her lips were thin, her chin pointed, and her nose small and straight. She had very long, perfectly straight, glossy black hair. It hung down her back, held at the nape by a shell comb. Li-Sung wore a simple, wide-sleeved silk dress buttoned high on the neck and reaching the floor. It was dark blue, with a lighter blue print of flowers. The dress was gathered at Li-Sung's tiny waist; her smallish bosom flared above, and thin hips curved out below.

"Who are you?" she asked, smiling gently, her lightly

12

bowed lips pulling back to reveal small white teeth.

He spoke, but no words came out. He could feel himself talking, his throat making the words, his mouth forming them. But no sound.

Li-Sung's smile broadened. She turned and poured some water from the china pitcher into a matching cup. With a strength that was surprising in the woman's slight frame, she helped raise his upper half with one arm, while bringing the cup to his lips with the other arm.

Hunter drank greedily, slurping. He spilled more than half the water, and he was embarrassed, but he could not help himself. The woman said nothing, only eased him back down when he was done.

"Now," she said pleasantly, "suppose you try again."

Hunter was fascinated by her barely discernible accent, almost as much as he was by her haunting beauty. "Jake Hunter," he croaked through a throat constricted by both lack of use and fluttering awe.

"Hello, Mr. Hunter," Li-Sung said.

"Hello, Miss Li-Sung."

"You may call me Li-Sung. You would consider it your first name. You Americans put your names backwards. So odd." She smiled.

"All right," he mumbled. Hunter licked his lips. "Where am I?" he asked carefully.

"The house of my father, Xiang Sen."

Hunter was perplexed.

"Do you remember anything?" Li-Sung asked.

He shook his head, gently lest he start it to throbbing again. "Not much. I was traveling a small road. Couldn't turn the wagon and go back. Rain. The wagon . . ." He trailed off.

But it seemed to jog his memory, and he shuddered. "I remember leaving Elk Grove," he said. "That's in Iowa. . . ."

Chapter 2

Jake Hunter hummed a mildly happy tune as he hunched over the oak plank side of the cabinet he was making. Long, thin curls of wood peeled up and away as he planed the soft wood. He heard the door open and clumping feet enter.

"Be with you in a minute," he said, without looking up.

The next thing he knew, the muzzle of a pistol was brushing his left ear, and he heard the thunderous click of the weapon being cocked. He froze, afraid to move.

A bead of sweat meandered through the gully between his eyes, down the broad, fleshy sweep of nose, and fell, splattering brightly on the wood a few inches under Hunter's face.

"I heard you was foolin' with my wife," a gnarly voice growled.

Hunter licked his suddenly dry lips. "I ain't fooled with no wife but my own," he said, voice cracking. *And not much with her,* he thought wryly.

"Ain't what my Melva tells me."

"Who?" Hunter asked. He had never heard the name before.

"My wife! Melva Scullet."

That last name rang a bell with Hunter. "Can I straighten up, Mr. Scullet?" he asked warily.

"Sure," Scullet wheezed. He could as easily kill Hunter standing as he could while the carpenter was bending over.

Hunter creaked straight up. He was fairly tall—about five-foot-ten—with a slim waist and wide, muscular shoulders. He had a long, angular face, with a thick nose and lips that curled up at the left corner. Soft brown eyes—almost womanish—stared out from under a heavy thatch of red-tinged sandy hair and matching bushy eyebrows. His hands—right one empty, the left still holding the plane—were large and powerful-looking.

Hunter was hatless inside, and he wore thick, well-used boots and heavy work pants. His cotton shirt had dark circles of sweat under the arms and small of the back. It was covered with dirt and clinging bits of sawdust. The sleeves were rolled up over the rope-like muscles of his forearms.

He was afraid, but less than before. He figured that if Scullet had meant to kill him right off, he would have done so. Standing tall now, Hunter thought he might be able to talk some sense into Darby Scullet.

Looking at the man, Hunter was suddenly not so sure. He had never met Scullet before, but had heard tales of him. Scullet was of medium height and very large around. He wore a ratty leather, wide-brim hat over filthy hair. One could not tell if his face was dirty, since ninety percent of it was covered by hair—and some shadow from the hat, from under which two dull eyes glared out. Other than that, all that poked through the forest was a bulbous, running nose, and a pudgy gash of a mouth barely covering bad teeth and fetid breath. The clothes were none too good either: worn black work boots pocked with holes, a pair of many-times-patched homespun trousers, and a coat that had once been the furred hide of a buffalo but now resembled the balding slope of a mountain. Scullet wore the coat wherever he went, whatever the weather.

15

Hunter shook his head. He had made it through three tough years of the Civil War alive—though not unwounded—and yet here he was apt to die at the hands of a crazed man jealous over a woman that no other man in his right mind would take after.

Melva Scullet was taller than her husband by several inches, and at least as round as he was. And she was every bit his equal as far as filth and degeneracy went. Hunter had not wanted to take the job, but he could, at the time, think of no way to turn her down. He was the only carpenter in the small town of Elk Grove, Iowa, and the corpulent Mrs. Scullet had wanted a fine hutch made. Hunter never asked why, though it seemed odd to him—the Scullet house was as dilapidated and worn through as its occupants. But she had the coin in hand to pay, and like everyone else these days, Hunter needed the money, so he took the job.

"Now, listen to me, Mr. Scullet," Hunter said carefully. Scullet was only two feet away, and the Colt Dragoon he was holding looked mighty big from Hunter's vantage point. "I don't know who told you there was something going on between me and your missus. But it ain't true."

"You callin' Melva a liar now?" Scullet growled.

"Certainly not," Hunter said, with as much dignity as he could muster. A dark look clouded Scullet's brutish face, and Hunter began to calculate his chances of making a move. They were not good, he decided, but he knew he had no other choice. He had to do something, since he was certain Scullet was going to go off half-cocked any minute now.

"I just think," Hunter said hastily, wanting to keep Scullet's attention focused on him and not on the Colt, "that maybe she was seeing something that wasn't really there, is all."

"Now you're sayin' Melva's crazy. That it?" Scullet snarled. He began raising the pistol toward eye level. "I'll teach you once an' for all not to defame my woman, you

16

no good . . ."

Hunter did not wait any longer. He lashed out with the plane in his left hand, praying that he would not miss. He didn't. The wood and metal tool clacked against the Colt, sending the pistol cartwheeling away in the air. The tool snagged on the gun, and it, too, went flying away to clatter on the floor.

Scullet was dumfounded, standing flat-footed, looking for all the world as if he was wondering where his pistol had suddenly gotten off to.

Hunter breathed a sigh of relief and then smashed the grungy jack-of-all-trades in the face with his fist.

Scullet's nose broke with a splintering sound, and blood poured from it down into his tobacco- and food-stained beard. But he showed little reaction other than to grunt once.

"Oh, Lord," Hunter muttered. He had really lambasted Scullet, and it had no effect. He ducked as Scullet launched a slow roundhouse punch at his head. The fist whooshed by, and Hunter came up inside Scullet's out-stretched arm, trying to ignore the reeking of Scullet's breath. He knew he was taking a risk, but he figured he had no other choice. He smashed his right fist into Scul-let's midsection three times, as hard as he could with the limited amount of space in which he had to work.

Scullet puffed as each blow landed, then started to bring the huge arm down and around, set to catch Hunter inside it like a bear trap. Sweating, worried, Hunter ducked out from the snare and slid two steps to the side, out of Scullet's reach.

The bearlike Scullet turned slowly, seemingly a little dazed, and Hunter began to wonder—and hope—that perhaps he had done at least some damage to the bulky man. He hurried around Scullet, whose movements were slow and studied. He launched a work boot at the back of one of Scullet's knees.

Scullet started to buckle, and Hunter raced in to grab

17

the man by the back of the ill-smelling coat. Straining, he marched Scullet the few steps toward the open door. Then, with all his strength, Hunter propelled the foul-tempered man outside, emphasizing the move with a boot to Scullet's broad rump.

Scullet staggered off the wood sidewalk that rose perhaps half a foot above the dusty ground beyond. A horse tied to the hitching rail there neighed loudly and tried to get away as the heavy man fell into the street.

Breathing heavily from the exertion, Hunter moved outside into the hard, bright sunshine. Puffs of white clouds drifted over the sleepy town. Hunter let Scullet get up, and then he began to pummel Scullet, his work-hardened hands landing regularly on Scullet's face and body.

Townsfolk, talking excitedly, moved up, watching, some with interest, others in horror. Hunter ignored them all as he continued his relentless beating of Scullet.

Neither man said a word, though Scullet was grunting now with every punch that landed. Hunter's breath rasped in and out, and sweat poured off his forehead, getting in his eyes. More than once Scullet got a brief respite as Hunter had to take a moment to wipe the perspiration away from his eyes.

Scullet finally toppled like a tree felled by a lumberman's ax. The handyman lay there, gasping for breath, pain throughout his body. Hunter stood waiting, trying to catch his own breath and control his raging temper. He was usually a calm man, not given to outbursts of fury. But he was too much of a man to let it pass easily when someone stuck a pistol in his ear, threatening to kill him while making wild—and false—accusations.

Hunter kicked Scullet in the teeth as the handyman tried to rise. The action snapped Scullet's head back, and it bounced in the dirt. He moved up to kick the downed Scullet again, but stopped when he heard a familiar voice: "You've done enough to him, Jake."

18

Hunter turned his head. "You don't know the full particulars, Marshal," he said lightly.

"That's true enough," Marshal Sam Palmer said. "But I don't need to stand here and watch you whale the tar out of old Darby here before I hear what you got to say. Now stand back away from him, Jake."

Hunter gave serious consideration to thumping Palmer, just for principle. Then he decided that would be foolish. He moved away from Scullet two steps and turned to face the marshal.

"Now you can tell me what this is all about, Jake." Palmer said, relaxed. He was another veteran of the Civil War, young, lean and hard. He was dressed simply in wool trousers tucked into plain knee-length boots, a cotton shirt, and faded, wide-brimmed hat. He didn't look like much, until you gazed into the cold, deep pools of blue eyes that seemed like ice.

"Well, Sam, I . . ." He stopped and gazed at Scullet when the beaten man groaned. He shook his head.

"I'm waitin', Jake."

Hunter looked around, as if seeing for the first time the crowd that had gathered. Most of the people were friendly toward him, but still their stares made him angry again. "I reckon I ain't in much of a mood to talk, Sam," Hunter said obstinately.

"That's a poor attitude, Jake."

Hunter shrugged. "Unless you're going to arrest me, and haul me before the judge, I reckon I don't have much to say."

"I hadn't planned on takin' you in, Jake. But I ain't completely against the idea, neither."

"You do what you have to, Marshal." Hunter heard another groan, and he turned to look at Scullet.

The handyman was sitting up, and opening his coat. Hunter grinned. The smile lasted mere seconds as he realized that Scullet was opening his coat to pull another gun. Hunter did not even hear Palmer, who was still threatening Hunter with jail.

"Watch it, Sam!" Hunter roared, suddenly shoving the marshal to the side.

Palmer roared in anger and reached for his Colt as he fell. But Hunter was no longer paying him any mind. He had spun toward Scullet and leaped. Scullet's pistol was loud even out here in the open, and Hunter thought he was dead for sure, as agony seared across the side of his neck.

But he was still moving, flying through the air—and conscious. He landed atop Scullet's chest and stomach with a thud, knocking the breath out of Scullet.

Hunter muttered curses as he grabbed Scullet by the large jug ears and began pounding the man's head on the ground, sending up small puffs of dust.

"Goddamn you," Scullet growled. He reached back with the pistol and smashed it into the side of Hunter's head.

Hunter moaned as lights exploded before his eyes. He fell to the side, fighting to remain conscious.

Scullet moved faster than anyone would have thought he could. He lurched to his feet and swung the pistol's muzzle toward Hunter. Panicking, Hunter jumped up, head swimming, black dots floating before his eyes, and kicked Scullet square in the crotch as hard as he could.

Scullet bellowed in pain, and his finger twitched on the trigger of the Colt, which fired a bullet harmlessly into the ground.

Thinking he would die—or at least pass out—at any minute, Hunter rushed in and punched Scullet several times in the mouth and nose. Scullet's head reared back, exposing his adam's apple. Ruthlessly, Hunter pounded it with his fist.

Scullet gargled and choked. Hunter hit him in the chin with an uppercut, knocking his head backward again. Scullet's back arched almost double and he sank down onto his knees. His Colt was forgotten.

"Move back, Jake!" Palmer ordered. He had gotten up and unlimbered his Colt. But Hunter was between him and his target.

Hunter ignored the marshal. He just snatched out the knife he always had strapped to his waist. Without thought, he whipped the blade across Scullet's throat.

Blood squirted from the gash in Scullet's neck, splattering Hunter's shirt. A woman in the crowd screamed. Then Scullet fell forward on his face, blood gushing streams into the dirt.

Hunter moved up cautiously and knelt. He yanked the pistol from Scullet's dying fingers and tossed it behind him, toward the marshal. Then he carefully wiped his blade on the back of Scullet's coat. Standing, he slid the knife back into its sheath. He watched a minute as Scullet fought for life. Scullet's breathing finally stopped, and Hunter turned to face Palmer.

Chapter 3

"You mind telling me now what that was all about, Jake?" Sam Palmer asked.

He and Hunter sat in the marshal's office. It was the day after Hunter had killed Darby Scullet on the main street of Elk Grove. After that incident, Palmer had spent some time dispersing the crowd and making sure the mess left behind by Scullet was cleaned up.

Hunter had gone back to his shop, but found quickly that he could not work. He closed up for the day, and strolled over to the Wandering Buffalo Saloon. He downed two quick shots of redeye before realizing that was not helping, either.

Reluctantly, Hunter headed for home. His wife, Lucille, would not live in a house behind the shop. She wanted her own place, away from his work, so Hunter had built them a comfortable, though small—something she never let him forget—home on the outskirts of Elk Grove.

"I hear that," Lucille Hunter scolded her husband before he had even closed the door to the house, "you have been fighting in the streets over another woman." Her voice was icy.

Her look matched the voice. It always had. Lucille Cutler was a shrewish woman—thin, with pursed lips and a heart to match. Hunter often wondered how he could have been foolish enough to marry this woman. He supposed it was loneliness.

After the Civil War ended and he had mustered out, he had gone back to his hometown in Pennsylvania. There he learned that his fiancée had died just weeks before. Diphtheria, they all told him. He nodded, and tried to go about his life as best he could. But it was of little use, and within a year he had packed up his tools in a small wagon and headed west.

He had had no particular destination in mind, but his wagon broke down not far from Elk Grove. He managed to make it into the town. As the wheelwright worked on the cart, he mentioned to Hunter that the town was without a good carpenter. Hunter shrugged. He had no place better to be, so he decided to stay on.

Several months later, he met Lucille Cutler. Several months after that, her parents decided to move on. Hunter, in need of a woman to call his own, abruptly asked the thin-lipped young woman to be his bride. To everyone's surprise—including his—she had agreed. He began to regret his decision almost as soon as she had given her consent.

The wedding was not the biggest thing Elk Grove had seen, but it still made Hunter quite uncomfortable. And his discomfort increased greatly as soon as the ceremony was over. Lucille turned from a chilly, distant, though somewhat likeable young woman to a cold, shrill crone. Hunter bore it as well as he could, occasionally availing himself of the services of one of the soiled doves who worked in the cribs behind the Wandering Buffalo Saloon.

But it was not an easy life for him. He was friendly and warm, if not very outgoing, and felt cheated by life with Lucille.

"Something like that," he mumbled.

"What do you mean, 'something like that'?" Lucille screeched.

"Darby Scullet thought I was messing around with his wife. Pulled a gun on me and was fixing to plug me." He shrugged. It was the best explanation he could give her, considering she wouldn't believe him no matter what he said.

"You were messing around with that ugly, dog-faced tramp?" Lucille said, with shrill harshness.

"No." Hunter sighed, tired of life.

"Then why did he . . ." Lucille started, voice rising in pitch.

"I don't know!" Hunter roared, shutting her off for once. More calmly, he added, "Somewhere he got that damnfool notion. Where, I don't know."

"He must've had some cause for thinking such," Lucille hissed. "Or else he wouldn't have gone after you with that gun."

Hunter snorted in disgust. It was just like Lucille to take the rantings of a half-crazed man as gospel, at the same time not believing her own husband.

"Well, I'm tired, beyond belief, of this poor life you've given me," Lucille roared, trying to make it into a whimper and failing dismally. "I've done all I could for you; I've gone out of my way, given you every courtesy, treated you with the utmost respect and . . ."

"Like hell!" Hunter was boiling again, and was having a very difficult time keeping his rage under some semblance of control. "You ain't done nothing but cause me grief since we've been married. You don't treat me like a husband, don't allow me any husbandly privileges, 'cept maybe once every couple months. I . . ."

"That all you do is think about *that?*" Her frosty voice was withering.

"I don't think about it at all when I'm around you," he retorted piercingly.

Lucille winced and screeched, "Why should I give myself to you in that way when you're more interested in doing such a vile thing with every other woman—strumpets all—in Elk Grove. You're worse than a rutting goat. You're an animal and . . ."

Hunter had had enough, and he did something he had long wanted to do but had not felt right in doing. He smacked Lucille. It was not as hard as he could give, but it sent her reeling backward to crash into the wood table.

Lucille stared at him in shock. Slowly her hand came up and touched her lip. The corner was split and bleeding. She glanced at the blood on her fingertips, eyes still stunned.

"I killed a man today," he said slowly, sadly. "And all because he was making foolish—and wrong—accusations. Maybe to you that doesn't mean much, but I get no joy out of it." He shook his head, feeling the weight of depression. "And I come home to my wife expecting maybe a little comforting, and all you can do is throw the same false accusations in my face. It ain't right, Lucille. It sure ain't."

He turned and left, leaving Lucille still braced against the table in shock. He headed for the Wandering Buffalo Saloon but decided before he got there that it was not a place he wanted to be right now. Instead, he went to his shop, where he worked hard, hoping the activity would loosen him up.

It worked a little, but not enough, and he finally just sat in his chair, feet up, and fell asleep. It left him with a crick in his neck and a sore back when he awoke in the morning. Testy, he ate breakfast at a restaurant, and then strolled to Palmer's office.

"So, do you mind telling me now what happened, Jake?" Palmer asked.

Hunter went through the story fast, flatly.

"He was a bad egg, all right," Palmer said, when Hunter had finished his narrative. "But I hate like hell to see such things in my town. It's usually so peaceful here."

"Not at my house," Hunter muttered.

"What?"

"Nothing."

"I reckon it was all self-defense, Jake," Palmer said with a shrug. "Ain't anyone but Melva going to miss that high-smellin' polecat. So you're free to go on about your business."

Hunter nodded and walked back to his shop. He spent the morning finishing the cabinet he had been working on yesterday when the trouble started. He skipped lunch, not feeling much like being with people.

Sometime in the afternoon, Marshal Palmer entered the shop. Hunter wiped the sweat off his face with a cotton rag. "What can I do for you, Sam?" he asked politely. But he didn't like this, since he figured Palmer was not bringing good tidings.

Palmer took off his hat and twirled it in his hands, looking almost embarrassed. "I hate to say this, Jake," he said finally, "but I'm going to have to ask you to leave Elk Grove."

"Why?"

"Yesterday's business turned out to be more troublesome than I had expected."

"How so?" Hunter sat as Palmer rolled and lighted a cigarette.

Palmer blew out a cloud of smoke before saying, "I didn't know this mornin' that Scullet's got a couple brothers. From what I hear, they're as crazy as he is. Maybe worse. They live down in southern Missouri. Somehow, Melva got word to them already."

"So?" Hunter asked. He was not afraid, even though he knew what was coming. Nor was he angry anymore. The thought of leaving Elk Grove was almost a pleasing one. The only thing that tempered it was the thought of it looking to everyone as though he had run.

"So, they're headin' this way, lookin' to avenge their dead brother."

"How many of 'em are there?"

"Three."

"We can take three of 'em."

"I could probably take 'em by myself. But I don't want that kind of thing in my town. You know that. Yesterday's killin' was more than enough excitement—and dyin'—for most folks around here. I ain't afraid of the Scullet boys, but I don't need to make unnecessary trouble for the folks in Elk Grove."

"Easier just to run me off, eh?"

Palmer nodded, no longer embarrassed. He had to think of the town and the safety of its residents first.

"You going to give me a deadline?" Hunter asked. He was angry now. The more he thought about running—as opposed to leaving—the angrier he became. He considered taking out Palmer now, and worrying about the Scullet brothers later. After he took care of them, he could leave town peacefully.

But that was, he knew, stupidity. The war had been over for three years now, and he could no longer think of great battles, and of facing the enemy bravely. He was just a carpenter; that was all.

"Tomorrow too soon?" Palmer asked hopefully.

"Reckon not. I've only got a few things to finish up. I can be gone by tomorrow afternoon."

"I'd appreciate it." Palmer dropped the cigarette butt on the wood floor and made sure he had smashed all signs of life from it with a boot toe. He turned for the door, then stopped and looked back. "I really do wish it could be another way, Jake," he said.

"Me, too."

Palmer left.

Hunter worked hard the rest of the day and into the night. He finished all the projects that were in the works before spreading a blanket down on the floor next to his workbench. He got a slightly better night's sleep, but was still crotchety in the morning.

After breakfast, he walked toward his house. It was

not something he looked forward to. He entered the house cautiously. Lucille sat at the table, a half-eaten plate of eggs and bacon sitting before her. Her hands were on a mug of coffee. She had woken recently, Hunter figured by the look of her. Her eyes were puffy with tiredness, and they were tinged with red, as if she had been crying. She still wore her nightdress—a shapeless mass of muslin over her bony body. A bruise discolored one side of her jaw. Hunter felt bad about that, but it was something that couldn't be undone.

"Come back to beat me some more?" Lucille asked defiantly.

"No," Hunter muttered guiltily. "Marshal Palmer's asked me to leave town."

"Why?" Lucille asked, startled.

Hunter explained. "So I'm fixing to leave today. Soon's I get everything squared away."

"And you expect to drag me with you?" Lucille asked in that piercingly grating voice of hers.

"You *are* my wife," he said simply. He didn't much give a hoot whether she came or not. Indeed, he was starting to think about how pleasant life would be without her.

"I'll seek a divorce and stay here before I go with you."

"You don't even know where I'm heading." He didn't, either, but that didn't matter.

"I don't care."

He nodded. "If that suits you."

"It does," Lucille said in a huff.

Hunter nodded. "Then I reckon I'll just gather up what's mine. You can have the house and such furniture that's in it. We've got several hundred dollars in the bank. You can have most of it; I'll just need a bit. When you go for your divorce, you can use the grounds that I deserted you, if it'll make it easier on you." He was trying to be contrite. There was no love lost between him and Lucille, but still, she had been his wife for more

28

than a year, and he felt he owed her something for that.

"It'll only be the truth," she said snippily.

"Yeah." Hunter sighed. "And they'll believe it easily, too," he jabbed. He went about gathering up what clothes and other personal items he had in the house, packing them in two small boxes. He carried them, one by one, back to his shop. There he packed his tools. As he did, he thought he would see if Palmer would sell the shop for him, but he decided to just let it go.

Packed, he strolled to the livery, where he harnessed up his big gray horse to the small buckboard. Then he drove to the general store and bought food and other supplies. After packing them on the wagon, he went back to the shop and loaded up his belongings and tools. He covered it all with a waterproof tarpaulin.

It was with some sadness, though not too much, that Hunter snapped the reins on the gray's back and rode slowly out of town. He nodded at Palmer, who stood outside his office watching Hunter leave.

Chapter 4

Hunter went only ten miles that day before pulling off in a clump of cottonwoods for the night. He made his camp quickly and soon was eating corn cakes and salted beef washed down with coffee.

When he was finished, he pulled out a small mirror and checked the wound on his neck. It was scabbed over and would not even leave much of a scar, he decided, though it was painful at the moment. He expected it would give him some trouble for a few days before the pain went away. But it was no worse than smacking his thumb with a hammer, something he had done more than once.

He put the mirror away, leaned back, fired up the old pipe he smoked occasionally, and sat thinking. The past day and a half had been a blur to him, from the moment Darby Scullett had entered his carpenter's shop until now.

Hunter had no idea where to go. He just knew he had to get out of Elk Grove quickly. He wasn't worried — not really. Just filled with a sense of uncertainty. He had to find some direction, he guessed, soon. Still, he realized, there was an undercurrent of joy beneath the surface. He felt a sense of freedom for the first time since before the war. It was refreshing.

He had left Elk Grove on the trail south, as if drawn

that way. But he was by no means sure he wanted to continue in that direction. For one thing, Scullet's brothers would be heading north along that trail, which was not something pleasant to contemplate. Hunter considered turning west, toward the new state of Nebraska, and perhaps beyond, to the Rocky Mountains. Maybe even all the way to Oregon.

But doing so would mean having to brave the fierce Sioux, and with them the Northern Cheyennes and Arapahos. And after them, the Crows and Blackfeet and . . .

No, Hunter told himself firmly, that would never do. He could, he guessed, head back east. But Pennsylvania held nothing for him now but sad and distant memories. North? He wondered. But that would lead him to a land where he heard there never was any summer at all. Iowa had been plenty cold and snowy enough for him.

Hunter had brought several pint bottles of whiskey with him, and he felt the need for a drink. He went to the canvas sack in which he had packed his few pieces of extra clothing, using the garments to wrap the fragile whiskey bottles. As he dug in the sack for a bottle, paper crinkled under his hand. He grinned and pulled out the paper, then dug back in for the whiskey.

Sitting with his back against a log, Hunter pulled the cork from the bottle and sipped. The amber liquid bit into his throat. He took another sip and set the bottle next to him. After relighting his pipe with a burning stick, he opened the crumpled sheet of paper.

It was a letter he had gotten from Kevin McSween, a friend and a man he had fought side-by-side with at Chancellorsville, Spotsylvania, and Gettysburg, and a dozen lesser-known places. The letter had been written the previous summer, but Hunter had received it only three months previously. He had planned to write back but had not gotten around to it.

He reread the letter, and suddenly was inspired. McSween had written colorfully about a place called Arizona Territory. He had talked about the glowing opportunities in the many mines, and the good farming and such in the territorial capital of Prescott. There would be, McSween had written, more work than Hunter could handle, since carpenters were mighty scarce in the area.

Yes, Hunter thought, sipping again, *this Arizona Territory might be just the place for me.* He corked the bottle and knocked the ashes from his pipe into the fire. Then he stretched out on his blanket.

Trying to keep from thinking about the journey he faced, he searched for sleep. It took a long time, but he finally managed.

After a breakfast of more corn cakes, with some bacon, Hunter packed his meager belongings and hitched the gray. But he could no longer keep the worries from surfacing. He would be facing a dangerous lengthy trek, through the lands of the Southern Cheyennes, probably still buzzing angrily about the massacre of some of their people down on Sand Creek four years ago; and the Comanches, perhaps; and Kiowas; and the Navajo; and the warlike, deadly Apaches.

Hunter shuddered, thinking about the last. He had heard stories about those Indians that could raise a man's hair on end. None of those stories had a happy ending. Hunter considered for just a moment turning around and heading eastward. Then he growled at himself and climbed onto the wagon. He had, however, taken the precaution of bringing out his Springfield rifle and loading it. Now he set the square, hard-leather pouch of the rifle's combustible paper cartridges, with molded balls, on the floorboard of the wagon, and rested the rifle across his lap.

"Come on, Reb," he said to the horse. He had thought more than once how ironic it was that he, a loyal member of the Union Army, proud Pennsylvanian, defender of liberty and the sovereignty of the Union, had a gray horse. It was how he had come up with the name. He had nothing against most of the Confederates. Most were honorable men fighting for something they believed in as passionately as he believed in the Union. He could not hate most of them. So, because of the horse's color, and the respect he had found for his old enemies, Hunter had called the horse Reb.

The gelding was a big, handsome animal, with heavy feet and a strong back. The horse was a fine, deep gray, mottled in places with a lighter silver. Reb was broken to the saddle as well as to the harness. Hunter felt lucky to have him.

Hunter pushed the horse some. It was already well into June, and Hunter was not certain how long it would take him to reach Arizona Territory. He had no desire to get caught out on the plains with winter coming on, as it sometimes did long before the summer had finally blazed itself out.

He followed the East Nishnabotna River southwestward. Four days later he came to the tumbling, muddy Missouri. It took two more days of looking, with Hunter growing angrier and more frustrated, until he found a spot where he thought he could make it safely across.

He spent another half a day spreading pitch over the wagon so it would float. He wrapped his rifle and ammunition in oiled cloth and lashed them and all his other belongings down in the back of the wagon. Then he had Reb ease the wagon into the swirling, chocolate-colored water. Hunter was tense as Reb strained to pull the wagon along the muddy bottom.

Suddenly they hit deeper water, and Reb, nostrils flared, swam hard. The wagon slid off into the deeper water, and the river's current caught it and shoved it sideways. Reb snorted and whinnied, straining against the harness.

"Hell and damnation," Hunter shouted. He dived off the wagon seat into the murky water and grabbed the side of the wagon. Kicking with all his might, he fought to shove the wagon back the way it should be.

Slowly the cart went along, and Hunter was thankful for Reb's strength. They swam on, man and horse, working together. With Reb pulling for all he was worth, and Hunter pushing as hard as he could, the wagon straightened out.

Hunter breathed a great sigh of relief as the wagon's front wheels hit the mostly solid bottom of the river. Then the back wheels caught. Hunter looked back over his shoulder, thinking they were lucky to have made it all that distance.

Breathing heavily, Hunter finally stood and began walking, the water only up to his chest. Within seconds he was up the short slope of riverbank. It was still quite warm, and his wet clothes served to cool him somewhat, though the boots were mighty uncomfortable.

A mile past the big river, he came to a small stand of cottonwoods next to a bubbling stream. He stripped down to his birthday suit, hanging his clothes on tree branches to dry, and then made his small camp. He whistled "Tenting on the Old Camp Ground," pleased with his humor. The sense of freedom he had felt since he had left Elk Grove had increased considerably.

He dressed in the only extra pair of pants he had, plus one of his two extra shirts. He put on clean, dry socks, but had no other shoes than his work boots. He was content, however, as he set about making a meal of venison, biscuits and coffee.

The sky was overcast in the morning as he hurried through breakfast. He hoped it would not rain, but even as he did so, he knew the hope was in vain. No sooner had he pulled out of camp than the rain started, pouring down in great, driving sheets of water accompanied by thunder that rolled across the wide, empty expanses. Lightning snapped and sizzled.

Hunter hunkered down into his oiled slicker, pulled his hat down as tight as it would go, and plodded along, listening to the sucking pop of Reb's every step. Within minutes of the storm's letting loose, Hunter was guiding the wagon through a brown ocean.

He knew the storm could not last forever, but he got no respite for several hours. When the storm did ease, the rain did not stop, and Hunter continued to splash through the muddy morass of prairie as the rain fell steadily.

Hunter swore as the wind picked up, cutting through his slicker to chill his flesh. He was cold, uncomfortable and not at all happy. And, worse, there was not a tree to be seen—nothing that he could use for shelter.

Then he saw some odd structures in the distance. He could not, for the life of him, figure out what they were, until it was too late for him to turn back. With a shrug of resignation, he drove the wagon slowly into the dreary Indian village. He did not know what tribe this was, and he did not much care. Besides, the place looked too poor to present much trouble. Looking at it, Hunter wondered how he could ever have been afraid of Indians. If these people were a representative sample, he thought, he would have nothing to worry about.

The lodges were brush and skin huts, whipped by the wind and beaten down by the rain. A few mangy curs barked, and there were several dilapidated racks for drying meat standing around.

Hunter spent the night in the shabby little village of Potawatomis, disgusted with the poor condition of the inhabitants, the filth, and odors. But it did keep him out of the drenching rain.

Still, he was plenty happy to ride off the next morning. A quarter of a mile away, he looked back, and shook his head. Hunter turned forward again, a sense of loneliness almost to the point of despair settling on his shoulders like a mantle. He hated to see any people in the shape the Potawatomis were in. He had seen some of the Confederates like that just after the war. They were so beaten down and bedraggled that they had lost all hope.

Within an hour of his leaving, it was raining again, an unceasing, heavy rain. Not the goose drownder of yesterday, but enough to keep his already gloomy spirits low.

Toward afternoon, the wind picked up again, and the rain began to taper off. Hunter heard an eerie roaring noise that never stopped. He knew what it was, but could not see it. The rain stopped, though it was still heavily overcast.

The roaring grew louder, and there was an odd calm in the air. Then Hunter saw a vague something moving in the far distance, off to his right. The wildly twisting funnel of a tornado churning crazily across the prairie toward him began to take shape in his vision. He had a gut-wrenching squeeze of fear as he realized the twister was bearing down on him.

"Giddap there, Reb," he shouted, snapping the reins.

Reb bolted forward, sensing the urgency in his master's voice. The wagon clattered ahead, bouncing uncontrollably on the muddy plains that might look as flat as a billard table but were far from it.

Hunter wrapped the reins around his left wrist so he would not lose them, and then he grabbed for the sides of the wagon and held on tightly. He was doing no good trying to drive the wagon; he figured he might as well make sure he stayed in the seat.

He watched with apprehensive fascination as the tornado howled toward him. There was not a tree or a bush to slow the raging monster of a storm. Hunter was not easily frightened. He had bravely faced death at the hands of screaming hordes of Confederate soldiers. But he had no control over a tornado.

He thought his neck would break, or his teeth jar loose from the hard bouncing on the unpadded wood seat of the wagon. He clenched his jaws shut. Then he spotted some trees, and he knew there must be a river or stream nearby.

"Go, Reb," he roared. He glanced at the tornado, and he felt sure it was a little behind him, as well as still off to the north a bit.

Ten minutes later, Reb neared the river with no signs of slowing down. The horse would have plunged straight into the water if Hunter had not recovered his senses enough to rear back, pulling on the reins with all the strength he could muster. "Stop, Reb!" he shouted.

The animal fought against it, but finally stopped, almost on his haunches, at another mighty tug from Hunter. Reb stood blowing, his great, gray sides heaving in and out like a giant bellows.

"Good boy, Reb," Hunter gasped. "All right, now, Reb, let's move into those trees. Slow." They weaved into the cottonwoods, and Hunter turned Reb until they were faced the way they had come.

The tornado sounded like two dozen locomotives. Hunter, still worried, climbed off the seat. He was shaking from the wild ride and the strain of trying to stop the wagon. He tied the reins to a stout tree and stood next to the foaming horse, stroking the side of the animal's long neck.

"Maybe the good Lord'll let us get through this one, Reb," Hunter said, more to calm himself than the horse. He could see the roaring twister plainly. The sound was deafening, and the change in atmospheric pressure stabbed at his ears. He felt as if someone were trying to poke a knife through each eardrum. He felt swallowed by the noise and the bulging pressure of the air.

The tornado was abreast of him now, several miles out on the prairie. The wind sucked and clawed at his clothes and whipped the sopping ends of his slicker in a frenzied dance.

Hunter stroked the horse, muttering softly. Reb's eyes rolled and he shuffled nervously, but he stood his ground.

Then the twister passed on, its weaving funnel chugging southward. It left behind a silence and stillness as painful as the noise and pressure had been. Hunter cracked his mouth and swallowed. His ears popped, and he felt immediate relief.

"Lord, that was something, wasn't it, Reb," he breathed. He continued to pat the horse, letting the animal calm down.

Chapter 5

Five days after waiting out the tornado, Hunter was sitting at a campfire near Council Grove, Kansas, eating with a group of sojourners.

It had not been an easy journey. The rain had fallen for two more days, accompanied every once in a while by hail and gale-like winds. He had made several cold, wet camps; forded three rain-swollen streams or rivers; and lost most of his meager supply of food when a prowling grizzly sent him scampering up the only cottonwood within miles.

Finally he had passed through a tent town where he replenished his supplies. He had ridden into this camp late this afternoon. He was welcomed by everyone, and sat to talk with Luther Pierce, the man who had been elected captain of this small wagon train of immigrants. Pierce's wife, Rachel, a nice though not very handsome woman, fed the two men well as they sat by the fire, talking.

"You're mighty lucky you found us," Pierce said gruffly.

"Reckon I am," Hunter said agreeably.

"Most folks are well on their way by now." Pierce grimaced. "We're so late settin' out, we couldn't even find us a proper guide."

"You're going on hope?" Hunter asked, looking at Pierce.

Luther Pierce was not a big man, but he had a commanding presence. He was in his forties, Hunter guessed, and balding at the crown of his head, Hunter saw when Pierce had pulled off his battered felt hat. Despite the heat, he wore wool pants and shirt, with thick pull-on boots. Dull brown eyes peered out from behind brass-rimmed spectacles.

"More like faith," Pierce said with a soft grin.

Hunter understood. "Mind if I ride along?" he asked quietly.

"Be glad to have another man, Mr. Hunter. As long as you obey all the rules."

Hunter nodded. "Three years in the army during the late unpleasantness accustomed me to taking orders, Mr. Pierce."

"I never fought in that war," Pierce said, in disappointment. "They said I was too old."

"Booshwa," Hunter muttered. Then, "Oops, pardon me, ma'am."

"It's all right, Mr. Hunter," Rachel Pierce said.

"We leave in the morning."

"I'll be ready, Mr. Pierce." Hunter finished his meal, thanked Rachel Pierce, and headed to his wagon. Dusk was long gone, and Hunter was quite tired, so he stretched out under his wagon to sleep.

He was one of the first up and had eaten by the time most of the others arose. He packed his supplies and harnessed Reb. Then he waited on his wagon. As he sat patiently, Hunter couldn't help but notice an attractive young woman with golden curls, well-padded figure and dirty face. She sashayed around, helping her family get ready. Hunter thought it a pleasant way to spend his idle time.

Pierce stopped by, riding a large, dark gray, exceedingly ugly mule. He had a new, rapid-firing, lever-action

40

Henry rifle across the saddle in front of him. Hunter had thought of buying one a while back, but decided against it since metal cartridges were still too hard to find. "I see you're ready, Mr. Hunter."

"Yessir."

"I hope you know how to use that Springfield of yours. We might have need of it." He looked only a little worried.

"We served each other well in the war," Hunter answered calmly.

"Good. You got any questions before we leave?"

Hunter grinned. "Who's that blond-haired young lady?" he pointed.

"Sarah Rogers. But I think she's been spoke for by Burl Baker," Pierce said evenly.

Hunter grinned. "Well, I just might have to see about that."

Pierce scowled. He did not need a love triangle interfering with this trip. Then he shrugged and forgot about it. Baker was a strapping young man, and could take care of himself. Pierce had more important things to worry about. He wheeled his mule and roared, "Let's roll!"

Those people who were not ready scrambled to finish their chores and get moving. Hunter clicked the reins and Reb pulled out, leading the procession. Hunter had no hankering to ride in the middle of the wagon train, sucking in dust with every breath. Rachel Pierce, driving her family's big Conestoga, pulled in behind him.

Hunter chafed at the slow progress the wagon train made, but he was grateful for the safety it provided. He took his meals at the Pierce family fire. The Pierces had eight children, from nineteen to four. The oldest two—a boy and a girl, they said—stayed behind, the son almost set to take a wife, the daughter already married a year.

After the first day, Pierce asked Jake to be the hunter for the travelers, a job Hunter enjoyed since it kept him off by himself.

That, however, limited the time he was able to spend with Sarah Rogers. Still, there were the evenings, and Hunter spoke with the fair-haired Miss Rogers as often as he could, usually under the glare of MacKenzie Rogers, Sarah's father; or Baker, the big, though innocent, young man who had been courting Sarah for some time.

Sarah was a delight, Hunter thought—tall, slender, full of joy and interest. After a week with the traveling wagon train, he began to think he might actually get serious about her.

The traveling company spent the July Fourth holiday taking a day's rest along the Arkansas River just past Pawnee Fork.

Hunter, after realizing that the Rogers and Baker families were determined to have Sarah celebrate with Burl that day, broke out his last pint bottle of whiskey. He sat off to himself in the shade of a cottonwood and polished it off, watching the festivities and listening to the music made with guitar, banjo, harmonica and fiddle.

Ten days later, just after they passed Cold Spring, Hunter rode in from hunting on the horse he had borrowed from Pierce. He tugged at a mule loaded with buffalo meat. "I ain't much on reading signs, Mr. Pierce," he said quietly, "but I got a feeling we ain't alone."

"Injins?" Pierce asked, looking around nervously.

Hunter shrugged. "I could just be imagining things, but I reckon a little extra caution won't hurt. From everything I've heard, we're either in Kiowa or Cheyenne country. They're allies, and I know the Cheyennes are on the prod."

Several hours later, with Hunter having taken back his wagon from Pierce's oldest son on the trip, they topped a ridge and started down the long, grassy slope. Hunter called to Pierce, and pointed to a cloud in the distance ahead. "See that, Luther?"

Pierce squinted against the glare of the blue sky topped with an orange glob of sun. "Dust," he said finally. "Injins, I guess." He nodded. "We need to get these wagons in a box so we can fend 'em off. Down there." Pierce pointed toward the bottom of the slope.

Hunter, who knew it was the best they could do defensively, nodded in agreement. "I'll head on down that way," he said. "You tell the others. Best make sure they hurry, though."

"Yep." Pierce trotted the mule back to alert each wagon driver.

Hunter looked behind him as Reb trotted ahead. The others were whipping their mule trains, urging them to as great a speed as possible on the rolling, rutted land.

Hunter stopped and waited. He looked toward the dust, and saw it was much nearer. This was going to be a close call, he thought.

Pierce's wagon rumbled up, and Hunter directed Rachel to pull it as close to Hunter's as possible. They hurriedly unhitched the team, and Hunter backed his wagon up to the covered wagon. One after another the wagons lined up, moved into place by sweating, cursing men guided by Hunter and Pierce, and pushed by fear.

As the Indians hove into view on the horizon, the men finished. Almost desperately they herded the women and children, and then the horses and mules, inside the rough box. Then they took their places.

Some of the women, no more frightened than their husbands or fathers, stood behind their men, cartridges or powderhorns, bullets and ramrods, at hand. They would reload as the men fired.

The children huddled amid the mules and horses in the center of the box. They were frightened; fragments of the scary stories of the horrible, savage Indians of the West flickered in their brains. Some youngsters whimpered and a few infants bawled, knowing that something in their so-young lives was not right. The women not on reload-

43

ing duty moved about, hugging where need be, offering a breast to a babe if possible.

Some older preteen boys moved among the animals, hoping to keep them calm so they would not bolt and possibly crush some people.

Hunter hurried toward the front of the box, facing the oncoming Indians. He carried his Springfield rifle, and he had strapped on his .44-caliber Remington army revolver. It was the first time he had had occasion to wear the pistol since the war, and its weight felt odd.

He found Sarah Rogers. "Miss Sarah," he said quietly. "I'd be obliged if you were to handle the reloading chores for me."

She looked uncertain. "But . . ."

"Your father's got your mother for such duties, and Burl's got his mother and two sisters old enough for such a chore. I got nobody."

She nodded tightly, worry and fear creasing her attractive face.

"Here." He handed her two leather cartridge cases— one for the rifle, one for the pistol. "Just stay down," he said.

Sarah nodded again. She was afraid to speak because her mouth was so dry. She just hoped she would be able to reload his guns; her hands were shaking and she was more frightened than she ever had been. She had never, ever, really, deep down inside, expected to come face-to-face with a bunch of wild savages. It left her cold inside.

Seeing Sarah's look of fear, Hunter said, "You'll do just fine, Miss Sarah. Don't you fret."

Sarah smiled, minutely relieved.

Hunter leaned on his wagon, watching the approaching Indians.

Luther Pierce was a few yards off to the left, his wife behind him, waiting stoically. She was a tall, stout, strong-looking woman, seemingly without fear. The two spoke quietly to each other, and Hunter smiled momentarily when he saw Rachel touch Luther's shoulder briefly. *If only I could find a woman like that,* Hunter thought wistfully. She was not the handsomest woman he had ever seen; indeed, Lucille, as scrawny as she was, was prettier. But there was something in the way Rachel looked at Luther, and the way she touched him and . . .

He shook the thoughts off as the Indians neared. "You know what they are, Luther?" he called over.

Pierce squinted, looking hard. "From the descriptions I was given, Jake, I'd say Kiowas. But I ain't sure."

The Indians closed rapidly, and Hunter realized his hands were sweating. He rubbed them on his pants leg, one at a time, shifting the rifle.

He was always this way at the start of a battle: butterflies in the stomach, an urgent need to make water, sweaty palms, arid mouth.

As soon as he fired the Springfield for the first time, calmness spread over Hunter like the cape of an officer's dress uniform.

Hunter handed his Springfield to Sarah and pulled his revolver. From all around him came the popping of rifles and pistols. Just as in many of the Civil War battles he had been in, men were firing as rapidly as they could, with no rhyme nor reason to it. As a result, they hit nothing. All they were doing was wasting powder and lead.

Hunter shook his head as he braced his right arm on the wagon. He sighted down the Remington's barrel and squeezed off a shot.

The Indians had swept across the prairie at a dead run toward the wagons. Some wore feathered war bonnets; others were bare headed. Most seemed to be wearing very little clothing, but they were moving so fast it was hard for Hunter to tell anything for certain.

The Indians had split, with half moving around one side of the wagon box, the others heading the other way. They raced around and around about fifty yards away,

45

firing arrows and once in a while a gun. Now and again one of the warriors would dart in toward the wagons, making a daring attempt to break through the line of defense. Half a dozen warriors had died in just such maneuvers.

The Indians never seemed to stop; they just raced around and around, sometimes daring the white men to shoot at them.

Hunter cocked the Remington and squeezed gently again. He shook his head in annoyance as he missed the Indian at whom he had fired.

"Rifle's loaded, Mr. Hunter," Sarah said.

Hunter nodded. He fired the pistol, and grinned tightly when he winged another Indian. He handed the pistol to Sarah. Grabbing his rifle, he took his time seeking target. He had learned long ago to use as much deliberation as he could. It made him a better marksman.

A short, bulging-bellied warrior stopped almost two hundred yards away. He sat surveying the battle, taking a moment to adjust the thong around his neck holding up a bone hairpipe breastplate.

"Just stay there another couple seconds," Hunter muttered to himself as he settled the Springfield into the hollow of his shoulder. He clicked back the hammer and adjusted the rear sight for the distance. His right index finger applied pressure.

There was a roar, and the rifle slammed against his shoulder. When the smoke cleared from his vision, Hunter saw the Indian lying on the ground behind his horse.

A scream made him and Sarah turn. "Lord!" Hunter breathed.

An Indian had leaped his horse through the gap between wagons, barely able to fit. He fell off the horse as the pinto burst into the enclosure, and landed hard on his rump. But he was up in a flash and racing toward the mules and horses — and children — in the center.

Sarah stood frozen, Hunter's pistol, reloaded, held out in his direction, her head facing the Indian.

Hunter darted toward the center of the box, grabbing his revolver from Sarah's almost numb fingers as he did. He shoved the weapon into the holster and snapped the flap shut over the top of it.

Mules brayed and lashed out with powerful hind legs. Horses whinnied and tried to bolt, but had nowhere to go. The women who had been in the relative safety of the animals scooped up infants and toddlers and ran for sanctuary, any sanctuary.

Several children maybe six or seven years old stood frozen in fear, not knowing what to do. Animals milled wildly, and Hunter caught just a glimpse of a ten-year-old boy trying to control the animals get kicked in the head by a mule. The boy went down, and Hunter lost sight of him in the swirling cloud of dust.

He tried not to think of it. There was no way the boy could survive in that rampaging melee of tons of flesh and iron-shod hooves.

A mule slammed into Hunter, spinning him and almost knocking him down. Hunter righted himself and ran again, his shoulder hurting where it had thumped against the mule's solid flank.

Dust clung to his throat and the inside of his mouth. It was hard to see, and Hunter ran almost by instinct. With a wild yell, he slammed his body into the warrior, knocking them both — and the five-year-old girl the Indian had grabbed — down.

The Indian was agile, and he sprang to his feet as the child ran, crying pitiably, toward her mother.

A sneer curled the warrior's face — painted with vertical stripes of ocher and black — as he charged the sprawled Jake Hunter. He drew a wood and stone war club and raised it high in anticipation.

Hunter was not surprised at how calm he was, or at

47

how everything seemed to move slowly. He was used to it. As the warrior swung the war club at his head, Hunter rolled sideways. The war club left a six-inch-deep dent in the grassy dirt where Hunter's head had been.

Hunter lashed out with his feet, catching the Indian at the back of both ankles. The warrior's feet were swept out from under him, and he landed on his back with a thump. His breath exploded out.

Spitting out a mouthful of dust, Hunter scrambled up and yanked out his knife, diving toward the Indian. The warrior had recovered enough to brace himself; one hand grabbed Hunter's knife arm.

They grappled. Sweat beaded on Hunter's face and dripped onto the Indian's. Their breath came in hard, rasping jerks. Hunter tried to gouge out one of the Indian's eyes with his left thumb, but the Indian darted his head out of the way and clamped his teeth on the appendage.

Hunter howled. With an extra burst of strength, he shoved his knife hand, and the Indian's, to the side, clearing a path. He reared back his head and butted the warrior's forehead with his own. He saw swirling dots in front of him as pain rippled through him, but he could tell the Indian was even more dazed than he was.

The Indian had unclamped his teeth from Hunter's thumb. Hunter balled his fist and punched the warrior in the face. The Indian grunted, and his grip weakened on Hunter's knife hand.

Hunter, unconcerned about the animals milling dangerously close, jammed his bleeding, swelling thumb into the Indian's right eye.

The Indian sucked in his breath. With a burst of effort, Hunter yanked his knife hand free. He plunged the blade forward and back, three times. With each thrust, he felt the blade pierce flesh, and once, bone. With each, the Indian's eyes widened with the pain.

"Die, by God, die!" Hunter hissed. He reared back for

48

another stab, hoping to end it. But it was not necessary. The Indian was not dead, but the glimmer of life was fading fast from his flat black eyes.

Panting, Hunter shoved himself off the Indian's body. Hunter's pants were covered with the dead warrior's blood, and there were several lines of red down his shirt.

Guns were still being fired all around, mules were braying, horses screaming, children yelling and crying, Indians shrieking war cries. Hunter staggered to his feet.

Another Indian burst through the squared ring of wagons. The horse landed, then darted forward. The Indian aimed his lance at a woman crouching by a wagon wheel nearby, clutching a months-old baby to her bosom. Her pinched face was streaked with dirt and tears.

Hunter yanked open the flap holster and snatched out the Remington. He prayed in that brief instant that his aim would be true. He snapped the revolver up, cocking it as he did. Then he fired.

There was a puff of powder smoke that obscured his vision for a moment. The Indian pony leaped ahead, riderless, and joined the other horses and mules. The Indian lay on the ground, two feet from the woman and infant, his lance inches from his right hand.

Hunter moved up cautiously, gun ready. The Indian's back was splattered with blood, and more was puddling under him. But he lifted his head and looked around. He saw his lance and his hand crept out for it. He grasped it and managed to get to hands and knees. He saw the woman, and his face, which Hunter could not see, frightened her more than any nightmare ever had.

"Don't," Hunter croaked.

Either the Indian did not hear him, or was of no mind to pay him heed, since he crept closer to the woman.

Hunter took two long strides and was next to the Indian. He put the muzzle of the Remington an inch from the back of the warrior's head and, without remorse, pulled the trigger.

49

The Indian's body jerked and fell, spasming. Hunter had seen worse in the war, but that didn't make this easy. The body stopped jerking and was still.

Hunter ran back toward his original post.

But the Indians had had enough. They were hightailing it across the prairie, having picked up what dead and wounded they could.

Chapter 6

As soon as the Indians were out of sight, Hunter yelled, "Captain, get some of the boys to haul them bodies out of here. There's no call for the women and young 'uns to have to see more than they have. And get some others to give those boys a hand controlling the animals."

Luther Pierce nodded. He handed his rifle to Rachel, and spoke softly to her for a moment. She nodded and touched his cheek unself-consciously.

"Goddamn, you were somethin', Jake," Pierce whispered as he hurried past Hunter, who shrugged.

Then Pierce moved about, shouting orders, trying to create some calm in the midst of all this chaos.

Sarah Rogers looked deathly white.

"You all right?" Hunter asked her, worried.

She nodded. "It's just all so . . . so . . ." She would not faint, she told herself firmly. But she sure wanted to. She sucked in several deep breaths, and felt steadied.

"I understand," Hunter said softly. "Well, I thank you for your help. Now you best go on and get back to your family."

She nodded and moved numbly off. Hunter watched, appreciating the gentle sway of her full hips, forgetting for a moment the battle that had just taken place. Perhaps, Hunter thought, Miss Sarah Rogers was the woman for him. He grinned and set about cleaning his weapons.

The boy who had been kicked by the mule and then trampled was the only fatality among the people of the wagon train. The death of Chas Baker—Burl's brother—shook the people. Burl seemed to be especially pained by it. In deference, Hunter decided he would not try courting Sarah for a spell.

As Luther Pierce directed the travelers in recovering themselves and setting up their camp, Hunter tied the bodies of the two Indians to their ponies.

"What're you aimin' to do?" Pierce asked, stopping by.

"Well, it don't seem right somehow to just dump 'em," Hunter said. "These boys fought well, and honorably, far's their ways go."

"So, what do you aim to do?" Pierce asked, hiking his eyebrows up in surprise.

Hunter shrugged. "Well, I've heard the Indians out this way will do whatever they can to get their dead back. I reckon that if I take 'em out a ways and send these ponies running, they'll get back to the Indians sooner or later. Might make 'em more peaceable toward us, if those Indians aim to seek revenge."

Pierce scratched the growing stubble on his chin. Then he nodded. "Can't hurt none, I guess. But these others might not like it much."

"The hell with 'em," Hunter growled. He was tired and drained. "I'll take care of it myself. That'll keep you out of it."

Pierce nodded thankfully.

Two miles from the camp, Hunter let the pintos go, sending them off with hard smacks on the rumps and encouraging yells. He sat a few minutes, watching the horses race across the plains, before turning back toward the wagons.

The group spent the rest of the day and all the next recovering some sense of equilibrium. Only the boy had been killed, but five others had wounds of varying sever-

52

ity.

Midway through the day after the battle, the Baker family laid Chas to rest, wrapping the youth's mutilated body in a quilt before burying him. Pierce said some words over the boy, and then led the group in singing a few hymns. There was little else they could do. Pierce sent the Baker family off and then assigned several men to fill in the hole and cover it with what rocks they could find. A small wood cross was pounded into the ground.

The following morning, Hunter packed slowly and then sat on the wagon, waiting. The camp was a bustle of activity as the people prepared to leave. Hunter was perplexed. He had tried speaking with Sarah briefly last night, and again this morning. But she had become decidedly cool toward him, and he did not know why.

Rachel Pierce pulled the heavy Conestoga up behind Hunter's small buckboard. She smiled at her man, displaying her pride in his taking charge. He smiled back and bellowed, "Let's roll!" Pierce turned his mule and trotted away.

That night they stayed outside Camp Nichols, where they felt safe. And there they learned that the Indians had, indeed, been Kiowas. The travelers also filled their water barrels, and made sure their animals were well watered before leaving the next morning. It was a mostly uneventful trip after that, with little trouble other than that expected — an occasional river that had to be forded; drenching rainstorms, sometimes bolstered by heavy hail; blistering heat; choking dust; lack of water; rattlesnakes and scorpions. Nothing out of the ordinary.

They ran into no more Indians, though there was a scare or two. Now that the railroad was making its way out here, the Santa Fe Trail no longer was a viable road for freight, though wagon trains of immigrants still used it.

Hunter kept his eyes on the deeply rutted tracks, worn into the soil by almost fifty years of use by the heavy wagons with their tons of cargo. Already, though, spur tracks for the railroad were seen on the section that once was the Cimarron Cutoff. They finally joined with the main segment of the trail, and saw more people, though it was still a lonely road they traveled. Still, there were towns now and again, and they could restock supplies or trade in a sore-footed mule for a fresh one, and such.

Hunter spent more time away from the plodding caravan, hunting, letting one of Pierce's sons drive his small wagon. Once or twice, when he was with the line of wagons, he caught Baker staring at him with dull, angry eyes. Hunter would smile grimly, irritatingly, at him and ride on.

The small wagon finally arrived in Las Vegas, New Mexico Territory. The immigrants had planned on going on to Santa Fe or beyond. But after arriving in Las Vegas, they took a vote. The majority elected to stay. Hunter didn't care much.

He was concerned, though, about Sarah Rogers, and the way she had been treating him. She had not come by to talk at all, and had remained cold toward him. He needed to know why.

He finally managed to get Sarah alone for a few moments. "I'd like to know why you've been so cold to me of late, Miss Sarah," he started. "We had some fine times, until . . ." He didn't want to say it.

"I have nothing to say to you, Mr. Hunter." She turned to leave, but Hunter grabbed her arm.

"Wait a minute," he said roughly, keeping a light grip on her arm. "We were getting along real well for a spell. But you've . . ."

"You let go of her, goddamn you," an angry Burl Baker snarled as he steamed up and yanked Sarah's arm out of Hunter's hand. He shoved her to the side. "Miss Sarah's gonna be my wife. She's consented."

"That true, Miss Sarah?" Hunter asked, ignoring Baker.

54

"Yes," she whispered.

"All you had to do was say so, Miss Sarah," Hunter said calmly, though he was acutely aware of Baker's presence. Baker was about the same height as Hunter, but broader of chest and shoulder. Hunter was only a few years older than the big, strong, dark-haired farm boy, but Hunter seemed infinitely older. Hunter was not afraid of Baker, but he was cautious. "I'd never of stood in your way. I was," he grinned, "fixing to ask you the same thing myself."

"You were?" she asked, eyes wide in surprise.

"Shut up," Baker snapped.

Hunter's anger peaked. "You best start treating her right, you lummox," he snapped. "She deserves better'n that."

"You ain't no better, that's for sure," Baker growled.

"Never said I was," Hunter said, perplexed.

"Maybe not, but you goddamn well think it." Baker's chest was heaving with emotion. "A show-off is what you are."

"What?" Hunter asked, startled and confused.

"It wasn't for you, my brother Chas'd still be alive."

Hunter was stunned by the stupidity of the statement.

"You should've stood your ground, instead of running around trying to build yourself up in Miss Sarah's eyes. . . ."

"You think that's why I went after those Indians?" Hunter was amazed.

"Damn right."

Hunter realized just how young and foolish Baker was. But at the same time, he realized that Baker saw him not merely as a threat, but a threat he could not counter. Hunter had been in the war, had shown in the fight with the Kiowas that he was brave and quick-thinking. Since he could not compete, Baker had got it into his mind that Hunter had, through false heroics, brought about the death of Chas Baker. And he had managed to convince Sarah of that.

"That what you think, Miss Sarah?" Hunter asked quietly.

"Yes." It was barely audible.

"Well, it ain't true," Hunter said sternly.

"You shut up talkin' to her," Baker said angrily. "You ain't fit to talk to such a good woman." He wanted to kill Hunter. He had thought of nothing else since Chas had died. But having seen how deadly Hunter was, Baker was afraid.

"You want to try stopping me," Hunter growled. "I'm here and ready." He waited, but Baker did nothing. Hunter turned. "It ain't true, Miss Sarah," he said sincerely. "It was that Kiowa jumping through that gap that set those mules off, not my running over that way. I hadn't of gotten over there right away, we would've lost a couple more people. Lord, that first Kiowa through had a-hold of a little girl by the time I got there. You got to believe that. You were watching."

She nodded slowly, but looked uncertain. She said nothing.

"That's all that's important to me," Hunter said. To Baker he added, "Best treat her right, son. And don't ever cross my path again." He turned and walked away, anger battling with frustration under the numbness. He felt useless and bereft of redeeming qualities. One woman dead of disease, another casting him off for no reason, and now a third choosing an inexperienced—and lying—young buck over him.

The next morning, Pierce asked, "You headin' on, Mr. Hunter?"

"Reckon so." Hunter found the town a dirty, muddy, forlorn place, and would not have stayed on here even if Sarah Rogers had consented to be his wife, which was something he had thought about.

"We'd like you to stay on with us, Mr. Hunter," Pierce said.

"I'm obliged, Luther. But I'm set on going to Arizona Territory.

It was a hot, rough journey as Hunter wound through the mountains. It turned into a hot, dusty trek as he crossed the wide, empty high desert. He rode toward what seemed to be a limitless, never-ending stretch of flat, sage-covered plains.

Hunter was a little nervous traveling by himself like this, especially after he pulled out of the mountains and onto the flats west of Albuquerque. But he saw no Navajos. Twice, though, he did spot groups of Apaches. Both times he managed to find a hiding place. His heart pounded as he watched them pass by, once through a screen of foliage from a dense thicket he had managed to force the wagon into, and the other from the depths of a cave in a sandstone mountain.

Almost two weeks out of Las Vegas he was moving along pretty well, unhampered by the slow, plodding covered wagons. He passed through a strange, fascinating land. To the south a short way was a land of chunky black lava. Just to the north was a long, squat mesa that ran for miles. In between was a flat plain of short, browned grass, sage, greasewood and mesquite. The plain was slashed by washes and small gullies.

The land began to change again, as it had frequently since Hunter had left Las Vegas. From the gnarly black lava and reddish-brown mesas, he moved into a land of soft sandstone mountains chopped through with holes, caves and indentations. He saw one, far to the north, that had a gigantic hole punched through it.

Hunter thought this land one of stark and startling beauty. It would go on and on, brown and blurry from the heat, as Hunter plodded along slowly, the land boring in its sameness. Then something would pop up like a hole in the rock, or the large cliffs to the south he had

57

observed through his old telescope. To Hunter, the cliffs looked as if they had been painted by the hand of God, using long, steady brush strokes to create the effect.

Hunter eventually pulled into Winslow, Arizona Territory. He was weary, and more than a little worried, thinking he might never make it to Prescott.

The next morning Hunter asked for directions to Prescott. He was given two options, and he chose the shorter though harsher of the two—south through Jack's Canyon.

Hunter dug deep to pay for supplies. He pocketed the two dollars he had left. That worried him, too. As soon as he had his supplies packed, and had filled up on a good restaurant breakfast, he rode out.

Several days later he found himself in the small, barren-looking town of Cartersville. In the town's only saloon, he asked, "Am I still on the right road for Prescott?"

The bartender, a scrawny, sallow man with bloodshot eyes and a vein-laced nose, grinned, showing blackened teeth. "Yeah."

"I just keep on this road?" Hunter asked, pointing out toward the street in front of the saloon. He was more than a little annoyed at the bartender's attitude.

"Yeah," the barkeep said.

"There's another way," a man said, sliding along the bar until he was standing next to Hunter. "You can save yourself a couple days—maybe more—if you take the Alton Cutoff."

Hunter grew angrier as he heard snickers and throttled chuckles.

"Take the road here out of town," the man said smoothly. "Two miles or so south, there's a fork. The main road goes more or less straight, due south. You take the road that cuts off to the right. It's a small road there, but it opens up considerable after a spell."

"Good road?" Hunter asked, trying to get a handle on

his anger.

"Hell, yes," the man said, to a chorus of chortled affirmatives. "Reckon there's a few rough spots here and about, like any road in these parts. But you can knock two, three days off the trip."

Hunter thought it over, certain he was being played for a fool, judging by the looks and reactions of the other men. Well, he decided, he would see when he got there. If the road looked likely, he would take it. He could always turn back and go back to the main road if the side trail faltered. He polished off the whiskey and thunked the glass down. "Obliged," he said gruffly, and thumped off.

It was still early when he came to the fork the next morning. He sat on the hard seat of the buckboard, looking from one road to the other. He was, he admitted, tired of traveling and would be more than happy to shorten his journey by any time he could. But he hesitated, the memory of stifled chuckles and mischievous grins fresh.

It started to rain. Big, soft drops pelted his worn felt hat, and fell with dull plops on the taut tarp covering his life's belongings in the back of the wagon. He reached under the tarpaulin, grabbed his slicker and pulled it on.

"Well, why not," he finally growled. He tugged the reins and clucked softly. The gray shook its shaggy mane and turned to the right.

The road was rough at first, and Hunter began to wonder if he had been foolish. But he persisted, and soon the road widened as it crossed an expansive flat covered by sage, cactus, mesquite, paloverde trees, and dying wildflowers. He relaxed, and even the rain could not dampen his spirits as he made his camp that night.

Two days later, he knew he had made a mistake. The road had wound into a deep forest of tall ponderosa pines, with small oaks, aspens and walnut trees here and there. Then the road headed downward, off the great

Mogollon Rim, the huge escarpment that slashed across a vast portion of the territory. The crooked trail cut through increasingly steep cliffs; it narrowed considerably.

Great slabs of red sandstone had tumbled down in places, occasionally nearly blocking the trail. But most had been smashed in the fall, and created a carpet of talus. The trail narrowed even more, until it was barely the width of the small wagon. The solid red wall rose on one side, and there was frequently nothing but a sheer drop-off on the other. Where there was no drop-off, the land sloped away at extremely sharp angles.

Hunter began to sweat despite the chilly drizzle and biting northern wind. It was nerve-wracking, and he felt the muscles in his neck and shoulders cramp as he fought to keep the wagon on the track.

He would have turned back hours ago, but there was no place wide enough for him to turn the wagon. He would have to stick it out, praying he would not meet someone coming the other way.

Hunter had edged the wagon over another in the endless series of rock piles, when a stone rolled under one of the vehicle's iron-bound wheels. He felt the wagon wheel bounce once, and when it came down, there was nothing under it.

"Damn!" he roared as he felt the wagon begin to topple over the lip of the cliff, pulled by the weight of his cargo. Reb whinnied in fear as Hunter slapped the reins on the animal's rump. The gray fought for footing and tried to pull the rig back up onto the slope. But it was too late. The wagon, pulling the squealing Reb with it, tumbled down into the nothingness.

31 Section Title... the again performance last dashed across
a... a pardon... haste... he... too... the... could... can car...
the can now saying... recalled... compared... hunters...
you...

Chapter 7

Xiang Li-Sung nodded sadly when Hunter had finished his tale. Her people certainly knew about adversity,
and she was sympathetic. "Well, you are in Tall Pine, a
town in Arizona Territory. Near a place called the
Mogollon Rim." Her accent mangled the difficult word,
but Hunter did not care. "My father found you at the
bottom of a gully, and brought you here. We have been
tending to you since then."

"There a doctor in town?"

"My father is a doctor." She looked angry and frustrated. "The people here don't want to believe that, so he
usually takes care only of our people."

Hunter was bursting with questions, and didn't know
which to ask first. He settled on, "There many Chinese—
you are Chinese, aren't you—in Tall Pine?"

"Yes, I am Chinese." She said it proudly. "There are
fifty or sixty of us in Tall Pine. Enough to see to our
own needs, and," she added almost viciously, "apparently
enough to make the white residents of Tall Pine nervous."

Hunter smiled, and it didn't hurt. "Don't count me
among those others," he said quietly.

She smiled, no longer angry. It dazzled him.

"How am I doing?"

"Well. My father says you are strong, and will recover."

61

He licked his lips again. He was nervous, and was not sure why. "How long have I been here?"

"Tomorrow will be two weeks since my father brought you back."

Hunter felt slightly relieved. "How'd I get here?"

"My father was riding out to hunt for roots and things that grow up on the Rim. Things we have not been able to grow with much success in our herb gardens here. Whenever anyone uses that trail—and that's not often— we always ride a horse; we never take wagons up there. He saw you down in the gully. He got help and between them they managed to get you up the hill, lift you into the saddle and lash you down. They walked back to town, leading my father's horse."

Hunter shuddered. Though he had been closer to death several times during the war, this was still too close for him. It unnerved him for a moment. "Reb?" he asked.

"What?"

"My horse. What happened to him?"

"My father said the horse was hurt very badly and could not be saved. He . . . put the animal out of its misery." She bowed slightly from the waist.

Hunter nodded sadly. He had loved that horse. It was a fine animal, strong and loyal. He felt again that sense of despair. Anyone—anything—he came into contact with soon was destroyed. He closed his eyes, fighting back tears of rage, frustration, pain and self-pity. But he vowed not to give in to the feelings.

"You must be tired," Li-Sung said, slight alarm in her voice. "You must rest some more. We will talk again later."

Hunter nodded, not opening his eyes. He heard the door open, and then close gently. *Stop it!* he ordered himself. *You cannot let this get the better of you. It's just life's way, is all*. The inner pain ebbed and drifted away after a time, and he felt sleep finally envelop him.

He didn't know whether he should call for someone when he awoke, so he lay, thirsty and hungry. The door opened and a small Chinese man entered. He was not very old, but Hunter could tell right off it was Li-Sung's father. His wide face was smooth, and very round, and his thick, graying hair hung in a long, braided pigtail down the back of his black frock coat. His pants matched the coat, and he wore plain black shoes that were highly shined. He had a thin gray beard and matching mustache, the long hairs of which curved around the corners of his mouth and dripped off his chin. He wore gold-rimmed glasses.

"How are you, young man?" he asked gruffly. His English was good, but his accent much thicker than his daughter's.

"Hungry." He looked embarrassed. "And I got to make water something awful."

Xiang nodded, unperturbed. He knelt and pulled a chamber pot from under the bed. He handed it to Hunter, and then headed for the door. Hunter felt better about that. But Xiang Sen did not go out. He only opened the door and said something in Chinese to someone in another room. Then he came back and stood at the side of the bed, gazing toward the window.

Hunter was still embarrassed, and it made it difficult for him to go. But he had to urinate so badly that he no longer cared that the man was standing there.

Hunter's flow almost stopped from acutely renewed embarrassment, however, when Li-Sung entered the room. But since he was still covered by the sheet, he managed to finish relieving himself into the pot, sighing greatly.

With a red face, he held the pot out toward Xiang, but the man ignored him. Li-Sung swept around her father and took the pot, making Hunter's face color even more. But Li-Sung seemed unembarrassed by it all. She took the pot and left the room.

"Are you better?" Xiang said.

"Some. Still hungrier'n a spring bear, though."

Xiang looked puzzled, then nodded in understanding. "Have you much pain?"

Hunter tested all his systems, moving his arms and legs. There was pain, some of it sharp, but none as bad as it had been the first time he had roused from his coma. The leg and ribs were the worst. "Nothing I can't live with," he said.

"Good." Xiang started checking over his wounds, pulling off the bandages as he did. He hummed and muttered and made sighing and snorting noises while he worked. If Hunter had not been in pain, he might have thought it humorous.

Before Xiang had finished, Li-Sung came back into the room, carrying the chamber pot; it dripped from the fresh scrubbing. She put it under the bed. A few minutes later, Xiang finished checking Hunter. He spoke to his daughter in Chinese. As the doctor began to leave, Hunter called out, "You think I can get some food, Doc?"

Xiang turned, and his lips lifted minutely. Hunter would learn over time that it was the closest the man ever came to smiling. "My daughter has instructions to feed you when she is done."

"Done what?" Hunter asked. But Xiang was gone. "Done what, Miss Xiang?" he asked again.

"Rebandaging you." She got fresh bandages, some pins and scissors from a lacquered chest of drawers. She dropped them on the bed and set about her work with little fuss and great efficiency.

When she finished, she put the scissors and extra pins away. Then she gathered up the old, soiled bandages. "I will be back in a moment," she said, and left. She returned quickly. "Can you get up at all?" she asked.

"Don't know," Hunter answered, shrugging his shoulders. "Why?"

Li-Sung shoved a chair from the wall to the side of the bed. "I must change your bedclothes," she said. "It will be easier if you can manage—with my help—to get into the chair."

"I'll try." Hunter was a little worried. Memories of his last attempt to get up flashed through his mind. "How'd you do it all the while I was out?" he asked, interested but knowing he was stalling.

"Some of our friends would come every day and lift you while I changed things."

Hunter nodded.

"Are you ready?" Li-Sung asked. She stood next to the bed and reached out to slide an arm under his armpits.

Her proximity and touch dazed Hunter. The woman had strength, and Hunter could feel the suppleness of her muscles in her arm. Li-Sung smelled of exotic perfume, and her breath was sweet. Her silk-covered breast brushed against his cheek near the ear as she bent. It thrilled him, and he could feel his body react.

"Wait!" he said hastily.

She slid her arm away and stood, looking alarmed. "Have I hurt you?" she asked, worried. She gazed at the floor, humbly.

"No," he said quickly. "I just wasn't quite ready." He tucked the top sheet around him as tightly as he could, knowing his face was red as a beet from the discomfiture he felt over his manly reaction to Li-Sung's closeness. He hoped she did not notice.

"All right," he finally said. "Reckon I'm ready." He hoped—no, prayed—that the sheet would come along, keeping him covered.

Li-Sung nodded and smiled. Hunter wasn't sure what to think of the smile. Had she noticed? he wondered. But she only slid her arm under his shoulders and armpits. "Whenever you're ready," she said.

Lord, Hunter thought, as the woman's nearness sent a thrill through him again. He steadied himself mentally, though with difficulty. "All right," he said.

He thrust up, and she lifted, once again displaying more strength than Hunter would have given her credit for. But up he came, swinging his legs around.

"Wait," he hissed as pain ripped through his chest.

Li-Sung stopped, letting Hunter sit on the edge of the bed and catch his breath. She spun and sat next to him, keeping an arm around his back so he would not fall.

Even through his pain, Hunter was excited by Li-Sung's touch. He enjoyed just sitting here with only a thin sheet separating her hand from his flesh. But he knew he could not stay there forever. "Let's go," he nodded.

He stood, with Li-Sung's help, on one leg, not putting any weight on the broken one. It was not as difficult as he had feared. Hopping, he managed to turn and let Li-Sung ease him down onto the chair. He welcomed the relief of sitting again.

Li-Sung set about pulling off the sweat-stained sheets and covers from the bed. Hunter studied the lithe young woman as she worked. He figured she was about twenty. He got a pretty good eyeful as she stretched and bent, though he could see nothing out of the ordinary. Still, her supple movements were mighty enticing.

Here was a woman he could enjoy totally, he thought. He sighed. But he knew he would never have such a woman. It was not in his stars.

Li-Sung finished putting the new covers on, then helped Hunter climb into the bed. He was still wearing the sheet for modesty. Li-Sung fought back a giggle. *Did he really think I was interested in what the sheet covered?* she wondered. *Why did all men feel they had something special there?* She sighed.

Of course, she thought, he was a rather handsome man, and even the injuries and bandages could not hide the long, lean lines of his body, or his hard muscles. She had accidentally seen more than she was supposed to once or twice when her father was ministering to Hunter. She had not been disappointed.

Hunter pulled the new covers up and then struggled to unwrap himself from the old sheet. When he did, he dropped it on the floor. He was sweating, and looked pale.

"Rest, now," Li-Sung said.

"But I'm hungry," he complained, and gulped as a wave of nausea gushed up his throat. He swallowed it back.

"Rest."

"No," Hunter said adamantly. "I'm hungry, and I need some food."

Li-Sung bowed from the waist, clasping her hands before her breast. "Yes," she said softly, and left.

Hunter rested on the pillows, and thought about all he had been through. He figured things couldn't get much worse for him than they had been of late. Indeed, they might even be looking up considerably. He was alive, he was comfortable, and there was a deliciously beautiful woman waiting on him.

Where was she, anyway? he wondered. She had been gone an awfully long time. Hunter began to suspect that Xiang Li-Sung was not planning to come back with some food. He considered getting up and chasing after her, to show her how hungry he really was. Then he realized he couldn't even get out of the bed by himself, let alone go wandering around.

He fell asleep.

Chapter 8

It was several weeks before Hunter managed to get up by himself and move around the room under his own power. He had wanted to try it the day after he first moved to the chair, but both Xiang Sen and his daughter were adamantly against it.

"Your leg must have time to heal," Xiang Sen said. "The bones must grow back together, and that takes many weeks."

Hunter acquiesced, and settled for having Li-Sung feed him a broth with some chunks of meat, which he assumed was pork, and many vegetables. It was tasty and filling, and he managed to get two bowls down. It strengthened him a bit, but it had something of a shaming effect on him.

The next morning he realized he needed to make a bowel movement. Li-Sung blandly handed him the chamber pot and returned some time later. With his face burning, Hunter gave her the pot to be emptied. After Li-Sung had left, Hunter thought with chagrin, *Well, pardner, you got no chance of ever getting close to her now.* It saddened him.

But Li-Sung never said anything, nor indicated that she was bothered by it, even after it became a regular occurrence.

Hunter never got over the embarrassment of having to have Li-Sung take out his fouled chamber pot each time, so he pestered Xiang Sen every day to be allowed to get up and move about.

Finally Xiang gave his permission. A young man named Wu Kwai—a large, pleasant-faced, pigtailed fellow who aspired to be Li Sen's assistant—was enlisted to aid. Wu was the one who had helped Xiang get the comatose Hunter into Tall Pine. With Wu's help, Hunter stood.

Hunter was woozy for a few moments, and silently gave thanks that Wu was holding him up. Once the spell passed, Hunter gingerly put some weight on the leg that had been broken. It held. He beamed with joy.

He soon found, though, that he had no strength left, and he could not stand for more than a few minutes. But he stayed up a little longer each day, and within three days, he forced himself to walk as far as the outhouse around back, and then return to the house. It gave him no little amount of pride to not have to depend on Li-Sung to handle such personal needs any longer.

Managing to get outside gave him a minor case of wanderlust. He knew he could not really go anywhere, nor did he have the strength to manage it. But he was tired of being cooped up in the small room, no matter how pleasant that room might be at times.

Li-Sung spent plenty of time in the room with him, talking. He often noticed bitterness in her voice, an unusual thing for someone who was generally deferential. So he asked about it one day.

She smiled sadly. "You do not know the ways of Tall Pine, Mr. Hunter," she said softly.

"Then tell me," he urged.

She sat in thought a few moments, giving Hunter a chance to study her perfect, finely chiseled face. Then she said, "Many of the Han—Chinese—men in Tall Pine came over to find the Gold Mountain."

"Gold Mountain?"

Li-Sung smiled. "You Americans called it the Gold Rush. In California."

In fits and starts, her emotions changing from joy or pride to bitterness or anger, Li-Sung explained how almost all the Chinese men had come to California alone, hoping to make their fortunes so they could either return to China and live better, or bring their families here.

What few women who had come in the early days virtually all were prostitutes, brought over by Chinese companies or powerful tong leaders.

Life for the men was, at first, quite good. The Chinese were welcomed; indeed, many were encouraged to come to America. Though some went into the gold fields, most were merchants.

But as people began to realize that not everyone was going to get rich in the gold fields, the tide began to turn against the Chinese.

Then railroad work came along. They faced much hardship at first, since the big Irishmen and Americans — Li-Sung looked almost scornfully at Hunter — thought the Chinese too small to do such work.

The Chinese easily proved they could surpass anyone else in such endeavors, but that did not gain them acceptance by the whites. Indeed, their ability to show up the whites, plus many habits — such as bathing regularly — that the whites thought odd, made the whites dislike and distrust the Chinese all the more.

As railroad work began to wind down, many Chinese headed back to China. Others went to the mines that were cropping up all through the mountainous West. Here, too, they outperformed their white counterparts. Still others found they got along quite well with Indian people and began living with some of the tribes.

Then there were those like Xiang Sen — who had come to America in 1851 alone and had brought his wife and young daughter over several years later — who decided it

70

was time to settle down. He and others had moved to Tall Pine.

At the time, five years previously, the population of Tall Pine had been less than a hundred. The Chinese were, if not actually welcomed, at least tolerated. But as the white population of Tall Pine grew—and as hatred and distrust of the Chinese spread across America—trouble cropped up.

Two years before, Tall Pine had passed a law restricting the Chinese to the north end of town. And several months later, they passed another law saying a Chinese could not testify against—or for—a white man in court.

"That's ridiculous," Hunter muttered.

"But true," Li-Sung said sadly. "And things are getting worse. Several of my people have been beaten." The anger she held in clouded her face. "One of the whites' favorite things is to cut either the pigtails off Chinese men—or their ears."

Hunter grimaced with disgust, and with shame. "I . . . could . . . I'd never . . ."

"I know," she said softly.

"You said your father brought over his wife and young daughter. Where's your mother?"

"She died several years ago," Li-Sung said, standing and leaving the room swiftly.

Hunter hated himself for upsetting her so, but the next day Li-Sung was back to talk with him, as if nothing had happened. He was happy about that, since he planned to make this wonderful woman his wife someday. But she kept her distance, and his hopes began to fade, until one day, when their conversation had flagged, and Li-Sung said, "Perhaps you will want to stay in Tall Pine."

Hunter was taken aback. It was the first time she had given any sign that she had feelings for him. He did not want to make too much out of the one small sentence, but he felt quite happy about it.

All he said was, "I'll see how I like the town." He had

not seen any of it beyond the Xiang house, yard and outhouse.

A week and a half after he had first put weight on his broken leg, he went out the front door, ready to take a look at Tall Pine. It was nearly winter, and this high up it was cold, even in the sunshine. The air was crisp and refreshing, and he sucked it into his lungs greedily. He shivered a little, despite his coat. It was new, as were his clothes. The day before, the Xiangs had gone to the small Chinatown mercantile — though Hunter did not know it — and bought him a new pair of black, heavy wool pants; a blue wool shirt; socks; boots; two bandannas; red longhandles; a thick, warm coat of rough leather lined with fur; even a new hat.

He had never known what had happened to his other clothes, the ones he had been wearing when he had the accident. He assumed Li-Sung had thrown them away since they must have been quite worn, as well as covered with dirt, mud and blood. He never asked.

The Xiangs had never asked for payment for the new clothes, nor for the time he had spent at their house, nor the food he had eaten, nor for the medical care. Hunter vowed he would pay them before he left — whenever that was.

The Chinese section was at the far north end of the town, which had been cut out of the thick forest of ponderosa pine. Tall Pine's one north-south street — Mogollon — was also the main street. It was lined with shops and stores, at least two saloons, and a bawdyhouse. Apache Street cut across Mogollon near the north end of Tall Pine; Navajo ran into Mogollon from the east but did not cross it; and Verde Street cut across Mogollon near the south end of town. Houses were scattered along the side streets on the east, and haphazardly out in fields on the west.

Hunter strolled down the east side of Mogollon Street, looking into store windows. The only buildings that sported wood sidewalks in front were Capper's Mercantile on the east and the Mogollon Saloon on the west. Hunter was grateful that was all there were. Even with the cane, he would have a devil of a time climbing up and down raised sidewalks.

An aroma caught Hunter's nose, and he stopped in front of the Navajo Restaurant, on the corner of Mogollon and Navajo Streets. The Xiangs had been feeding him well, even if many of the foods were alien to him. He had a real hankering for some beefsteak. There was no reason not to indulge himself, so he went inside.

He tried to ignore the stares everyone leveled at him. It had been the same way during his entire slow journey down the street. He took off his coat and hung it on the chair before sitting, still under the watchful glares of numerous eyes.

A heavyset, middle-aged woman waddled over and growled, "What do you want?"

Hunter stared at her in surprise for a moment. Then he said coolly, "Have I done something to offend you, ma'am?"

"What makes you think such a thing?" The woman was plainly uncomfortable.

"Well, I've been stared at since I started my walk a little while ago. There ain't a person in here who can keep his or her eyes off me. And I sit down here nice and peaceable and you come snarling at me like I've done something terrible to get your goat." Sarcasm oozed from the words.

"Naw, you ain't done nothin'," the woman babbled. "You're just a new face in town is all." She was still ill at ease.

"Well, that's nice to know," Hunter muttered.

"Did you want to order something?"

Hunter was about at the end of his patience. "No,

73

ma'am," he said evenly. "I just come in for the scenery, and the warm, homelike atmosphere," he added sarcastically.

The woman stood still, knowing she had been insulted but unable to respond.

"However," Hunter added smoothly, "since I'm here, I reckon I will order a small lunch. Give me a beefsteak. The biggest you got. I want it bloody on the inside, and black on the outside. Some beans—Mexican-style, if you can manage it—and a mess of taters."

"Somethin' to drink?" the woman asked, recovering.

"Coffee. Hot, black and thick enough to float the blacksmith's anvil."

Hunter was feeling a bit better about himself after having won a round with the waitress—probably the owner's wife, he thought. So he could ignore the remark he heard behind him: "Reckon them Chinks ain't feedin' him very well."

He seethed inside. So *that* was the problem, he concluded. Everyone wanted a good look at the unfortunate soul who had been befriended by the heathen Chinese. So they stared. It irked him, but there was little he could do about it. Still, it gave him some small sense of what the Chinese lived with every day. And it was not a pleasant feeling at all.

When he finished his meal, he shoved the plates away, wishing he had his small pipe. It would be the perfect conclusion to such a fine meal. Despite the surly service, the meal had been excellent, and he felt renewed inside. Still, he thought it would have been nice to have had the pipe.

Suddenly a cigar appeared before his face. He looked up to see a man standing, holding the cigar out toward him. The man was medium tall, and strong looking. He wore a mouse-brown hat, plain wool pants, and a brown wool shirt—with a star on the chest.

Hunter took the cigar and bit off the tip. He stuffed

74

the cigar in his mouth. The lawman scraped a match along the table and held it out toward him. Hunter got the tobacco lighted, and leaned back, nodding thanks.

The lawman sat, saying, "I'm Sheriff Russ Webster. And you?"

"Jake Hunter."

"Well, Mr. Hunter, what are you doing here in Tall Pine?"

"That's a damnfool question, Sheriff. And I don't take you for a fool."

Webster almost grinned. "Fair enough. I know how you got here. I'd like to know what your plans are, now that you're here."

Hunter blew out a stream of smoke. Then he shrugged. "Ain't given it much thought. I've been a touch under the weather of late, you understand," he said, in understatement.

"What were you doin' on Fool's Trail?"

Hunter grinned. "An appropriate name, I'd say. Got suckered into it by some boys over to Cartersville."

"You ain't the first," Webster allowed, though his face remained stony.

"Reckon I won't be the last, either." His jollity dropped. "Unless I make a stop back there one day, and introduce those boys to some manners."

"You do such things often, Mr. Hunter?"

"What?"

"Teach manners to pranksters."

"No, sir. But I don't mind making an exception when the prank damn near kills me. I lost a damn good horse, too. Worth considerably more than those boys who thought such a thing might be funny."

Webster shrugged. It meant nothing to him. "If it eases your mind any, that ain't the only reason it's called the Fool's Trail."

"Oh?"

"The only ones use that trail are fools—or Chinee.

75

Some folks think the two are one and the same."

Hunter glared at Webster but said nothing. Still, there was suddenly a sour taste in his mouth.

"Where were you heading?" the sheriff asked, after a moment.

"You ask a heap of questions, Sheriff."

"It's my job."

"Ain't the job of no sheriff I know to pry into a man's affairs for no reason."

"Maybe I got a reason." The sheriff's eyes glittered harshly.

Hunter was unfazed. He did not consider himself a fighter, just a normal man with a normal man's desires, hopes, and fears. If he had time to sit and contemplate danger, he might conjure up all kinds of fears that were hard to force back down, until the fighting started. But when it came on suddenly, he was as cool as a mountain spring.

"And that is?" he asked.

Webster stared hard at Hunter, apparently, Hunter thought, to frighten him.

"Just keep your nose clean while you're in Tall Pine, Mr. Hunter," Webster snapped.

"Or?" Hunter grinned. It came out more like a sneer.

"Or I'll run you out so fast it'll make your boot heels smoke."

"Well," Hunter said, his insulting grin widening, "I do believe I'm impressed, Sheriff." The contempt in his words was thick.

"You mess with me, boy, and I'll break you in two."

Hunter chuckled, making the sheriff's face flame red. "You need to learn to relax, Sheriff," Hunter said, puffing away on his cigar. "Such choler ain't healthy."

"You just keep in mind what I told you, Mr. Hunter, or you'll be the one in poor health."

"I'll see what I can do," Hunter said icily. He stood and put on his coat. "Well, Sheriff, I'd love to just spend the rest of the day here chatting with you, but a man in my condition gets around slowly." He limped outside and turned south. He strolled along.

A few doors down, Hunter stopped to look in the window of a milliner's shop. Out of the corner of his eye he could see Webster leave the restaurant and stand staring down Mogollon Street at him. Hunter grinned at his reflection in the window and continued his journey.

Chapter 9

Hunter crossed Mogollon Street at Verde and began a slow progress up the west side, soon realizing he had undertaken too much for his first day outside in almost two months. He stopped frequently, and walked even more slowly.

As he approached the Mogollon Saloon, he perked up. The saloon was the biggest building in Tall Pine. The two-story adobe building with the wood facade was large and square. The foot-high boardwalk ran the width of the front and the length of each side. The entire sidewalk was covered by a wood canopy braced by numerous poles. A staircase went up the south side to the second floor. A pair of swinging doors rested in the exact center of the front.

"Why not," Hunter muttered. He climbed up on the sidewalk and entered the saloon. It was smaller inside than it had looked from outside. Running almost the full length of the back wall was the bar itself. It, like the rest of the saloon, was plain, serviceable. Hunter was surprised to see no bartender. He supposed the barkeep was upstairs—there was a staircase in each corner of the back—sporting with one of the girls up there.

To his right, four cowboys were playing billiards. The rest of the room was dotted with tables, about half of which were filled. Some of the men at them were drinking and talking. Others were gambling.

As Hunter neared the bar, a man who had been bent over behind it popped up. Hunter was startled, not only by the man's sudden appearance, but also by his size.

The bartender was the biggest man Hunter had ever seen, about six-and-a-half feet tall and more than two hundred fifty pounds, Hunter guessed. His light red hair was slicked straight back from the forehead. A matching moustache was waxed so the ends curled up joyfully. His hands were the size of large hams. He wore a clean white shirt, the sleeves held at each large bicep by a black garter. He also wore a crisp white apron spread across the abundant chest and midsection.

"Can I help you?" the bartender asked, his voice seemingly thunderous.

Hunter stood speechless for a few moments.

The bartender grinned. "Say, you're that fellah old Joe Chang found up on Fool's Trail and brought in, ain't you?" He slapped a shot glass on the bar, pulled the cork on a bottle, and filled the glass. "Well, I reckon you can use somethin' to wet your whistle. This here drink's on me, sort of to welcome you to Tall Pine."

Hunter lifted the glass and jerked its contents down his throat in one action. He stood a moment, waiting for the heat to kick in; then the rosy warmth spread through his belly. He set the glass down. "Thanks," he said gratefully.

"See, I told you all you needed was to cut the dust a bit." He thrust out one of his monstrous hands. "I'm Linc Stone, owner, and usual bartender, of the Mogollon Saloon."

Hunter shook the hand, worried that his own might be crushed. But Stone was used to it. Stone poured Hunter another shot and then left to serve someone else. Hunter stood, almost trembling from the weakness brought on by his exertions.

Suddenly he heard someone say, "Well, well, well, look

at what we got here, boys." He was a medium man in most ways: medium height, medium weight, about thirty years old; medium handsome, if one thought a leering, insolent face handsome; greasy hair of medium length and nondescript coloration.

He and five other men crowded near Hunter at the bar. They were, for the most part, well under the influence of several shots too many of redeye. All were dressed poorly, their clothes showing signs of wear, as well as lack of care. But all were armed with well-oiled Colts, except one, who wore a pair of Starr revolvers.

The first man shoved his face into Hunter's, and Hunter recoiled from the man's rank, liquor-clogged breath. "Hey," the man slurred, "you must be that new pet of them Chinee."

The others crowded around, annoying Hunter to no end.

"He looks like a normal man," another of the men said. "Reckon there must be somethin' different inside him, since he likes them Chinamen so much."

Hunter stared at the man, a rodentlike little man with buck teeth, squinty eyes, a long, beaked nose and pointed chin.

"It ain't China *men* I like so much, Rat," Hunter said quietly. "It's China *women*."

The six others were dumbstruck for a moment before the first one laughed. The others soon joined in.

"Pass another round around over here, Linc," the first man said.

"Let's see your cash, Quint," Stone said, lumbering over.

Quint Boyd pulled several coins from a vest pocket, and dropped them on the bar, where they rattled. "That enough?" he asked in a surly tone.

"It'll do." The bartender left to get the drinks.

"What do you mean callin' me Rat?" the grungy little man asked, thrusting forward toward Hunter.

"It's what you look like," Hunter said calmly. He almost wished he was wearing his Remington. But it was with his other gear somewhere along the Fool's Trail. Besides, he realized, he was no gunfighter, and wearing a pistol probably would only antagonize this bunch.

"Why, you . . ." the little man huffed. "My name's Oakley Skagg, and you'd darned well better learn that in a hurry."

"And if I don't?" Hunter asked nonchalantly. He unobtrusively dropped his right hand to his knife, and let it rest on the hilt.

"I'll shoot you full of holes."

"You don't watch it," Boyd said, as he and the others laughed, "this man's likely to pull you over his knee and give you a good, sound whuppin'." Five of the seven men standing at the bar were swept up in gales of laughter. Only Hunter and Skagg were not.

"I'll kill you, too," Skagg roared. "I'll kill all a ya. You'll all be flower fodder when I get done with ya." His eyes were red and wild, and spittle flickered from his mouth.

"Pipe down, runt," Boyd snapped. "Ain't it bad enough for this damn fool to have to put up with the Chinks all the day? He don't need you aggervatin' the situation. Ain't that right, mister? Say, what is your name, anyway?"

"Jake."

"Jake what? Jake Chow? Ling? Ding-Ding?" His wit overwhelmed him and his companions to the point where they were nearly helpless with laughter.

Linc Stone returned with a bottle and several shot glasses. "You want another, Jake?" he asked.

"Nope. Got to get going."

"Stay a while," Boyd said, around his rumbling chuckles. "Next one's on me."

Hunter knew better than to argue with half a dozen armed men. "I'll have a beer this time, Mr. Stone," he said quietly.

"Comin' right up," Stone growled.

"I reckon if I'm going to be drinking with you boys, I ought to know who you are. I'm Jake Hunter."

Boyd nodded. "I'm Quint Boyd." He pointed to the rodentlike little man. "Oakley you already know." He identified the others as Barney Crane, the man with the two Starrs; Dolph Connor, a brooding, almost hunchbacked man with a perpetual scowl; Dell O'Rourke, a very tall, almost emaciated man whose gangly arms reminded Hunter of an ape's; and Grant Simon, a bearded brute with a vicious, scarred face.

Hunter nodded to each, not happy.

"I reckon," Boyd said with a leer, "that you're anxious to get back to all your yellow joy girls, ain't you, Jake?" He dropped his voice. "Tell me, Jake," he said in a loud whisper, getting close enough to make Hunter irritable, "how are them slanty-eyed fillies, anyway?"

Rage started in Hunter's stomach and headed upward, like lava reaching for the open cone of a volcano. Hunter clamped a lid on it just before he erupted. He seethed silently a few minutes, letting the anger settle down into his stomach and bubble quietly.

"Well, Mr. Boyd . . ."

"You can call me Quint," Boyd said magnanimously. He grinned, but it did little to improve Hunter's disposition.

"Well, Quint," Hunter said in what he hoped was a sincere, comradely tone, "they're different."

"Like how?" Crane asked, jaw slack.

"Shut up, Barney," Boyd said. "Let the man talk."

All of them had eyes bright with lecherous interest. Hunter wanted to grin, but he forced himself not to. He knew no more about Chinese women than these six, but he had an active imagination—and common sense. He knew full well Chinese women would be no different from any other women. But these boys wanted to hear

82

what they already believed about Chinese women, and Hunter was going to oblige.

"Well . . ." Hunter paused to look around, as if to make sure that no one else was listening in to learn of these secrets. "They look pretty much like regular women when they're dressed."

" 'Cept for them damn slanty eyes," O'Rourke said, in hushed tones.

"Right. But once you get 'em undressed . . ." Hunter was warming to the task.

"Yeah?" Skagg said. He was nearly slobbering over himself.

"What?" another asked.

"Well, it"—he winked—"is different, if you know what I mean." From the corner of his eye, he saw Linc Stone grinning so widely he seemed likely to burst.

"Diff'rent how?" Crane asked. He, like his five companions, was slack-jawed.

"Well, I don't know if I should say," Hunter said in a voice barely above a whisper.

"Why not?" Boyd demanded.

"Them Chinese are strange folk, as you boys well know. And they often guard their secrets well. I'd purely hate to have some of their hatchetmen sent after me for giving things away."

"We'll look after you," Crane said. He was, Hunter figured, as stupid as he looked. The slack-jawed look seemed right for him, somehow, and that was almost frightening to Hunter.

"Gee, I don't know, boys," Hunter waffled. He drank some beer.

"There ain't none of them Chink hatchetmen here, Hunter," Boyd said, in a distinctly unfriendly tone. "Besides, we know how to deal with old John Chinaman in Tall Pine. Don't you fret about that. Now, we're right here, and we aim to hear what you got to say." He tapped the Colt on his left hip.

"Well," Hunter said, in mock stiffness, "if you're going to threaten me, I reckon I'll have to tell." He looked around conspiratorially once more. "Well, boys, them China women have theirs . . . You boys know what I mean," Hunter added with a sly wink — "slanted — going sideways!" He half turned so he was facing the bar. He lifted his mug, but found he could not drink, since he was trying desperately not to burst out laughing.

Linc Stone, standing nearby, seemed ready to split wide open from holding in his laughter.

From the six men there was nothing but a stunned silence. Then one let out an astonished, "Goddamn," drawing the word out.

"I told you boys it weren't a good idea to fool with them yellow women," Simon said. "It ain't right. They ain't right."

They turned as one to stare across the saloon at Joy Fung, one of the two Chinese prostitutes that worked in Stone's place. Joy and the other, Merry Chow, belonged to Pete Tong, the old man of the Chinese district. Tong got a portion of all the two women's earnings, and the two women did quite well at the Mogollon Saloon. They were tiny, beautiful and fragile-looking, like dolls. The ranchmen, cowboys and miners from the area liked that. More than that, they liked the two women's deference to men.

But Boyd and his companions feared people they did not understand. They had heard that Oriental women were trained from birth to please men, but none was brave enough to try to find out.

Unbeknown to the six men standing around Hunter, several other men had thought something might be up, and had eased closer. Now they were also trying hard to keep from laughing. But it was of no use. Stone was first to crack, the laughter exploding out of him like steam from a locomotive. The others standing nearby quickly let loose, relieved at being able to do so.

And then the story spread like wildfire around the room, and before a minute had passed, everyone was in the saloon—except Boyd and his companions—was laughing loudly. Joy Fung and Merry Chow thought it quite funny.

"What the . . . ?" Boyd muttered, any sense of fun he might have had falling off his face to crash on the floor.

"We been had," Dolph Connor muttered darkly.

"You been lyin' to us?" Boyd demanded of Hunter, who was laughing now with all the rest.

"Now, what do you think?"

"I don't take kindly to bein' made a fool of," Boyd said, in barely controlled rage.

"Then maybe you ought not to make it so easy," Hunter said calmly. But he had stopped laughing, and he was more alert.

"I should've known," Boyd sputtered, "that a stinkin' boot-licker for the goddamn Celestials would've lied to real folk."

It was Hunter's turn to be furious. He had had about as much of these oafs as he could take. And he was annoyed at having to back down to the six of them because he was outnumbered and outarmed. He was tired and the pain was seeping back into his limbs. He had done far too much for a man just off what might easily have been his deathbed. He wanted nothing more than to get back to the Xiang residence and rest his weary, aching bones.

"Real folk don't talk like fools," Hunter said, turning to face Boyd and the others.

"Real folk don't kowtow to yellow scum, either," Boyd said in fury.

"Your humors could stand a heap of improvement, Boyd; you know that," Hunter said, not asking, but telling.

"You gonna do the improvin'?" Boyd asked with a sneer.

Hunter shrugged. He had a hand on his mug, still half full of beer. Suddenly he whipped it up and flung the contents at Boyd. The liquid splattered across the gunman's face and dripped off his stubborn chin.

"Don't know as if I could help you improve yourself any," Hunter said calmly, though he was tense, waiting. "But maybe that'll help you cool down."

Boyd's eyes bulged so much they looked as if they were going to pop out of his head. He moved back a few steps, and his minions parted for him and spread out a bit into the saloon, where they would all have room.

Six men went for the guns at the same time; then a thunderous roar echoed in the room. All seven men craned their necks. Linc Stone stood behind the bar, a smoking double-barrel shotgun in one hand and a pistol in the other. The second hammer of the scattergun was pulled back.

"I reckon you six boys have had your fun, Quint. Now leave Mr. Hunter alone."

Six pairs of deadly, flat eyes stared harshly at the bartender, who gazed back, unconcerned. Then Boyd said slowly, "You ain't seen the last of us, Stone."

Stone shrugged. "Skedaddle. All of you."

The six stared for a moment more before turning and stomping out of the saloon.

"Thanks," Hunter said, as Stone uncocked the shotgun and put it and the pistol away under the bar.

"It was nothin'." He poured Hunter another beer. "Best stay here a bit and let them either leave town, or cool off."

Hunter nodded and sipped from the mug.

"Those boys are gonna be trouble for you, I reckon," Stone said.

Hunter shrugged. "I've seen trouble before. But what about you? Won't they come against you?"

Stone laughed. "They might think they're tough, but they know better than to come against me. They do, it'll be the end of 'em real fast."

A cockroach skittered across the bar. One of Stone's massive hands flashed out and slammed down, squashing the roach. The bartender wiped his hand, and then the bar, with a rag. The message was clear to Hunter.

Chapter 10

"I'd be obliged if you was to take me to where I crashed my wagon, Mr. Xiang," Hunter said.

It was two and a half weeks since he had first ventured outside the Xiang home and into town. Since then, he had gone out regularly and strolled through town, picking up speed each day. Within a week, he was hiking into the surrounding hills, including part of the way up Fool's Trail, which angled down into town from the northeast at the division between Tall Pine and Chinatown.

Hunter was feeling much better now, and was almost back to full strength. It was October, and the nights were cold, though the days sometimes had a little heat to them. There had been a dusting of snow several times, but nothing much.

More than once, Hunter thought about his friend Kevin McSween, and of trying to get to Prescott to start life anew. But with winter so close, he would not make it. He would be dead inside a week. He had no supplies, no wagon and no horse. He would not get far in the best of weather. In winter he wouldn't get ten miles.

Beyond that—and much more important to him—he owed these Chinese people far too much, both in cash and in things not so material. They had saved his life, taken him in as if he were one of them, tended and mended him. All without asking for anything. He felt he had to pay them back. He thought he could do that, at least in some measure, through his carpentry work. But to do that he must have his tools.

So he quietly asked Xiang Sen—who the white residents of Tall Pine called Joe Chang. Few of the white townsfolk could pronounce the Chinese names, and most were just plain too lazy to learn the Chinese names, anyway.

Xiang nodded. "We will go tomorrow," he said. "You can walk far enough?"

"How far is it?"

"Eight miles, maybe. Each way."

"I can make it."

The next morning, Li-Sung made them a lunch to pack along. Xiang went first, leading his horse. Hunter brought up the rear. Xiang set a strong pace, but Hunter had no trouble keeping up, despite the fact that the trail sloped sharply upward and the thick coating of talus made walking difficult.

As they marched, Hunter thought about Li-Sung. He felt a bit more comfortable around her since he had been able to get up and around. But her ethereal beauty still tended to keep him off balance. He wanted her for his own, but had no idea how to go about courting her. He had tried asking her out on picnics or just strolls through town. But she had always rebuffed these advances. Politely, to be sure, but rejection, just the same.

Still, he had learned that she had no suitors among her own people. That had seemed strange to him at first—another question in a series of perplexities.

He had to admit to himself, though, that Xiang Li-Sung was another reason he was staying in Tall Pine, at least for the time being. He had lost his Miriam to diptheria; he had lost Lucille—if he had ever even had her—to her own oddities; and he had lost Sarah Rogers, before having a real chance to get her, to an inexperienced young man.

Hunter was determined not to let Li-Sung get away, if there was any chance at all of making her his own. Until he found out for certain that there was not, he would stay here and work at it.

It took several hours for him and Xiang to get to the spot where the accident had occurred. Hunter felt a little apprehension as he stood on the trail looking down at the remains of his wagon. But he had to go down there.

"You stay up here, Mr. Xiang," he said. "I'll wrap a rope around me and work my way down there." He realized that while he had been staring into the pit, Xiang had carefully turned the horse on the narrow trail.

The Chinese nodded, getting a rope. He dallied one end around the pack saddle and handed the other to Hunter.

He slid and scrabbled down the steep slope, knocking his knees and elbows on trees and sharp rocks. He wondered how Xiang and Wu had ever pulled his inert form up this slope, despite Wu's obvious strength. Then he was down at the wagon.

The cart was wrecked. All along, he had secretly harbored a hope that it would be salvageable, even though he knew in his heart it was hopeless. He was mostly unaffected in finding that he had known right all along.

The loss of Reb, though, hurt him. He found the horse's skull nearby as he prowled around, staggering on the sharp incline. He found a few other bones, too, but most had been carted off by wolves, or maybe bears.

Well, Jake, he thought, *there's no more time for dallying.* He found his rifle, which had been flung off when he fell over the side. The stock was scratched and nicked, and the barrel pitted from the rain and dew, but with a little work it would be usable again. He laid it aside and sought out his personal belongings. Most had been scattered in the tumble. The few extra clothes he had were rotted through, and all the food was gone. But he found the Remington, in the holster, still wrapped in oil cloth, and in fine condition. He also managed to find his pouches of paper cartridges—though he didn't know if they would be any good now—and caps, as well as powder and lead.

His toolbox had miraculously remained intact, though it was battered. He had trouble prying it open, but when he did, he was quite pleased to see that everything was in fine shape. A little filing on some rust spots, he figured, and a coating of preserving oil, and they would be good as new.

He slammed the box shut, and stood. His possessions amounted to precious little, but as long as he had his tools, he could make a living in the world. With some rawhide thongs he had stuck in his coat pocket, he tied the rifle, pistol, cartridge cases, and other small possesions between two boards from the wagon.

Hunter balanced the small load on his right shoulder, holding it in place with that hand. "Keep the rope taut, Mr. Xiang," he yelled.

When he saw the old Chinese nod, Hunter started up the hill, pulling himself on the rope, which Xiang kept tight by sliding the dally along the rear crosspiece of the pack saddle.

At the top, Hunter set the bundle down. "Ain't much, is it?" he mused aloud.

"More than some have," Xiang said.

"Thanks to you." He paused, looking at the sky. Thunderheads were building to the north, scudding on the wind. It was growing chilly.

"We should hurry," Xiang Sen said, though he did not seem at all eager to be on his way back. He seemed to Hunter to be quite at peace.

Hunter nodded. "There's only one more load—my tools." He started back down the hill.

91

At the bottom he paused to stare at the box of tools for a moment. It would be the supreme test of how well he had recovered. He had not wanted to express his concerns to Xiang. He took a couple of deep breaths and then bent. With a grunt, he hauled up the heavy box full of metal tools and got it onto his shoulder.

He felt the rope around his waist tighten, and he smiled. Xiang was quite efficient. Hunter dug in his heels and shoved forward, grunting with the strain. But Xiang kept the rope tight, and after a short while, Hunter felt himself almost pulled along. He glanced upward and saw the horse walking slowly down the trail, Xiang guiding it carefully to help pull Hunter up the slope without jerking the man off his feet.

At the top at last, Hunter eased the crate down, and breathed heavily. He felt almost weightless. Xiang backed the horse up to him. "You are not a common man, Mr. Hunter," the Chinese said.

"Oh?" Hunter wheezed.

"So much effort for some tools."

"These tools are my livelihood," Hunter said simply, almost recovered in his breathing.

"Tools can be bought."

Hunter shrugged. How could he explain that these tools meant more to him than simply instruments of his trade, when he could not even explain it to himself.

"Do you own a razor, Mr. Xiang?" he asked suddenly.

"Yes," Xiang answered, startled.

"Do you like it?"

"Yes."

"Would you give it to me? As a gift?"

"I . . ." he paused. "I will buy you one at the store," he said stiffly, bowing.

"That ain't the point," Hunter said earnestly. "Why won't you give it to me?"

"Because I . . ." Xiang felt quite uncomfortable.

"You could buy another for yourself," Hunter pressed.

"Yes, but . . ." It just did not seem right to him.

"You won't do it because it's your razor. It fits your hand; it fits your face. You're used to it, and would feel mighty uncomfortable with another. Right?"

"Yes," Xiang acquiesced. Understanding dawned on him. "So, this is the way you feel about your tools?"

Hunter nodded, shrugging and grinning apologetically. "They fit me. I can get others, but these are mine," he said simply.

"As I said," Xiang said with unflappable dignity, "an uncommon man." He placed his hands together in front of his chest and bowed slightly.

"Uncommon enough to be welcomed into your family?" Hunter blurted out, startling himself even more than Xiang.

"And how?" Xiang might have been surprised, but he had an uncanny ability to sound bored all the time.

In for a penny, in for a pound, Hunter thought. He could not turn back now. "Would you take exception if I was to start courting your daughter?"

Xiang stared at Hunter, his face expressionless. "Has she encouraged you in this?"

"No, sir. And if she takes exception to it, I'll not continue. I was just asking your permission to give it a go." He grinned disarmingly.

"You are not of our people," Xiang said seriously.

Hunter thought he might be treading on mighty thin ice here. "And you are not of mine."

Xiang's face cracked minutely, which Hunter now knew was a smile. Xiang liked this young white man. He was strong, intelligent, inquisitive, courageous, and seemingly unprejudiced. But one could never be sure. He might be looking for the exotic, the different, a conquest among a people so different from his own.

Xiang had been in this land for many years now, and

had become much accustomed to American ways. Still, some of his heritage remained, and deep down he wanted to keep his lineage pure, untainted by any white blood, no matter who the man. He also knew that to make his way through this land, he often had to make compromises, and if he wanted a better life for his grandchildren, this would be one way to accomplish it—if the bigoted whites who seemed so abundant would allow it. And, he thought distastefully, if the bigoted members of his own people would allow it. There were plenty of those, too, though few would admit it.

For a few moments, Xiang almost regretted having saved Hunter. This brash young American was only complicating his life. At his age, all Xiang wanted anymore was a life filled with peace and serenity. Though an agnostic as far as most deities went, Xiang tried to follow the teaching of Confucius, as written in *Mirror of the Mind,* a book most Chinese read.

"I will have to give it thought," he said, finally. Perhaps this was the best way—put off a decision and perhaps Hunter would forget about it. Or maybe decide to leave Tall Pine of his own accord.

Hunter nodded. He had a thousand things he wanted to say, but he knew this was not the time to say them. "Hold that horse steady," he said gruffly, bending to hoist the heavy box of tools onto the pack saddle. The two men lashed it down, and then added the small bundle of personal belongings.

As they started down the trail, snow began falling lightly. Hunter silently enjoyed it.

Over the next several weeks, Hunter worked hard, doing woodwork for the Chinese community. Most of the whites in Tall Pine still distrusted him, and some even openly reviled him, because of his close ties to the hated Chinese. Hunter—in those times he was not angry about the blindness of the whites in Tall Pine—thought it odd that the people of Tall Pine would let the Chinese do their laundry, cook their food, grow their vegetables or do any number of other jobs for them, but yet would not accept them. It made no sense to Hunter.

Hunter kept his thoughts to himself, though, and worked hard. Eventually a few brave white souls commissioned work from him. When they did, the quality of his work began to be noticed. That, and the fact that he was the only carpenter within miles of Tall Pine, led more whites to begin coming to him for whatever work they needed. Usually, at least at first, his white customers would come after dark or before dawn, since many did not want their neighbors to see them in Chinatown.

Hunter enjoyed working, and he was happy he was so busy. One reason was the money he made. He tried paying back Xiang for their efforts and help. But neither Xiang nor his daughter would accept any cash, so Hunter began depositing it in the First Union Bank of Tall Pine in their name.

Another reason he was happy with the volume of work he had was that it kept him from thinking about Li-Sung too much. Xiang had never answered his question about courting, and Li-Sung had not encouraged him, so he bided his time, thankful that his work kept his mind occupied. Except at night.

He was still staying at the Xiang house, working out of a shed in the back, but the proximity of the woman was occasionally torture for him. More than once he swore he would put her out of his mind until spring, and then be on his way. But he knew he was lying to himself. He could not leave there until he was sure he could not have her.

So he worked, saving his money, planning to get a place of his own when he could. Making his burden a little lighter was the fact that some of the townspeople were warming to him. It also helped that he had not seen

Quint Boyd and his pals since their altercation in the Mogollon Saloon.

The Mogollon Saloon had become Hunter's hangout in town. It was a good place for him to get away from the pressures of work and his thoughts of Li-Sung. Linc Stone was a friendly, boisterous man, not given to letting anyone stay blue for too long. He was, more often than not, a perfect antidote for Hunter's depression.

Chapter 11

Winter hung heavy over Tall Pine. Snow from drifts and shoveling was piled deep alongside buildings. Mogollon Street was mostly clear of deep snow, kept that way by the constant traffic of horses, people and wagons. The temperatures were frigid, but not much worse than Hunter had experienced.

Hunter was kept busy with his carpentry. With winter here, people found they needed doors rehung or better fitted, cabinets made, and furniture built or repaired. It was a time most of the people in the high country of the Mogollon Rim slowed down—except those like Hunter, and Linc Stone. Most folks were content to stay inside.

Hunter did not mind. He had always been a man who liked to work. By Christmas, he was thinking of getting his own place to live, as well as opening a shop of his own in town.

Staying in Tall Pine was becoming less and less likely for Hunter. Xiang had said nothing to Hunter about allowing the carpenter to court his daughter, and Hunter did not think it right that he bring up the subject again. Nor had Li-Sung given Hunter any indication that she might welcome his attentions. It was all very frustrating for Hunter.

In addition, he felt like a real outcast in Tall Pine. He did not fit in anywhere. Both the whites and the Chinese

97

were suspicious of him—the townsfolk for his association with the foreigners, the Chinese for the color of his skin. The situation was becoming untenable for him.

He decided on Christmas Eve that if the situation in the Xiang household, at least concerning him, remained the same by the time the snow cleared enough to make traveling possible, he would buy a new wagon and set out for Prescott. In the meantime, he would save his money. He thought that in less than a month he would be able to afford a house and a shop of his own.

Christmas morning dawned cold and clear, and he was not sure what to do with himself. The Chinese were not planning to celebrate. Their big celebration—to ring in their new year—would take place in a few weeks—late January or maybe early February, Li-Sung had told him. So he finally dressed in his only suit, bought a few weeks previously, and answered the call of the church bells. He was uncomfortable sitting on the hard church bench, listening to the boring imprecations of the Reverend Hudson, and he wondered why he had done it. He decided he had done it because of some benighted desire to fit in.

As soon as the service was over, he headed for the Mogollon Saloon. Before he even reached the bar, Stone had a shot and a beer waiting for him.

"I saw you goin' into the church a while ago. Reckon you can use these."

Hunter said nothing. He only tossed back the shot and then thunked the glass down.

Stone grinned. "Reckon I was right. Here," he added, refilling the glass, "have another."

Hunter jerked that one back, too, and then washed it down with several mouthfuls of beer. He set the mug down and wiped the foam from his mouth with the back of a hand. "You, my friend, were never more right," Hunter said earnestly.

Stone laughed, making a sound that was quite reminiscent of an avalanche.

"What're you planning to do for a Christmas celebration?" Hunter asked.

Stone waved his arms around. "You're lookin' at it. I'll be here well past the wee hours."

"It don't look so busy."

"Give it another couple hours. Once all the boys get out of church and have paid their respects to their womenfolk by oohin' and ahin' over the Christmas goose, they'll head here."

"Need help?" Hunter asked suddenly.

Stone looked at him, eyebrows peaked in surprise. "Ain't you got nothin' to do?"

"Nope." Hunter shrugged.

"Hell, I can always use extra help on a day like this. Finish up your beer and then go change. We don't want you to go messin' up your fine suit," he said, with a false sneer.

"I ain't got a woman to chase after me about such things," Hunter said. "Unlike some unfortunate fellows I know." He grinned ingratiatingly.

"Aaaahh," Stone growled. He stomped away.

Hunter laughed. Stone's wife, Polly, looked like a doll next to the huge bar owner. She was barely five feet tall and couldn't have weighed more than ninety pounds. But her flaming red hair gave some indication of her temperament. She was not mean-spirited, but she did have a feisty nature.

Polly Stone held solid sway over her husband, but would not admit it. He, on the other hand, would joke that she kept him on a pretty tight rein. It probably was true, but only because he allowed it. His love for her was as deep as the Grand Canyon. It put considerable power in Polly's hands. By the same token, she loved him every bit as much, and so would never misuse that power. It was a marriage made in heaven. Hunter envied Stone considerably for it.

He finished the beer slowly and walked home. Anyone looking at him would never suspect he had been in such a bad accident so recently. He, however, could feel it. He had thought he was back to one hundred percent of health, but he still could tell he was not. These cold days would make his leg ache; and there were times when he was working that his ribs would send a sharp twinge shooting through him. He sometimes wondered if he would ever get fully back to the way he had been before the accident.

He strode purposefully through the living room of the Xiang house, heading toward his room. Both Xiangs sat in the living room. Sen looked up from his book and nodded. Li-Sung glanced up from her sewing, and Hunter thought for a few moments that she had looked at him with interest. By the time he got to his room, he figured that what she had expressed was curiosity, surprise to see him in a suit. It was the first time, after all.

Hunter changed quickly into denim pants and wool shirt, and left. The wind was biting, blowing down off the Rim, and considerable cloud cover had moved in. Both served to drop the temperature even lower, and Hunter figured it was hardly above zero.

Stone gave Hunter an apron. It took Hunter several minutes to figure out how to wrap the tie around his waist to get it just right. When he finally did, Stone said, "There ain't much to this job, just a lot of work."

He showed Hunter that there were bottles of whiskey under the bar at regular intervals, as well as other bottles on the shelves behind them. He turned toward the shelves. "Once in a while, some damn fool like Fortney Simms . . ."

"Who's he?"

"The banker. Ain't you met him?"

"Nope. I bank there regular, but I reckon he don't figure I'm worth his time."

"That and the fact that, like most other folks in Tall

100

Pine, he don't like Chinese. Anyway, every once in a while, somebody like him'll come in and want some fancy rookus juice. We ain't got much high-falutin' stuff, but what we do have is here on the shelves. I don't reckon you'll have to worry much over it."

He quickly showed Hunter where the taps for the beer were. And where the shotguns were under the bar. There were three. "So you'll never be far from one, if trouble comes."

Hunter nodded. "You don't mind if I hope I don't have to use one, do you?"

"Nope. But they're there in case you need 'em. You got a belt gun?"

"No," Hunter lied.

"Want one?"

"Nope. I got my knife, if I need something close up. And I can handle myself with my fists pretty well."

Stone nodded. "Fine by me. But don't let trouble get too far before you haul out one of them scatterguns. Those things have a way of coolin' down a hot-tempered dude in a hurry." He grinned. "*If* you need to fire one of 'em to get some quiet, aim it up and toward the front door." He pointed. "I'd sure as hell hate to lose one of the girls—or one of the customers."

"Got you."

"Harry down there needs some help," Stone said, aiming a finger at a customer down the bar. "Do your duty."

Hunter nodded.

It stayed slow for another hour, but then picked up steadily. Hunter soon found he had little time to think about what he was doing. He just slapped beers and shots and glasses and bottles on the bar, and scooped up dirty ones to give them a quick dunking in some dirty water before pressing them back into service. He found it quite interesting at times, trying to dodge Stone and his two other helpers, brothers Carter and Will Hawes. But they managed.

During a slack period, Stone came up to Hunter and asked, "Hungry, Jake?"

"Reckon so." He had been too busy to think about it, but with the mention of it, he realized his stomach was empty. He had last eaten at breakfast, and it was now late afternoon, maybe early evening.

"Take off your apron, put on your coat and come with me."

"You taking me over to the restaurant instead of paying me?" Hunter asked, pretending to sneer at Stone's largess.

"Just shut your trap and do like I told you," Stone growled.

Hunter shrugged and did so. He followed Stone out the doors. They marched quickly, Hunter having a little trouble keeping up with Stone's long stride, across Mogollon Street and north to Apache. They turned east on Apache.

Stone opened the gate in front of a large stone and brick house. "What's this?" Hunter asked.

"My house," Stone growled.

Hunter found that Polly Stone was quite a cook—probably one of the reasons her husband stayed such a large man. And she was as pleasant company as a man could want. Hunter managed to keep from grinning with joy as he noticed the obvious caring that flowed between these two people, though neither tried to show it. His joy was tempered by envy.

"I don't want no thanks from you, Jake," Stone said in a growl as the two men headed back out into the cold. A light snow was falling through the darkness.

"Wouldn't think of it," Hunter said, with a grin. He felt quite good.

The saloon was in full roar when they got back and the two quickly jumped into the fray. Two hours later, it slowed again, and Stone let Carter and Will leave for a quick dinner. After those two returned, the pace of the saloon never seemed to slacken.

Hunter saw the saloon as a blur of glasses, unidentifiable faces, colorful shirts, and bottles. He had never worked so hard. And the noise! It seemed as if there was one continuous rumble. Words, arguments, the piano — nothing was distinguishable in the raucous babble.

Suddenly, as he was breezing along the inside of the bar, trying to avoid his fellow workers, a shot glass grazed his forehead and crashed into bottles lining the back wall. Two shattered. He finally stopped, realizing someone must have thrown the glass.

He turned, anger flushing his face. He felt his forehead, and his fingers came away with a bit of blood. He was just nicked, but it irritated him to no end.

"Who threw the glass?" he shouted.

No one paid him any heed, if indeed he could even be heard. His frustration and anger were growing geometrically. Several men at the bar were shouting for service, their eyes drunken and demanding. It angered him all the more.

"Let's see how you boys like this," he muttered to himself.

Hunter grabbed a shotgun from under the bar and fired both barrels in succession, remembering Stone's admonition as to where to aim.

Silence came rapidly as the thunderous double blast faded. People stared around, wondering what was going on.

"All right," Hunter said roughly, setting the shotgun down, "which one of you clods threw a glass at me?"

"I did," a burly man in a thick wool shirt said.

"What'd you do that for?" Hunter asked, surprised.

"I wanted another drink and was gettin' no service."

"Somebody would've got there soon enough."

"Maybe," the man said, as he and his companion chuckled. "But it got your attention."

"You might not be too happy now that you got it,"

Hunter snarled.

"You fixin' to come after me?" He laughed, amused. "Well, come ahead. I'd be more than obliged to clean your plow for you, boy."

Hunter glanced at Stone. The big man was standing with a wide grin on his face. "Your call, Jake," he said.

Hunter smiled and began to untie his apron.

Chapter 12

The betting was heavy by the time Hunter dropped his apron. Stone and the Hawes brothers were collecting action as quickly as they could. Even some of the working girls on the floor of the saloon got into the fun of it all.

Hunter heard someone say, "I'll put ten dollars on Big Walt." He did not know whether to laugh or be angry, as the action was quickly swept up. He decided to do neither.

Hunter slapped his hands down on the bar. Using them for leverage, he swung his feet up and over.

Big Walt was faster than Hunter had thought, and managed to nip his head out of the way as Hunter's booted feet sailed over the bar. Hunter had not really thought he had much of a chance of catching the man by surprise, but he figured it was worth a try. Hunter landed on his feet, and spun, fists up, ready in case Big Walt was coming at him already.

But Walt was standing with his arms across the big, round chest. He spat out a wad of tobacco into a nearby spittoon. "Well, lookee here," he said in a tone that mocked Hunter. "The boy seems ready to fight."

Hunter relaxed a bit and dropped his hands. He shrugged and grinned, biting back his anger. "Well, if I'd of known you weren't of a mood, I would've stayed behind the bar."

"Wearin' your apron, I reckon. Come to think of it, you did look fetchin' in it."

"I'd never of took you for that kind of fellow," Hunter said in derision. "But if that's what you're looking for, I reckon your pardner there would be a far sight more obliging than me. You two do make such a pretty pair."

The other man's eyes snapped fire, and he started to come after Hunter.

Walt stopped him, murmuring, "He's mine, Stefan. You can have what's left of him." Walt was grinning, but it was tight, stretching the muscles of his face. To Hunter he said, "No, thanks. I was just commentin' on how *natural* you looked wearin' that there apron."

"Linc's wearin' one, too. I reckon he'd be obliged to you for such a compliment." Hunter grinned when he saw the worry that flickered across Walt's face.

"I'll pass." He looked a little nervous.

Hunter's irritation was growing again. "Looks like you're about to pass on about everything."

"What the hell's that mean?" Walt asked, surly.

"You been jawin' at me for five minutes now. You didn't want to fight, you shouldn't of called me out. If it's a quilting bee you're of a mind to join, you can find one down to old Mabel's house." He sneered.

Walt's fists came up, and he sneered. "You asked for it, boy. I'm gonna whup you good." He advanced.

Hunter lifted his fists, unworried. "About the only thing you're going to do, Walt, is talk me to death." He moved to his right, his fists making small circles in the air in front of his face.

Walt lunged, coming in with a swooping right fist. Hunter almost laughed as he jerked his head out of the way and snapped in two left jabs that connected with Walt's nose. Walt's head snapped back a bit, and a trickle of blood slithered out the right nostril.

People were shouting encouragement to both men.

Even the women who had been in rooms upstairs had come out, with their customers, to stand at the rail and watch. The noise was loud, but Hunter did not hear it; his concentration was focused on the blocky man before him.

Walt made the same move again, with identical results: a whooshing miss with his right fist, and then the sharp pain of a couple of snap punches to the nose. It hurt only a little, but it angered him.

He decided to try the other way, whipping in a great roundhouse left. This time Hunter blocked it with his right hand. His left moved in a blur, thudding into Walt's ample stomach. Walt's breath popped out, but he recovered quickly. He was no boxer, but now that his opponent was within his grasp, he figured it put a different light on matters.

Walt butted Hunter's chin with his forehead. The blow knocked Hunter backward, stumbling and finally falling. He reached up to touch his jaw. He was furious, made all the more so as Walt stood with his hands on his hips and laughed.

Hunter pushed himself up. He wiped away the bit of blood from his split lip. His eyes were hard. His fists rose again.

"Whoa, pard," Walt said expansively, "now I'm *really* worried." His laughter belied the statement.

His smile dropped abruptly as Hunter moved in, his fists flying. Walt never had a chance. He hoped to be able to grab Hunter and hold him, crush him with his bulk and strength, but he found now that wherever he moved there was another fist. He began to wonder, as he tried to cover his head, if Hunter had not grown several extra arms when he hadn't been looking for a moment.

Covering his head did no good. Hunter just shifted his attack to Walt's midsection. Walt tried to cover that area, thus opening up his face and head again. Hands hardened by years of steady use of a hammer and plane and

107

ax thumped Walt whenever—and wherever—an inch of flesh was revealed.

The blows began to tell, each hurting. Walt's eyes puffed up, and there were cuts on each cheekbone. His nose bled steadily, and his ribs ached. Walt's fractured nose made breathing difficult. He flailed out wildly, hoping to connect with a few punches. Perhaps that would give him a moment's peace so he could catch his breath and maybe mount a counterattack.

But Hunter blocked each punch and continued his relentless assault. Then suddenly he stopped.

Walt stood, weaving, amazed that he was no longer being pummeled. He never saw the haymaker Hunter threw.

The audience did, and was silent during its short flight toward Walt's jaw. The crowd gasped as the punch landed. Walt's eyes clouded over, and his whole frame seemed to shake for a moment. Then his eyes rolled upward, and he crashed straight over on his back.

An excited babbling arose from the gathered masses, and money changed hands, accompanied by much mostly good-natured bantering about the misfortunes of the losers.

Hunter rubbed the knuckles of his right hand. They were split, and would ache like the devil in the morning, but right now he did not care. He stayed there smirking a few moments.

Stefan knelt by his partner and lifted Walt's head. Walt was not out, but he was as near to it as he'd ever be. Stefan glared at Hunter.

Hunger grinned nastily down at him. "I've got more'n enough left for you, Stefan," he snarled. "You want a piece of me, just come on. But I'll warn you now, I'm in an ill humor and of no mood to go lightly."

"Help me here, boys," Stefan said roughly, trying to lift Walt. Three men bent to help him, and they soon got Walt up and carried him out.

"Here," Stone said with a huge grin, as Hunter walked around behind the bar. He held out some bills.

"What's this?"

"I figured I'd pay you five dollars for your work here today. So"—he shrugged, still smiling—"I took five dollars and bet it on you."

"What for?" Hunter asked, surprised. He did not care about the money so much; it was just that the whole thing seemed so foolish.

"Nobody thought you had much of a chance. Except me. So I got good odds on you. We both did well." He was laughing.

"Damn fool," Hunter snapped, but he was secretly pleased. He took the money and shoved it into his pocket. He bent and retrieved his apron. "We got work to do," he said.

Indeed, they did. Thirsty men, many with new winnings in their hands, were lined up three and four deep the entire length of the bar. Hunter, Stone and the Hawes brothers jumped to serve them.

Hunter was exhausted the next morning, and slept late, much to Li-Sung's chagrin. "Well, I'm sorry," he said, when she slammed plates of eggs and bacon down in front of him, "but I was out late." He felt guilty about having slept late, but thought he deserved it. And it annoyed him that he thought he had to explain to her.

"You shouldn't stay out in saloons all night," Li-Sung snapped.

"But I was working," he protested.

She was facing the stove. Now she turned to face him. "Working?" she said, angry. "Is that what you call drinking and fighting?"

"Wasn't much of a fight," he said lamely. "But I was working. Honest." Damn, he hated acting this way. She didn't deserve an explanation. And even if he was going to give one, he didn't have to sound so whiny about it.

But Li-Sung had turned a stiff back to him again.

"Ahhh," he mumbled, angry. He tore into his breakfast.

They did not speak of it again, but Li-Sung retained a definitely chilly air toward him. Hunter suffered in silence, taking his meals quietly with the Xiangs, but speaking little. He spent as much time as he could in the shed behind the home, working, even in the cold of the night when the old potbellied stove did little to warm the place. And he took to spending more time than was usual for him in the Mogollon Saloon.

New Year's Eve arrived, and Hunter found himself looking forward to it. First off, the whole town would be celebrating. But also, it marked the beginning of a new year, meaning it was only a few more months before he could be on his way. He had decided not to stay in Tall Pine any longer than necessary.

Hunter arrived at the Mogollon Saloon early, but the place was going full blast.

"Want to work again?" Stone roared over the cacophony. He slammed a bottle on the bar, and a mug full of beer. "I could use the help."

Hunter shook his head. "I had enough last week."

Stone nodded and moved off. Carter and Will Hawes were racing around trying to keep everyone's glass filled. Hunter emptied half the mug of beer in one long gulp. With it in one hand, and the bottle in the other, he shoved through the crowd at the bar. He broke through and almost had some breathing room. He searched around for an empty table, or even an empty chair. There were none.

"Lonesome, sweetheart?" a voice asked.

He grinned when he saw Crooked-Eye Sal. No one knew her real name. She had acquired the working-girl moniker because she was cross-eyed. It was a little disconcerting sometimes, looking at her, but other than her eyes, she was a reasonably good-looking, well-constructed woman. She wore only a thin cotton shift that did little to conceal her charms. Her rouge and lipstick

110

were smeared, and her hair, done up in some kind of bun, was starting to fall.

"Reckon I am," Hunter said. He had not thought about it before, but it had been a long time since he had had a woman. He seemed to have been saving himself in the hope that he could win over Li-Sung. But now that that seemed out of the question, he could see no reason to hold off.

"Let's head on upstairs," she said.

They did, and as the door to her room shut out the noise, she leaned back against the door and sighed. "Lordy, it's *loco* down there." She grinned at him. "I hope you're lookin' for more than just a quick poke."

He raised his eyebrows.

"I've had my share of customers for one day. If you're of a mind—and got the cash," she added, with a greedy smile, "I'd as soon spend the night in here."

"Suppose I ain't got the cash?" Hunter asked, with a grin.

"We'll work somethin' out," Crooked-Eye Sal said. She moved away from the door, shucking the shift as she did. She stood naked before him and reached for the whiskey bottle, taking a long swallow. "Whoo," she said, "that gets the old ticker pumpin'." She paused, looking up into his eyes. "Well, pard?"

Hunter set his mug on the small table. As he undressed, rather embarrassed under the woman's bored gaze, Sal sipped from the bottle. She was unconcerned about her own nudity.

"Nice," she said, when he was as naked as she. He blushed. She laughed, her voice husky. She set the bottle on the small table next to the bed, and then lay down. "Well, come on," she said, boredom in her voice again.

He paused before moving to the end of the bed. "You can enjoy this, too, you know," he said.

She stared at him in surprise for a few moments. Then she smiled—a real smile this time, not a tart's false smile.

She looked younger and more vulnerable when she did it. "Reckon I can, pard—er—I mean, Jake."

He nodded and climbed onto the bed beside her, as she watched him with wide eyes and an eager expression.

"This ain't necessary, you know," she whispered.

"What ain't?" He stroked her along one smooth white flank.

"Bein' nice to me."

"Maybe not," he admitted, running his hard hands along her body. "But it's a heap better'n a quick hoot and holler."

She sighed and relaxed.

Chapter 13

Hunter awoke with a monumental hangover. The inside of his skull reverberated with the crashing and roaring; his stomach rocked and swayed like a rowboat on a tidal wave; his mouth tasted as if he had eaten a skunk — hair, smell and all. His tongue was furry, his vision blurred, and he trembled when he sat up.

He groaned when he stood, and bit back the bile that rose from his roiling, sour belly. Doing so made his stomach lurch again. Crooked-Eye Sal murmured in her sleep. Hunter looked at her, and was disappointed that he did not get more pleasure out of seeing her. She was still nude, and the covers had fallen off. She lay on her side, back toward him. She looked almost innocent that way. But Hunter was too sick to get much of a thrill out of the sight.

They had polished off the bottle of whiskey Hunter had brought up with them the night before. Then Hunter had stumbled into his pants and boots and staggered downstairs to return with another. That one went down much slower than the first, but disappear it did, though Hunter and Sal did manage to make love twice more before they polished off the last of the redeye. At last they fell soundly into drunken sleep.

Hunter took a step, then another. He knew right off that there was no way he was going to be able to dress himself and make it to the privy. He shuffled to the window as fast as he could and wrenched it open. He leaned out, over the alley, and let himself vomit. It was no fun while it was happening, but when he was done with the dry, heaving retching, he felt considerably better. Not terrific, but somewhat better.

He shivered in the bracing bite of the wind and the frigid temperatures. Sal coughed lightly, and he looked at her. He almost grinned. Sal's skin was goose-bumpy, and she reached out for the quilt while still asleep.

He walked gingerly to the bed and covered Sal, sort of regretting it. He made water in the chamber pot and then dumped it out the window. He began to think he might survive the morning. Hunter shut the window; the cold air had helped clear his head a bit, but more than a few minutes of it was too much. Shivering, he quickly crawled under the covers, snuggling against Sal's warm back. She murmured and wiggled her bottom into him.

Hunter had no idea what time it was when he awoke again, but Sal was staring at him from barely six inches away. "How ya doin'?" she asked, with a lopsided smile.

"Reckon I'll live," he said quietly. "Though I ain't exactly certain yet that I want to." His head still hurt, but it did not feel as if the First Cavalry's marching band was encamped and practicing there. "You?"

"I'll be fine." Indeed, Sal seemed none the worse for wear. "But you had a head start on that first bottle, and tended to hog the second one more than you should've."

He said nothing, ashamed.

"We did do it up brown last night, didn't we?" Sal said, smiling, though lust smoldered in her eyes. Her left hand stroked his hair and shoulder.

"I'll say." The soft touch of Sal's hand was mighty pleasing. He worried about offending her with his whiskey-laden breath, but she was in no better shape as far as that went. They sort of canceled each other out.

"I ain't done somethin' like that in a coon's age," Sal

114

said. Her body moved closer to his, brushing front to front.

"Me, either," Hunter admitted. He was beginning to react to the sultry movements and heat of Sal's body. "I ain't so sure I got enough dimes to pay for all this celebratin', though." He did, but he would hate to have to spend so much.

"New Year's Special," Sal said. It was not that she had a heart of gold or anything so foolish. It was just that every once in a while a girl, even one in her profession, liked to let her hair down and enjoy herself, just for the fun of it. She certainly did not love Hunter, but he was handsome, clean and considerate. She had no regrets about spending a wanton night of abandon with him—and not charging. She only had to pay Stone for the room. The rest was hers to keep, so no one was being hurt by it.

"Just like now," she added quietly. Her soft brown eyes bored into his, only inches away. "If you're willin' to give a poor girl a poke of a mornin'."

"Only if you'll let me buy you breakfast after."

Hunter and Crooked-Eye Sal walked down the stairs slowly, still feeling the effects of last night's frolic, though they were not so badly off as they had been.

Sal had some tooth-cleaning powder in her room, and they both had availed themselves of it. Sal had sneaked into two different rooms down the hall for pitchers of water, managing not to wake her compatriots, who were sleeping off last night's revelry. While Hunter washed off in the cold water Sal had poured into the basin, Sal had gone off to filch a pitcherful for herself.

Then, with more than a little reluctance, they dressed and headed out. As they started down the stairs, Sal said, "Lordy, look at this place."

Hunter laughed. He had seen battlefields that looked

better than this after the fighting. Whiskey and beer were puddled all over the floor; tables and chairs were overturned; broken glass was mixed with the little sawdust remaining. The Hawes brothers, under the stern direction of the huge Linc Stone, were busy cleaning.

"Mornin'," Stone shouted, beaming at them.

The sound hurt Hunter's head, but he would not let on. "Morning," he said, trying to make it sound cheerful.

"You kids have a good time?" Stone asked with an almost lecherous grin.

"You'll never know, you old goat," Sal said breezily. She liked Stone, and she knew the feeling was mutual. Not that they had ever done anything. Stone wouldn't think of it, though Sal would've been more than willing. But Stone loved his wife too much for such doings, and so Sal had to content herself with others—like the amiable Jake Hunter. She decided it wasn't all that much of a sacrifice.

Hunter was used to such banter around army campfires or in a saloon, when there were only men around. He was a little shocked that Stone used it in the presence of a woman, even one of Sal's profession. But he said nothing. He and Sal were at the bottom of the stairs, and Sal stopped, looking around at the carnage.

"Want to help clean up?" Stone asked.

"Not on your life," Sal answered, with a grin.

"How about you, Jake?"

"Reckon not," Hunter said, managing a grin.

"I ought to make you," Stone said, with a small laugh. "Unless you can prove to me it was someone else hangin' out Sal's window early this mornin' pukin' his brains out down the side of my buildin'. *And,* emptyin' a chamber pot right after it." He tried to look severe and couldn't.

"Must've been," Hunter said jovially, getting into the spirit of it a little. "I certainly wouldn't do such things." He chuckled.

"Well, if you see him, tell him he better get his butt

over here and start cleanin' up," Stone said. He waved as he joined the Hawes brothers in the work.

Hunter and Sal enjoyed a pleasant breakfast at the Navajo Restaurant, chatting idly. Hunter walked the woman back to the Mogollon Saloon and left her at the door. He didn't know quite what to say as they stood for a moment in the freezing air outside the door. Finally he just said, "Thanks, Sal, I . . ."

"You don't need to say anything, Jake."

"Sure I can't pay you?" He looked a little forlorn.

"You don't owe me *anything*," she said.

Hunter was relieved. He had worried that perhaps Crooked-Eye Sal was falling for him. He had enough trouble with women without getting too involved with a Cyprian.

"Well," he said, rather formally, "I had a smart time. I hope you got some enjoyment out of it."

Sal giggled at his cresftallen, hangdog look. "You bet I did, sweetheart." She got serious. "I mean that, Jake. It was a fine time. It ain't often I get a chance to cut the wolf loose like that, and it's a pleasure to be able to do so." She searched his face. "Just don't go readin' too much into it, all right?" She grinned.

He returned the smile. "Yes, ma'am," he said.

As he turned to walk away, Sal said, "Y'all come back now, hear?"

He whirled to face her again, grinning. He couldn't resist saying, "I reckon you'll charge me five times normal to make up for your largess."

"Ten," she said, with a throaty laugh, swirling inside.

Hunter pulled the coat a little closer around him, realizing he was cold. Then he headed toward home. He was much relieved to find that the Xiangs were not home. He did not think he could face Li-Sung right now. He changed into work clothes and headed out to the shed. In between rubbing his hands to ward off the cold, he kindled a fire in the stove. When it was going, he set

117

about working.

But he was distracted, mostly by the hangover that lingered in his system. But images of Crooked-Eye Sal kept flickering before him. Nearly all of the images were lewd ones, and he was somewhat shamed by that.

"Ahh," he growled at himself finally. He tossed down his tools and put out the lanterns. He headed back into the house, and fully clothed except for boots, hat and coat, he crawled into the bed for a nap.

Hunter was as hungry as a starving wolf when he awoke. Light was streaming through the cracks at the sides of the curtains, so it was still daylight. He stuffed his feet into his boots and wandered toward the kitchen. Li-Sung was there.

"Afternoon," he said politely.

If he had thought Li-Sung was cool to him the last time he had gone on a bender, this time she was downright frosty. At least her back was. He reckoned it at about five degrees cooler than the well-below-freezing temperatures outside. She refused to look at him or answer him.

It angered him. "Will you be long in here?" he asked, trying to match her coldness. "If you are, I can come by later and fix myself something to eat."

"Not long," Li-Sung said, icicles dripping from the two sharp words.

"Thank you," Hunter said sarcastically. He poured a cup of coffee and sat at the table. He watched her as she worked at whatever it was she was doing at the counter. All he could see was her back, and the short, sharp, jerky motions her arms made as she worked. But even at that, he was taken in by her.

He shook his head in annoyance at himself. It wasn't right for a man to feel this way about any woman, he told himself silently. In his mind he smiled, and thought, *Li-Sung ain't just any woman*. And therein lay his problem.

118

She turned, holding a platter of a food unfamiliar to Hunter. Her look was one of controlled rage—and sadness. Hunter was shocked. She walked toward the other room, her back rigid, her face set.

"Li-Sung," Hunter said softly as he passed him.

She stopped. She did not look at him or say anything. But at least she had stopped. She stared straight ahead.

Hunter looked up at her. "What have I done to offend you, Li-Sung?" he asked quietly.

"Nothing." The word was clipped, and as sharp as a dagger.

"Then why are you acting like this?" He was befuddled. He could think of nothing he had done to offend her. Perhaps her father had finally gotten around to telling her that Hunter wanted to court her, and she was displeased with the idea.

"You should know."

"But I don't." He half turned in the chair, his coffee forgotten. "I swear I don't."

Li-Sung shrugged her slim shoulders. She wore a heavy, simple cotton dress, and had her hair pulled back into a long, braided pigtail, exposing her small, shell-like ears and smooth, finely crafted cheeks.

Hunter nodded, though Li-Sung did not see it; his mind was made up. He looked toward the floor. "I'll be movin' out soon, Li-Sung," he said, as quietly as before. "Tomorrow, maybe the day after. I've had my eye on a little shop. I was going to wait to take it and set up my shop, but I reckon now's a good time for it."

Li-Sung said nothing, surprising him. He had expected her to say *something*. He looked up.

She was crying silently. Her thin shoulders shook, and tears coursed down the smooth skin of her cheeks, dripping off the edge of her jaw. She sniffled, and her full lower lip quivered with the emotion.

"What's wrong now?" he asked, torn between exasperation and a gut-rending feeling of guilt.

Still she said nothing. "Well, that's what you want, ain't it?" he asked, voice rising in annoyance and frustration.

"No," she whispered. Then she hurried out of the room, leaving Hunter sitting there with his mouth agape. He was more confused than ever.

Chapter 14

Li-Sung made herself scarce—at least to Hunter—for the most part over the next several days. Hunter divided his time between the makeshift shop in the shed back of the Xiang house and dickering over the building he hoped to get for a shop. While he worked, he fluctuated between wondering just what was going on and trying not to think about any of it.

Li-Sung still made the meals, but as soon as Hunter came in to eat—if he did—she would disappear. Hunter was confused. She had said she didn't want him to move out, yet she would not talk to him, or even look at him.

"That's the way it is with women," Stone told him the night after. Hunter was in the virtually empty Mogollon Saloon sipping at a beer. He finally had to get it off his chest, and unloaded on Stone. The big, gruff Stone had laughed and then made the statement.

"That don't help me much," Hunter growled, unhappy.

"Well, what do you expect?" Stone rumbled jovially.

"I expected you to say something useful. Something that'd help me out of this pickle."

"You want something useful? Hell, why didn't you say so? I thought you just wanted to unburden your poor soul on me." Stone scratched his bulbous nose. "Best thing I can tell you is to head upstairs, find Crooked-Eye and give her a royal good poke." He chuckled at the

121

animosity spreading across Hunter's face. "Of course, if you had any gumption, you'd go back to Joe Chang's, find his daughter, set her butt down, and tell her just how you feel."

"That's part of the trouble, Linc," Hunter groused. "I don't *know* how I feel about her."

"Booshwa," Stone snorted, his humor seemingly unceasing. "You got yourself a high-falutin' case of hankerin' for that woman. It's as plain as the nose on your face."

Hunter made a rude noise with his lips, but that did not stop the good-natured Linc Stone, who added, "And, if what you told me about what she said is true, I reckon she's set to cast her line for you. She might have a funny way of showin' it, but I reckon it's true."

How could I be so stupid? Hunter thought. It was so simple. But he had been so blinded by worry and wonder that he could not see it. "Thanks, Linc," he said gratefully. He drained his beer and headed out into the bitter cold.

It was snowing again, and he was a little sick of all the snow. It was piled in great, heaping mounds all over the town. People had regularly shoveled off their roofs, making some mounds. Others built up from drifts or the rudimentary plowing the officials of Tall Pine tried to ensure was done to at least keep Mogollon Street clear.

As he walked, head down, Hunter tried to frame in his mind the words he would speak to Li-Sung as soon as he tracked her down. So absorbed was he that he was not watching where he was going. He bumped into someone. "Sorry," he mumbled, looking up.

"Well, well, if it ain't that old Chink-lovin' son of a bitch," Quint Boyd said.

"Boyd," Hunter snapped, tensing, more from irritation than fear.

"Looks like you're in a mighty big hurry," Boyd snapped. "Headin' off to one of your *slanty* fillies?" His

122

tone had taken a nasty turn.

"It ain't any of your concern," Hunter tried going around the man, but a hand on his shoulder stopped him. Hunter looked from Boyd to his five cronies. Like Boyd, they all had their gunbelts wrapped around their waists outside their coats.

"Now, wait just a minute," Boyd said, trying to affect some note of camaraderie in his voice. "Me and the boys been out ridin' them cold, hard ranges for a couple months. We got back here just this mornin'. And who's one of the first boys we see? Our old friend Jake Hunter. And he wants to run off. Now, I ask you, boys, is that right?"

The others chorused nope behind him.

"Now, I reckon we ought to march down to the Mogollon Saloon and have us a few snorts to celebrate our renewed friendship." His eyes were hard, and he tried to pull Hunter around and march him off.

But Hunter was having none of it. He did not budge. He did stare levelly into Boyd's eyes and say quietly, "You know, Boyd, I've had saddle sores that were less of a pain in the butt than you."

Boyd's eyes bulged as the five other men laughed. "Son of a bitch!" he breathed in anger, shoving Hunter away with the hand on his shoulder. "Ain't nobody says something like that to me," he said, as he pulled his Colt pistol.

Hunter smirked at him. He was nervous, with a kernel of fear in his stomach. "What're you going to do, Boyd, shoot me down over an insult?" he said, with a sneer. Then he nodded. "Yep, I figured you for that kind of yellow-bellied sheepherder."

Boyd was livid; the others laughed some more. People began to gather alongside buildings, watching, wondering.

"Yeah," Hunter said, pushing, "I expect you could easy shoot me down, and then go on and tell all the girls

123

of the line over at the saloon what a hardcase you are. You so shrunk up that you got to take it out on somebody 'cause none of the girls'll have anything to do with you? That your problem, Boyd?" His tone was mocking.

Boyd was shaking with the rage that steamed inside him, ready to explode. He cocked the Colt.

"Don't do it, Quint," Dell O'Rourke said sharply.

"Why?" Boyd ask, his voice a rasping snarl.

" 'Cause he ain't armed, you damned fool. You gun him down and they'll likely hang you, me and the others, too, soon's they can get a rope from Capper's store. He might be just some Chink-lovin' son of a bitch, but he ain't a Chinee. He's white. And that'll cause no end of troubles for us if you just go and gun him down out in the street like this."

Boyd's rage colored his face, and he stood stock-still except for the trembling in his muscles. He finally managed to uncock the pistol. Suddenly he screamed and lashed out with the Colt.

Hunter, who had looked relaxed but was keyed up in anticipation of something happening, snapped his right arm up. His forearm collided with Boyd's, blocking the blow. Then the pistol sailed free, missing Hunter's head by inches. It landed in the snow a dozen feet away.

At the same time, Hunter's left hand came up in a powerful uppercut, slamming into Boyd's stomach, which was well padded by his coat. Still, Boyd's breath popped out. Hunter reared back and came back with another uppercut that crashed into Boyd's stubbled face.

Boyd's head snapped up and he staggered backward, hat flying off. His feet slipped on the new snow and he fell on his tailbone, wincing at the pain.

"Had enough yet?" Hunter asked calmly.

"I'm just gettin' started, goddamnit," Boyd said harshly, as he stood. He rubbed his jaw and then wiggled it, making sure it was not broken. "That was a damnfool thing to do, Hunter."

"Don't seem that way to me," Hunter said with false joviality. "Then again, I ain't the one just been knocked on his butt in the snow." He grinned. "Reckon you've just got a different view of things from there."

He half expected Boyd to charge wildly. Boyd seemed the type, with his volatile temper. But the bully surprised Hunter, and came at him slowly, fists up. Hunter grinned at him again. This he could handle, Hunter figured. He slowly pulled off his coat, despite the bitterness of the day. He was not comfortable bound up in the heavy garment. It restricted his movements.

Fighting a southpaw was a new experience for Hunter. It threw his timing off, and allowed Boyd to get in a few good punches where a right-hander would not have been able to land any.

Still, Boyd was not in Hunter's class in fisticuffs, and Boyd was still hampered by his coat. Hunter took several blows, but gave back two or three telling shots for each punch he received.

Soon Hunter was jabbing and punching Boyd in the face almost at will. On occasions he would give Boyd a bit of relief by pounding his midsection and sides. Boyd wheezed; his nose and mouth were bleeding, and his right eye was puffed almost shut.

Hunter, on the other hand, was mostly unscathed. He had a small cut on the left side of his jaw, and he knew there was a big bruise building over the lower ribs in his right side.

He ducked and bobbed, lashing out with fast fists. A hard, straight punch to the jaw sent Boyd reeling. Hunter gave him no quarter. He moved in, slinging punches, driving Boyd back, until Boyd was up against a hitching rail.

Hunter pounded Boyd without mercy, slamming mighty rights and lefts into Boyd's face and head. Boyd sagged.

Hunter grabbed Boyd by the coat front, pulled him

forward, and then spun, shoving Boyd toward the middle of the street. Boyd staggered before crumpling. He was still conscious, but all the fight seemed to have gone out of him.

Hunter walked up to loom over the fallen man. "I'd be obliged, Boyd," he said, panting, "if you was to never step foot in my path again."

Hunter turned, and Boyd kicked out, his boots catching Hunter behind the right knee. Hunter buckled and fell. He cursed, but got his hands in front of him to break the fall. He rolled as soon as he hit.

Boyd stumbled up and tried to leap toward the falling Hunter. But he was too beaten down to move fast enough. He landed hard as Hunter was pushing himself up. Hunter was furious. He walked up to Boyd, who was on hands and knees, facing away from Hunter, trying to get up.

Boyd made a tempting target with his rump up in the air like that, Hunter thought. But that would never do. Hunter moved along Boyd's side and reached down. He grabbed Boyd's hair and pulled. Boyd yelped, but rose, with the aid of Hunter's tugging.

Keeping his grip, Hunter stepped around so he was facing Boyd. "What am I going to do with you, Quint?" he asked, in the manner of a schoolteacher talking to an unruly pupil.

"Go to hell, Hunter."

Hunter let go of Boyd's hair. "You have such a way with words, Boyd." Hunter hit him—a short, quick jab to the face. It connected solidly. If Boyd's nose had not been broken earlier, it certainly had been this time.

Boyd stumbled backward three steps, shock dulling his eyes. He fell.

Hunter took a step toward Boyd, intending to finish the man off. Beyond the fallen Boyd, he could see Simon reaching for his Colt. Hunter turned to the side, his boot slipping a bit on the snow. He shoved off, running a few

126

steps and then diving. He heard Simon's gun fire, and saw the bullet kick up snow just in front of him as he landed on his belly and slid along the snow.

He felt a sharp, quick pain across his calf at the same time that he heard Simon's gun again. Hunter's fingers grasped wildly as he slid. He came to a stop, thankful that he had managed to grab Boyd's fallen pistol in the slide. He rolled, curled and twisted, going from right angles to the gunman to being flat on his belly, facing Simon.

Grant Simon fired again, cursing at having missed twice. The third bullet plowed into the frozen earth just in front of Hunter, sending up a small shower of snow and fresh horse manure.

As he thumbed back the hammer of the pistol, Hunter prayed the powder had not gotten wet, or that the cap had not fallen off. He fired, cocked and fired, cocked and fired.

The wind whipped away the cloud of powder smoke pretty quickly, but things were still a bit blurry before Hunter's eyes. As things cleared, he saw Simon on the ground. He glaced to his left. Boyd was still lying there, but all his other friends were gone.

Hunter stood and brushed the snow off his shirt and trousers. He walked cautiously over and looked down at Grant Simon. The man was dead, three holes welling blood over the front of his coat. Hunter had no remorse.

He headed toward Boyd, as townsfolk gathered to stare at the two men on the ground. Hunter lifted the Colt and fired up in the air until the hammer was clicking. He stopped next to Boyd and stood a moment, looking down. Boyd was barely conscious. Hunter dropped the revolver on Boyd's chest.

He turned and walked away, scooping up his coat and hat along the way.

A few minutes later, he was in his room at the Xiang house. Li-Sung came in after knocking. "I heard what happened," she said, looking worried. "Are you all right?"

"Yep." Hunter nodded. He dropped the coat on the bed and twisted to look around the calf of his pants.

"You're hurt!"

"Just a scratch."

"It must be cleaned."

"I can do it."

"No." She left. In a few minutes she was back, bearing a basin of water, some fresh cloth and some bottles of herbs and powders. "On the bed," she ordered.

Knowing he could not get out of it, Hunter lay face-down on the bed. Li-Sung cut the back of his pants, baring the bloody groove across the calf. "It bad?" he asked.

"No." Li-Sung set about cleaning the wound.

Hunter sucked in his breath. When the initial pain faded, he said, "We got to talk, Li-Sung."

"I know."

"I . . ." A knock interrupted him. "Who is it?"

"Sheriff Webster."

"What do you want?"

"Got to talk to you, Jake."

"Come on in," Hunter said, with a sigh.

Chapter 15

Sheriff Russ Webster came in. He pulled a chair from near the wall and set it down next to the bed, facing Hunter's head. He looked uncomfortable. Hunter rested his chin on the thumb sides of his fists and stared balefully at Webster. He had been at the point of getting things straight with Li-Sung. He was not happy that the sheriff had interfered.

"All right, Jake, tell me what happened," Webster said gruffly.

Hunter did. It did not take long.

"That it?" Webster asked when Hunter had stopped talking.

"Yep."

"I don't like people bein' shot down in the middle of the street in my town, Jake." Hunter looked unconcerned. "But I reckon there's no one gonna grieve over Grant Simon." Webster sighed. "I don't see as any laws've been broke here," he said, in a tone that made it obvious he wished there was some reason to take Hunter in. His dislike for Hunter—and the Chinese—was evident.

The sheriff stood and put the chair back where he had found it. Li-Sung finished wrapping the bandage around the poultice on Hunter's leg. "Done," she said quietly.

Hunter rolled until he was sitting on the bed, watching as Webster headed for the door. Webster looked back at Hunter. "Just don't make a habit of such things," he warned, before clumping out.

"He looks like he has a sour stomach all the time," Li-Sung said, not at all playfully.

"He probably does," Hunter said in distraction. "I'm glad he's gone," he added eagerly.

"Me, too," Li-Sung whispered.

"Now, as I was saying . . ."

Xiang Sen entered the room, and Hunter thought he would explode. Would there be no end to these interruptions?

"You are all right?" Xiang asked.

"Yep," Hunter said sharply.

"Good." He turned to Li-Sung. "Daughter, you are needed at the Zhou home."

"Right away, Father," Xiang said, with proper deference. She gathered her supplies and hurried out of the room.

Hunter stared at the Chinese doctor, angry. Xiang's face was bland, allowing no one to read it. Without another word, he left.

"Damned interfering old coot," Hunter mumbled.

He stayed in his room the rest of the day, waiting for Li-Sung to return. But she had not returned even by morning. Hunter, angry and depressed about it all, walked to Capper's Mercantile and bought new pants—heavy-duty work trousers of ducking material—and a new wool shirt.

As he was leaving the store, Webster moved up alongside him. "Mornin', Jake."

"Sheriff," Hunter said, angry.

"I'd appreciate it if you could stop by my office for a few moments."

Hunter tensed, sensing danger. "There a problem?" he asked tightly.

"Nope." It was not friendly, and Hunter was suspicious.

"If you aim to arrest me, Sheriff, you can do it here."

"I ain't gonna arrest you."

Hunter nodded.

A few doors up, they entered the sheriff's office. "Take a seat, Jake," Webster said.

When Hunter did, the sheriff handed him a cup of coffee. He got one for himself and sat in his chair at the desk, facing Hunter. "I didn't want to say nothin' in front of . . . Miss Chang," he started. He had an odd expression on his face. He sipped. "But I just wanted to warn you to watch out for Quint Boyd and his boys."

"I ain't afraid of them, Sheriff."

"That ain't what I meant."

Hunter looked quizzically at Webster. "What's that supposed to mean, Sheriff?" he asked gruffly, thinking he knew.

"Quint and his pals are old hands in Tall Pine, if you catch my drift."

"You telling me I ought to keep my distance from Boyd?" Hunter asked, furious.

"If you know what's good for you, Hunter." Webster looked nonchalant.

Hunter's rage built until he thought he would burst from its pressure. "I don't reckon," he said through tight lips, "that you've made the same sort of offer to Boyd."

"And why would I do that, Mr. Hunter?" Webster asked, gazing levelly at Hunter.

"Only seems fair," Hunter hissed.

"You're a newcomer here, Mr. Hunter," Webster said, as if explaining things to a slow child. "There's a heap of things you don't understand about this town—and the people in it. One of 'em is that I like a quiet town, Mr. Hunter. A place where a man can raise his family up in wholesome surroundings. I don't cotton to gunplay on the main street, nor fellers thumpin' each other out in

131

public."

"You got something to say, Sheriff," Hunter snapped, "you'd be a heap better off spitting it out, instead of dancing around it."

Annoyance colored Webster's face. "All right, Mr. Hunter," he said, in growing anger. "If that's the way you want it." He paused, then said blandly, "Every time you see Boyd, there's trouble. I don't cotton to such things, you understand."

"I never started no trouble, Sheriff," Hunter said tightly, holding himself in check.

"Never said you did. . . ."

"Not directly."

Webster shrugged. "It don't matter even if Boyd or one of the others is startin' things. You're always involved. They're old hands here; I told you that. You ain't. And I'd be obliged if you were to leave Tall Pine."

Hunter sat with a hard grin frozen on his face. "You running me out, Sheriff?" he asked, in clipped tones.

"Such a thing'd be against the law, Mr. Hunter," Webster said unctuously. "But if you was to *choose* to ride on . . ." He lifted his hands, palm upward, and shrugged.

"Why would I do that?" Hunter said, trying to make this as difficult as possible for the sheriff.

"For your safety," Webster said vapidly.

"Am I in danger?" Hunter asked mockingly.

"Well," Webster said, shrugging again. "Quint Boyd and his boys are probably gunnin' for you and all."

"He's a bully and a craven coward. He comes after me, I'll plant his butt in the bone orchard."

"He's got his boys. And he might get more help."

Hunter thought he might know where that help would come from. "Why don't you just run him out of town next time he shows up?" Hunter asked sharply.

"He ain't done nothin' wrong," Webster whined.

"Neither have I."

132

"You're the cause of all these troubles."

"How so?" Hunter muttered, fighting for control. He had a great desire to wring the sheriff's neck.

"Well," Webster began. He paused a moment, reflectively, "Well, to be honest, Mr. Hunter, it's the company you keep. If you know what I mean."

Hunter sat, bewildered. Did Webster have something against Linc Stone? he wondered. Then it hit him, and he felt the rage explode inside like a starburst. He was quiet until he had calmed down. "The Chinese found me and saved my butt, Sheriff," he finally said, through clenched teeth. "If that's what you call keeping the wrong company, well . . ." His rage would not let him continue.

Webster could not even see Hunter's anger, or perhaps he was just blind to it. "Exactly," he muttered. "They did you all right, of course, by findin' you and nursin' you back to health. But, well, I mean, to continue stayin' there, consortin' with their women, workin' for them. Well, it just ain't right, you know, a white man subjugatin' himself to them yellow heathens like that. It ain't the natural way of things."

Hunter couldn't quite believe what he was hearing. He stood, fury almost getting the better of him. "I reckon I got no more to say to you, Sheriff," he muttered.

Hunter clumped over to the Mogollon Saloon, still enraged.

"What's eatin' at you?" Stone asked.

"Just had a chat with the sheriff," Hunter spat out. "Most enlightening."

"What'd he say?"

"Mostly to get out of town."

Stone laughed. "That's what's got you all worked up? Hell."

"It's because I'm living with the Chinese."

"You mean," Stone asked with some incredulity, "that you just found out Russ Webster don't like the Chinese?"

"Bah. Seems like he likes Quint Boyd a heap, too."

133

Stone grinned. "Does seem odd, don't it?"

"Sure does. Hell, they're just a bunch of damnfool cowpokes."

"That's what a lot of folks think."

Hunter cocked his eyebrows at the bartender. "They something other than what they claim to be?"

"You seen them of late? Before yesterday, I mean."

"Not in a couple months. Boyd said yesterday that they been ridin' for the ranches."

"More like ridin' the owlhoot trail."

"You sure?" It set Hunter to wondering. He finished his beer.

"Yes, I'm sure."

"And you're telling me Webster's mixed up in that with them?" Hunter asked skeptically.

"Don't know if he's mixed up in it. But he knows it's going on, and he turns the other cheek to it."

"Why don't somebody do something about it?" Hunter felt his irritation growing.

"Reckon not too many people know. The federal marshals don't get down this way too often. Most people around here ignore it. Boyd usually heads somewhere else to do his deeds, so people in Tall Pine don't care."

"So Boyd really is some kind of hardcase, eh?"

"Yep."

"You think he'll come gunning for me?" Hunter did not seem greatly concerned.

"Good chance of it. Simon's been riding with him a long time. He'll not be in the best of humor about seeing Simon up in the bone orchard. Plus there's the fact that you went and whaled the tar out of him right out on Mogollon Street. I don't expect that'll give him saintly feelin's toward you." Stone grinned.

Hunter nodded, none too concerned. He left the saloon and stomped to the Xiang house. He was still angry, though Stone's infectious humor had helped that anger abate a little. His humor did not improve much when he found that Li-Sung was still not home. He put on his new pants and shirt and headed out again. He felt it time, even if he did think he now had a chance to court Li-Sung, to get his own shop, if not his own place to live. If Boyd was planning to come for him, Hunter did not want to endanger the Xiangs—or any of the other Chinese.

Though he had known it for some time, it became sharply clear to him only now just how ingrained the hatred against the Chinese was here. He had known he was not well-thought-of by many townsfolk, and that many of the people who dealt with him did so simply because of his work. Many barely concealed their distaste when they had to deal with him.

But not until now had he become conscious of the underlying tension in the town between the two groups of people. He began to wonder if perhaps he wasn't sitting on a powder keg that was about ready to explode.

Hunter had been dickering with a townsman, Emory Fairhaven, for a place he could use as a shop. Fairhaven was asking too much for it, but Hunter decided he would take it, no matter what the cost, to protect the Xiangs. He quickly clinched the deal on the place—on the corner of Mogollon and Apaches Streets, catty-corner from the Mogollon Saloon. It had two rooms—one out front that he could use as a shop, and another at back outfitted as living quarters.

He realized, as he concluded the deal, that Fairhaven was selling to him simply because he thought he was helping Hunter escape from the confines of the Chinese life and people. If Hunter hadn't been so angry, he might have thought it funny.

The shop took shape quickly, and in less than a week he had his sign hanging out front and was operating out of the shop.

Then Li-Sung walked into the shop one morning. She looked sad, and Hunter thought she might have been crying. "Are you alone?" she asked, her voice quavering with worry.

He made a pretense of looking around. "I don't see anyone else," he said, trying to affect good cheer.

"Don't patronize me," Li-Sung said, almost pleading.

"Sorry," Hunter answered, a little shaken. "What makes you think there'd be anyone else here?" The look on her face told him, and he felt shamed. "I'm alone," he mumbled.

"Can you close the shop a little while?"

His stomach lurched and his heart jumped. Finally, he figured, he would have a chance to talk to her, get things set right. "Sure." He paused a heartbeat, then asked, "Ain't you afraid people'll talk?"

"People will talk about me and my people no matter what I — or we — do."

Hunter nodded sadly. Still, the excitement of having her here infected him. He hurriedly locked the door, hung his "Closed" sign in the window and pulled the curtains over it. He turned and started to say something.

But Li-Sung came to him, seeming to glide across the floor. Her small hands pulled his head down, and then her lips were on his.

He was startled.

Li-Sung pulled back an inch and said into his breath, "Don't talk." She took his hand and turned toward his room at the back, tugging him along. He went willingly, if confusedly; hopefully, if just a bit fearfully.

Chapter 16

"You wanted to talk to me?" Li-Sung asked after the world had calmed down for her and Hunter. They were lying on Hunter's small, rumpled bed together, with their clothes jumbled heaps on the floor.

Hunter rested with the upper part of his back braced against the pillow on the rough headboard. Li-Sung lay in the crook of his arm, the covers pulled up almost to her breasts. Her shiny black hair was spread across much of Hunter's chest. She looked very content, and as if she belonged there.

"Yes." He gulped.

"What did you want to say?" She almost giggled as she sensed his discomfiture.

He thought for a few minutes, enjoying the view of Li-Sung. There was no need to hurry his answer. They had plenty of time. Slowly a grin started, and then spread. "Well, I had wanted to see about courting you, Li-Sung. But I reckon we've gotten past that problem."

She smiled, and stretched, catlike. Hunter loved the sinuous movement of her body, and he felt a warm glow growing. "Reckon we are," she said in a voice like velvet. "But," she added playfully, "don't think this is an everyday occurrence."

"I won't," he said nonchalantly, but his stomach lurched.

"What else did you want to say?"

"I ain't sure," Hunter confessed. All the while he had been trying to sit her down for a talk, he had known what he had to say. But now that the time was here, it seemed as if he had lost all capacity for thought and speech.

"Can't think of anything?" Li-Sung asked sleepily. She was warm and comfortable.

"Well," he said, an unknown sort of fear gripping him, "I wanted to tell you I love you." The sense of relief that washed over him at having gotten it out in the open was tempered by concern that he might be rejected. Even though they were lying here nude together after just having made love, he had that fear. It was irrational, he knew, but it existed nonetheless.

"I love you, Jake," she said, tears staining her soft cheeks.

Hunter could feel the tears on his abdomen. "You're crying," he said, befuddled. Hunter did not know what to do. Women were beyond his understanding. "Why?" he asked quietly.

"Because I love you," Li-Sung blubbered. "And because you love me." The tears and sobbing slowed.

"But . . ."

"I know that sounds stupid," she said. She sat up and rummaged around in her clothes on the floor next to the bed. She came up with a cotton hankie and wiped her eyes, and then blew her nose, rather indelicately for such a small woman, Hunter thought.

"I understand," Hunter said. "It's nice." He paused. "But . . . I thought you . . . ." He shook his head. "I thought you didn't even like me," he finally stammered.

"Why did you think that?"

"You wouldn't talk to me half the time. Wouldn't even acknowledge me. I had asked your father if it would be all right to court you. He never gave me an

138

answer. And when you'd hardly let on that I existed, well ... Lord, I thought you hated me for sure."

"I loved you for a long time, Jake Hunter. My father told me what you asked. I was eager for you to court me. But then I thought about it." She sniffled. "I put you off because . . ." she started to weep softly. ". . . because . . . for your safety."

"What?" he asked, confused.

"You didn't — still don't — really understand the way life is here in Tall Pine for my people. We are used to it. But I could see no reason for you to suffer."

"I've suffered before," Hunter said huffily, angry that she would think she had to protect him.

"You have seen already how some of the people here treat you — just for living with us. After we rescued you. Can you even imagine the hate they would heap on you if you had courted — and maybe even married — me?"

"I would face every man in town out on Mogollon Street to save your honor — or your father's," he said simply. "I ain't much for words, Li-Sung," he said earnestly. "At least, not most times. But you are a finer woman than I could've ever dreamed of having." He knew he was being maudlin, but he could not stop it. "You're probably far better than I deserve."

"Don't say that," she hissed.

She turned to face him, and he was struck by the sheer elegant beauty of her. She was like a perfect, delicate flower, able to withstand some of the strongest elements in nature, but so easily crushed with injudicious treatment.

"Well, it's true," he said. "I fell in love with you the first time I saw you. But I was scared of it all."

"Why?" she asked, her slanted almond eyes widening. Her small, pointed breasts rose and fell with her breathing, made ragged by the just-ended sobbing. She was surprised at the thought of a big American man being afraid to love a woman, but the Americans did have many strange ways.

"Well, first off, I figured you were too good for me. Too beautiful. And"—he paused—"well, there's my past, too."

He explained as quickly and as unemotionally as he could about his previous fiancée, and Lucille. "It left me a little gun-shy," he added ruefully. "To tell you the truth, Li-Sung, I ain't even sure Lucille's even followed through on the divorce. It might make things sticky for us. . . ." He trailed off.

"It doesn't make a difference," she said, staring at him.

He smiled. "Well, anyway, I wanted to be proper about such things. I don't really know how your people go about these things and . . ."

"Many of us don't know much about the old ways," Li-Sung said softly. "Some are trying to become more like the people here."

He nodded. "Well, I had wanted to do it right, by your lights. So when your father took me to get my things lost in the accident, I asked him if he'd mind me courting you. He said he'd have to think about it. He never gave me an answer."

Li-Sung looked stricken. "I told him that I would be honored to have you court me," she said, lowering her eyes. "He asked me to think about it. I did, and realized your well-being was in danger, so . . ."

He sat back, breathing harshly, as if he could rid himself of his anger by expelling it forcefully. When he calmed down, he said quietly, "If we could only make up for lost chances in our lives."

For the first time, Hunter saw Li-Sung angry. Her face and chest flushed with it, giving her an interesting coloration. But she calmed down. "Yes," she mumbled. "But we cannot. Nothing is so fleeting as the passing of an opportune moment." She smiled wanly.

"That from that book your father's always reading?"

"Yes."

Hunter nodded. "There is one thing, though, that bothers me. You've been cool toward me for a while — I guess since your father told you what I'd asked. But the last week or so, you've really been even more distant. Like you didn't seem to even know I existed."

Li-Sung smiled bittersweetly. "I hated you for a time," she said, with a touch of bitterness.

"Why?" he asked, shocked.

"Because of what you did on your New Year's Eve."

"What, got drunk? I admit it was foolish, but . . ." The look on her face stopped him. "You know about . . ." He suddenly felt funny about mentioning Crooked-Eye Sal.

"Yes." It was almost a moan. "It was not the first time, either, was it?" She seemed heartbroken.

"Yes, it was," he said honestly. "Since I've been here I've had my hopes set on courting you, but that was right about the time I figured you had no interest in me. So, when the opportunity came along, I . . . well, I joined in all the celebrating and . . ."

"First time?" Li-Sung asked, surprised.

"Yes, ma'am."

It was her turn to look shamed. She steepled her hands before her breasts and bowed in supplication. "I thought . . . I had heard . . ." She stopped and sighed, also regretting missed chances. Still, there was the future, and they seemed to have gotten things worked out.

"It doesn't matter now," he said.

"Have I shown you that I no longer hate you?" she asked, tense.

"Yes, ma'am." He beamed.

"Good," she said, relaxing.

141

"But . . ." He paused, not sure whether he should ask, but finally deciding he had to know. "But why'd you do this?"

She was suddenly aware of her nudity, and didn't know whether to hide her head in embarrassment or to chuckle. She wanted to laugh, but she thought that might offend him. Nor did she know what to say, so she opted for the truth. "I wanted to show you," she said nervously, but with a firm voice, "that I wanted you. And, that I was as good as *she*." The last word dripped with derision.

"Better," he said, starting to smile. "Far, far better."

Li-Sung scrabbled up and kissed him when she arrived at his face.

"What do we do now?" he asked with a grin.

"What do you think?" she asked, nibbling on his lower lip.

"All right," Hunter asked when he could finally breathe properly again, *"now* what do we do? About life I mean?"

"You come courting me," Li-Sung said dreamily.

"Ain't we gone a little far for that?"

"Maybe." She was almost asleep; she was that comfortable. "But," she added, as she wiggled a bit, trying to burrow into his skin, "we need to keep up appearances for the town."

"You weren't worried about appearances a bit ago," he said.

"My part of town," she said simply.

He nodded, feeling like a fool. "I hate to say this, Li-Sung," he said, "but I reckon you best get going, or people'll talk."

"Let them talk."

"Your father, too?"

She looked up, alarm undimmed by the epicanthic folds of her eyes. "No," she said firmly. "Not him. He has tried in many ways to become like an American, but he still has many of the old ways."

"Not all the old ways are bad," Hunter said quietly. "Your people have some good ways. They're just different from American ways. A lot of people hate what they don't understand."

Li-Sung nodded. Then she smiled. "Yes, I better go." She stood and stretched, making sure Hunter got a good eyeful. Then she lazily pulled on her silk clothes, facing Hunter, letting him watch.

And he did, hardly even blinking during the entire performance. Then he dressed, quickly, almost ashamed to put on a show for Li-Sung as she had done for him. She looked a little disappointed, but would not let it tear down her good feelings.

She stepped up and kissed him hard, before they headed for the door. As she left the shop, uncaring about any eyes that might be on her, she looked properly demure in her thick wool shawl.

Hunter shook his head, not quite sure this was real. He opened the curtains and set about working again.

That night he called at the Xiang house. He was greeted at the door by Li-Sung. She ushered him in, and he sat in the stuffy living room facing Xiang Sen. The Chinese man said nothing, so Hunter matched the silence, until Li-Sung mercifully called them to dinner.

It was a strained affair, with hardly a word spoken, though with the looks Hunter and Li-Sung traded, they did not need words. Hunter wanted to say something to Xiang, but he didn't know what, so he kept quiet. Soon after the meal, Xiang went off to his room, and Li-Sung and Hunter sat in the living room, talking. They said little of consequence; all the important things they had to say to each other they had said that afternoon.

It was that way each night for more than a week. And then one night, Hunter sat at a feast such as he had never seen. Afterward, Li-Sung spent the evening cleaning.

Xiang and Hunter sat in the living room. Hunter sensed the old Chinese wanted to talk to him but did not know how to start.

"What's going on, Mr. Xiang?" Hunter asked, actually curious. "That meal wasn't normal for your household. And now Li-Sung . . ." He waved an arm in the woman's direction.

The doctor looked at him before the upper lip lifted slightly, indicating a smile. "Tomorrow is New Year," he said almost happily.

"Big doings?"

"Yes, yes," Xiang said, head bobbing eagerly. "The start of the new year is very important to my people. Our meal tonight is an indication of a new beginning. So is my daughter's cleaning. Everything is cleaned for the new year. All debts are paid, obligations fixed, so that all might start with a clean paper."

Hunter felt bad. "Then I'll have to get to the bank first thing in the morning," he said earnestly.

"For what?" Xiang asked, surprised.

"If all debts must be paid, I ain't aimin' to welch on mine. I owe you—and Li-Sung—a heap. I aim to pay back in full, though I reckon paying in full'd be impossible. But I'll do what I can."

"I did not say that so you would think you had to pay us back," Xiang muttered, almost insulted. "I do not want your money."

"But . . ."

"No," Xiang said, stomping off to his room.

"I've done it now, ain't I?" Hunter asked as Li-Sung came up to him and kissed him.

"No," she whispered. "He is just a proud man. He had hoped to tell you of our celebration, but with his poor command of your language, he found it difficult. He is shamed now, that you would think he was accusing you of owing something."

"But I . . ."

"It's all right," Li-Sung said, placing a soft hand across his mouth. "It is fine. Now you better go. I have many things to do."

With all the racket coming from the firecrackers, music, singing and celebrating in Chinatown the next day, Hunter found it too difficult to work, so he strolled to the Mogollon Saloon. He stood chatting with Linc Stone while he sipped at a beer. The huge bartender ribbed Hunter considerably, knowing the carpenter was happier than he had ever seen him, but not knowing why. He tried, through friendly banter, to draw Hunter out, but he could not do it. That, however, did not slow the running commentary of ribaldry.

Noise grew outside, and, curious, they looked toward the saloon's swinging doors. Suddenly ten Chinese men burst breathlessly into the saloon. Each wore loose black pants, wooden shoes, silk caps, and wool coats that looked incongruous with the rest of their clothes. All were frightened.

"Trouble's brewin'," Stone said, though he did not looked concerned.

"What're you going to do?" Hunter asked, finishing his beer.

Stone got him another. When he returned, he said, "Nothin'—at least until I find out what the deal is."

The Chinese had stopped by the door, peered out, and then scuttled toward the bar along the back wall.

"You're losing all your other customers," Hunter

said.

Stone let go his hearty laugh. "All two of them. This ain't been one of my busiest days." He looked at the Chinese, who stared at the big man in some fear. Stone nodded toward two tables not far from the bar. The Chinese sat, casting worried glances toward the door.

The noise from outside seemed to be growing. No longer grinning, Stone said with a little irony, "I'll be right back. Got to take care of my new customers."

Chapter 17

The Chinese were sitting quietly, nervously, at two tables. "What're you boys doin' in here?" Stone asked, as he thumped up to them.

"Nothing," one said.

"Look, Wang, I never said your people couldn't come in here. And I know your people are celebratin'. But by the looks of things, there's trouble comin'. Now, what're you doin' in here?"

"Several men were chasing us," Charlie Wang said quietly. "We came in here to get away from them."

"Why here?"

Wang sat stolidly, not planning to answer. The man next to him—Stone knew him only as Bill Ching—bent close to Wang's ear and spoke rapidly in the whining tone of his native language. A moment later, Wang looked up at Stone. "We thought you might help us."

"Why'd you think that?" Stone asked, curious.

"You have never insulted my people," Wang said stiffly.

Stone grunted, then asked, "You got a mob after you?"

"There were several men," Wang repeated.

"There were many by the time we came here," Ching added.

"What brought this on?"

Wang said nothing, until Ching leaned over and talked to him in Chinese again. Wang nodded. "You know of Wing Lo?" he asked Stone.

"Jimmy Wing? Sure."

"Some of your fellows came to our festival this morning. They found Wing Lo and dragged him away and beat him to death."

"Wasn't my fellows, pal."

Wang shrugged. To him, all whites were the same.

"You go see Sheriff Webster about it?" Stone asked.

"Yes." Wang said tightly, staring straight ahead.

"No help, though, eh?" He had known, but thought he should bring it into the open.

"No." Wang was angry, but under control.

"When we came out of his office, others were waiting for us," the soft-spoken Chinese said. "A left-handed man was leading them."

"Quint Boyd?"

"Yes."

"So you thought comin' in my saloon's gonna help you somehow?"

"Yes."

"Why?"

Wang glared at him. He was no friendlier than before, but some of the others seemed to be. "It was thought you would not object. Some of my people think you," he added, with a look of disgust, "might be sympathetic."

"You don't?" Stone asked, a spark of anger darkening his face.

"No," Wang said stiffly.

Stone fumed for a moment. Then he flashed his normal grin. "You ought to pay more heed to your elders, Wang. They know a lot more'n you do."

"Are you going to throw us out?" Wang asked, looking up at Stone's huge face. He was surprised.

"Nah. But I'm losin' a heap of business. You're

148

gonna sit here, you're gonna have to order somethin'."
He tried to grin again, but wasn't having much luck
with it. The thought of Jimmy Wing's death, and the
sight of one of the Chinese men with his pigtail rudely
lopped off, was not at all funny.

"We will have beer," Wang said with distaste.

Stone served them and went back to the bar across
from Hunter.

"I better go see what our gentlemen callers outside
want," Stone said. The noise from outside had been
growing steadily.

"What's going on, Linc?" Hunter asked.

Stone explained it quickly.

"Ain't you worried?" Hunter asked.

"Not yet."

"Things could get interesting." He sounded worried,
but mobs always made him nervous.

"Yes, sir, they could."

Stone grabbed a scattergun and a Colt, setting both
on the bar. He bent again and brought out a shoulder
holster. He strapped it on and dropped the Colt in it
after making sure the pistol was loaded. He cracked the
shotgun to check that, too.

"This won't take but a minute," he said confidently.

"Want help?"

"Nah." Stone marched off and shoved through the
doors.

Hunter waited a moment, then set his beer down. He
looked at the Chinese. He was not sure whether he felt
hatred, sympathy or revulsion for the men, who sat
stoically. He walked toward the swinging doors and
stood just inside, watching.

Stone stood on the edge of the wood sidewalk, shot-
gun cradled in the crook of his arm, facing the crowd.
There were maybe two dozen people—including Quint
Boyd, Dell O'Rourke, Dolph Connor and Oakley
Skagg. Boyd was in front, egging on the crowd, whip-

ping up the passions of their bigotry. He was trying to get them worked up enough to storm the saloon and drag the Chinese out.

"Quiet down!" Stone bellowed. His voice, usually as loud and deep as a foghorn, boomed out into the cold air, accompanied by a billowing cloud of vapor. Everyone finally obeyed, almost stunned at the voice.

"You folks got no business here—unless you fixin' to come in and have a drink," Stone roared, his tone letting them know he was not about to back down.

"Not with them Chinks there," someone shouted.

"Yeah," Boyd shouted cockily. "What's the idea of lettin' them celestial heathens in your place anyway, Stone? It ain't right, is it, folks?"

There was a roar of "No!" behind him, and he grinned like a cat who had just caught the world's fattest rat.

Stone turned a malevolent stare on Boyd. The gunman's face was still a blend of mottled purple, flat yellow and shimmering blue. "Seems to me," the big bartender said, with a grin, "that you're a fine one to talk about the color of a man's skin, seein's how you look."

There were several chuckles from the crowd, and Stone thought Boyd might have flushed in embarrassment and anger. But it was hard to tell, with Boyd's face as colorful as it was.

"You can't get out of answerin' to the people of Tall Pine for this, Stone," Boyd said haughtily. "It goes against all reason."

"Didn't know you had any, Boyd."

"What?"

"Reason." Stone surveyed the crowd for a moment. "Now all of you listen to me. This here clod"—he pointed to Boyd—"ain't doin' nothin' but tryin' to stir up trouble where there ain't any. I don't like it, and you ought not to be listenin' to him."

He saw no reason to try to explain to this rabble that the mob killing of one of the Chinese was what led to this, and more mob rule would only worsen matters. Most of the people in Tall Pine were bigoted against the Chinese, but not usually willing to go out of their way to cause those people undue trouble. Only when some fool like Boyd got them worked up were they of a mind to cause trouble.

"This here is my saloon," Stone roared. His face was hard, and he looked like a towering, angry god of ancient Rome. "I'll let in it anyone I damned well please. Right now it suits me to serve beer to a bunch of Chinese. Any of you want to join us, I'll be happy to serve you, too. Any of you don't like that idea, you're invited to go on down to the Verde Saloon."

The Verde Saloon, at the south end of town, was an odorous place with a nasty owner. The place was never clean, the few girls who worked there were shabby, the drinks were watered down, and the small regular clientele was unpleasant.

Hunter stood inside, listening. He was impressed by Stone's words, but two things bothered him: One was that Sheriff Webster was standing near his office, watching, but not doing anything. The other was something Hunter could not put his finger on.

After a few minutes, it dawned on him. He saw only three of Boyd's cronies. There should've been one more. He realized the other could have gone off on his own or been shot, or maybe was just lying drunk somewhere. But Hunter didn't think any of those things likely.

He stuck his head over the top of the swinging door and peered left, then right. As Stone continued trying to disperse the crowd, Hunter kept up his vigil.

"But let me warn you folks that this ain't gonna end here," Stone said. "The Chinese ain't happy that you fools killed Jimmy Wing. They might think to start demandin' some rights."

"Chinee got no rights, Stone," Skagg said.

"*You* ain't gonna have a *life* you open your flap to say somethin' stupid again."

Hunter saw Boyd's missing comrade. Barney Crane had crept around the corner of the building to Hunter's right. He was sliding slowly along with his back to the wall. He had one of his two Starr pistols in his hand, but it was not cocked. Hunter waited.

"They plannin' somethin'?" someone shouted from the crowd. The voice was nervous.

"I ain't sure. Just 'cause I let 'em in my saloon don't make me their bosom pal. But I reckon if they decided to stop doin' laundry and some of their other work, this town'd fall apart."

That set the crowd stirring. Boyd and his three companions tried to regain control of the crowd, but they were having a hard time. Most of the people had no stomach for lynchings—or for facing Linc Stone and his scattergun.

At the edge of the swinging doors, Crane stepped forward, lifting his pistol to crack Stone on the head. Hunter pushed out the door. He tried to be silent, though he supposed that with all the noise from the crowd it wouldn't matter much. As he stepped outside, he pulled his hammer from a loop in his overalls.

Just before Crane could hit Stone with his pistol butt, Hunter thumped Crane on the head with the hammer. Crane fell against Stone's broad back, startling the big bartender a little. The Starr dropped on the sidewalk and bounced into the snowy street. Crane continued falling to the side, landing heavily next to Stone on the edge of the sidewalk.

The crowd, whose view had been blocked by Stone's immense size, gasped as Hunter stepped from behind Stone, putting his hammer away. His face was tight. He knelt and pulled out Crane's other revolver. He stood, looking small next to Stone. But his face was just as determined. He put one boot on Crane and shoved, rolling him off into the street.

Boyd glared at him, hate narrowing his button eyes.

"If your folks've had your fun," Stone growled, his voice sounding like a cave-in, "go on about your business."

Stone and Hunter watched as the crowd began drifting apart. Little knots of people moved off, talking, arguing, muttering to each other.

"You saw that Webster just stood and watched without offering to help, didn't you, Linc?" Hunter asked.

"Yep. It don't surprise me none. I told you Webster's got no likin' for the Chinese."

"I learned that not long ago." Hunter pulled the caps off the Starr and tossed the gun down. It landed on Crane's stomach as Boyd, Connor, O'Rourke and Skagg arrived near their friend.

Crane was not completely out, but his eyes were glazed, and he was helpless. "Get him," Boyd snarled, and spun to walk away. As Skagg grabbed Crane's pistols, the other three hauled Crane up and started carrying him away.

"Thanks, Jake," Stone said as they turned and headed back into the saloon.

"Wasn't nothing."

"Yeah, it was."

"Nah. Hell, this's just another burr under Boyd's saddle blanket."

"Reckon' you're right." Stone stowed the shotgun away, then pulled off the shoulder holster and put that away, too. "Still, I'm obliged." He poured a beer for Hunter. "It's on the house." He got himself one and raised it in a toast to Hunter, who responded.

Crooked-Eye Sal came up, smiling. "What'd he do to make him such a hero, Linc?" she asked.

"Saved my hide. One of Boyd's boys was about to

buffalo me, when Jake here whacked him good with his hammer."

"I should've let him hit you," Hunter mumbled, embarrassed. "Wouldn't've hurt your hard head any."

Stone laughed, and Sal giggled. "And all you got out of it was a free beer?" she asked in mock horror. "See, I told you Linc was a miserly sort."

Hunter grinned, as did Stone, who took no offense.

"Well, I got something better to reward you with, if you're of a mind to," Sal said with a warm, welcoming smile.

Hunter smiled back, but said, "Reckon not right now, Sal." He felt bad. Sal was attractive, and she did know how to pleasure a man, that was sure. But now there was Li-Sung.

Sal looked surprised, almost hurt.

"I just stopped in for a beer," Hunter said hastily, not wanting to hurt her feelings. "Then I got caught up in all this. I got three days' worth of work settin' back in my shop that's got to be done today. I ain't got time for a poke."

Sal brightened a little. "Another time, then," she said, still slightly wounded.

"Yeah."

"You courtin' Joe Chang's girl finally?" Stone asked as Sal moved off toward the stairs.

"Yep." Hunter felt as though he would burst with pride and good fortune.

"Well, you old devil," Stone joshed.

Hunter made a rude noise at Stone, though he grinned.

Stone walked to the table where the Chinese still sat. "Mob's broke up," he said offhandedly. "But you boys best set a spell to make sure. And watch yourselves when you leave. I wouldn't put it past a couple of those bastards to backshoot one of you."

Wang was silent, angry, bitter that he had had to

154

come here and seek protection from this—or any—white man.

But a relieved Ching said, "Thank you, Mr. Stone."

"Sure," Stone said, with a shrug. He wandered back to the bar, confused. He had nothing against the Chinese, but he knew that if they made a habit of coming into his saloon, they would soon be his only customers.

He shrugged in his mind. If that happened, he could always pack up and head somewhere else. He was not the kind of man who worried over such things.

Hunter polished off his beer and set the mug down. "Well, see you later, Linc."

"Yeah. And, thanks again, Jake. I'm obliged to you."

Hunter shrugged and headed out.

Chapter 18

Hunter had gotten the idea for the sawmill just before Christmas. He had let it simmer past New Year's
and a couple of weeks past the day the Chinese entered
the Mogollon Saloon. There was no longer a question
that he would stay in Tall Pine—at least for a while.
He hated most of the people of the town, because of
their prejudices and their lack of feelings. But he loved
Xiang Li-Sung, and that was enough to make him stay.

He cleaned up after work each night—a habit he had
picked up from Xiang. The Chinese doctor had told
him that bathing every day was characteristic of his
people. Indeed, even the railroad workers had managed
to keep hot water going so that all could bathe after a
day of hard work. The Americans had laughed at
them, but the Chinese persevered, thinking the Americans uncouth louts.

So Hunter had picked up the habit, and found he
enjoyed it, even when the weather was cold. After
cleaning himself, he would go to the Xiang house,
where he often would eat dinner, prepared and served
by an obsequious, though beaming, Li-Sung. Her father
usually was impassive, but Hunter began to realize that
the Chinese man liked having him around, especially
after Hunter had helped Linc Stone stand up to the
mob in front of the saloon.

Xiang had some difficulties with all this. He liked Hunter, thought him a brave, stalwart, honest and hard-working young man. Still, he was not Chinese, and that troubled Xiang greatly. Xiang was torn inside himself. He was proud of his Chinese heritage, and wanted to keep it alive not only in himself, but also in his child and in any grandchildren he might be blessed with. On the other hand, he knew that to stay in this country and really make his way, he would have to adapt more to the ways of those rough-edged, heathen Americans.

The main stumbling block was that he knew, deep down, that the Americans would never accept the Chinese, no matter how much the Chinese adapted to American ways. It seemed to Xiang most times that the Americans simply refused to have any dealings with those they considered different, or worse—inferior—which was anyone who had any color to his skin.

It was a problem that was splitting the Chinese community in Tall Pine. Some wanted to fight for their rights, and become like the Americans; others wanted to retain all the old ways. Still others wanted to fade into the background, unnoticed by anyone. It led to rifts that were not always invisible to outsiders, but were real—and hurtful.

Because of his closeness with the Xiangs, and some of the other Chinese, Hunter could sense this. It was troubling to him. He loved Xiang Li-Sung, and planned to ask her to marry him, but he knew she was torn. And he liked Xiang Sen, and wanted to help his prospective father-in-law, but he did not know how. He sought solace in his work, and in his exploring of Li-Sung. Xiang tried to find answers in his copy of the Confucian book *Mirror of the Mind*. But its proverbs and wisdom seemed to be failing him this time.

At times Xiang stoically accepted Hunter's presence at the house every night, knowing the young man was courting his daughter, and not liking it. After all,

Hunter was not Chinese.

At other times he was glad Hunter was there. Still, it was not his way to openly acknowledge the budding relationship.

Hunter learned to accept that in Xiang. He understood the man's torment. He also understood that his future father-in-law had accepted him in his heart, if not in the eyes of the Chinese community.

Li-Sung seemed to be mostly unaffected by the abyss within her community. She wanted to be an American—if that was what Hunter wanted. She would become Mexican, if that was what Hunter asked. She remained loyal and faithful to her father, treating him with the utmost respect, as was proper. But Hunter had taken her heart, and she was pledged to him, even if the words had not been spoken.

Once or twice a week, Li-Sung would stroll to Hunter's shop-house. She never said when she would come by; she just suddenly showed up. Hunter loved those times, and the suspense kept him in a constant state of excitement. Li-Sung knew that, and secretly enjoyed that little power she had over him.

She was troubled, sometimes, about such actions. This was not the way of her own people, nor was it the way of the Americans. But in her own study of *Mirror of the Mind,* she had come to realize that what she and Hunter had was beautiful and that they broke no laws of any deity that she could see. It soothed her most times to think that way, although at other times she was convinced she was deluding herself.

When she arrived, Hunter would shut up the shop, using a new sign he had had printed up saying "Closed for lunch. Back soon." They would retire to his small, cluttered room at the back. And there they would explore each other—their minds after their bodies.

After an hour, Li-Sung would dress, putting on a lascivious show for Hunter, until she was covered and looked perfectly demure. Then he would let her out, reopen the shop, and try to work the rest of the day with thoughts, sights, and scents of her clouding his mind.

His thinking seemed to be taken up by only two things other than Li-Sung these days. One was Boyd, who Hunter knew would be back sooner or later. He was not afraid, but he was not happy with the waiting, watching, always trying to be on guard. The other was the thought of building a sawmill.

There was, he had known since he had woken up and stepped outside in Tall Pine for the first time, an abundance of huge ponderosa pines. There were oaks and walnut trees interspersed among them, which would give him something different to use for special projects, but mostly he would use the pine. He could make cabinets and all kinds of furniture from it. And he could make planking for houses.

He could not believe someone had not done this before, not with the supply of pines in the area. It would save everyone the time and trouble of packing materials up from Mazatzal, or even as far away as Prescott or Phoenix. That and the weather had kept him from proceeding. He figured that if he had thought of it, surely someone else had, too, and failed, or there would be a sawmill in Tall Pine.

But finally he decided that he would give it a go. One morning in early February, he gathered up his courage, put on his only suit, walked to the First Union Bank of Tall Pine, and asked to see Fortney Simms, the banker.

"What can I do for you, Mr. Hunter?" Simms asked. He was tall, white-haired and courtly. His voice was stentorian, and he was every inch a banker. He also was none too thrilled to see Jake Hunter. Still, since Hunter was banking regularly, he thought it wise at least to exhibit some form of civility to the man.

159

"I'd like a loan," Hunter said, embarrassed. He had never done this before, and did not like the idea.

Simms's eyebrows rose. "Oh?" he asked, "And for what?"

"Well"—Hunter licked his lips—"I've been pretty busy in the shop, and all. And, well . . ." He took a breath and plunged. "I figured what we really needed here is a sawmill. . . ."

Simms did an excellent job of covering his surprise. It was a good idea, he thought. Now all he had to do was reject Hunter's request, lend himself the money instead, have it built and hire someone to run it for him. He could make a fortune. Besides, he'd be damned if he'd loan money to this Chinese-loving newcomer.

"I reckon that with a sawmill, I could do even better," Hunter said. "I could pay you back pretty quick and all."

"Hmmm," Simms said, in a thoughtful manner. "And just how would you power this sawmill, Mr. Hunter?"

"Well, I thought . . ." Suddenly Hunter clamped his lips shut. He was suspicious. He wasn't sure why. Simms hadn't asked anything out of the ordinary, nor had there been anything in the banker's manner to tip him off. He suddenly just got gun-shy about saying too much. Maybe he was just nervous about the whole thing. He was no fool; he would watch what he said.

"I ain't sure yet," he said lamely, though trying to sound convincing. "I figured that once I got the money, I'd head off somewhere I could get what I needed, and see what was offered. That might make my determination. I got some ideas, but, well . . ." He shrugged.

"I understand," Simms lied blandly. "Well, how much do you need, do you think?"

Hunter gave him a figure he thought would be enough to meet all needs, and yet not break him if things took longer than he figured to get going.

"Not an unreasonable amount," Simms said. He steepled his fingers in front of his face, and sat in deep thought. *Not at all unreasonable,* Simms thought. *But give yourself maybe twenty percent more, to ensure all goes well.*

"Indeed," he finally said, "not at all unreasonable."

Hunter felt excitement growing inside as he thought he was about to achieve his goal.

"But, even so, I'm afraid I must deny your request." Simms looked as sympathetic as he could manage. It wasn't much, especially with the gray, bristling eyebrows, deep-buried eyes and almost cadaverous face with the large white muttonchops.

Hunter was shocked. "Why?" he asked, growing angry.

"Several factors are involved here, Mr. Hunter," Simms said. He thought perhaps he had gone too far. One never knew with someone like Hunter.

"Like?" Hunter's face was hard and unforgiving.

"Well," Simms said unctuously, "for one thing, I assume you have no collateral. If you do, you have not mentioned it, and I know of no holdings you have."

"My shop and house," Hunter said shortly. "And there'd be the sawmill itself."

"Indeed." Simms sniffed, almost offended. "And how am I to know that you won't take the money, say you are riding to Mazatzal to get the equipment you will need, and just keep riding? Oh, no, Mr. Hunter. I have investors and depositors to think about. They have entrusted me with their hard-earned monies, and I must see they are safeguarded."

"But the shop . . ."

"Not enough."

"Supposing I come up with some collateral?" He had no idea of how or where he could do that, but he wanted to miss no chance.

"Well, there are other factors. You haven't been around Tall Pine long. And your arrival, as well as

161

your early accommodations here, were, shall we say, less than . . ." He paused, searching for the right word. ". . . auspicious." That might not be the word he wanted, but the exact word might set Hunter to raving, for all he knew.

"Auspicious?" Hunter questioned, surprised. "I was brought in unconscious. I . . ." He stopped and glared. "Oh, I see," he muttered.

"Indeed," Simms said, his voice oily.

Hunter stood, his face red from his rising temper. "Well, good day, Mr. Simms," he said, with tightly controlled anger.

"I'm sorry," Simms lied, standing and extending his hand.

"Sorry, my butt," Hunter snarled, ignoring the hand.

Simms blanched and his hand fell to his desk. "Well, then," he said, highly offended, "I would think our business is concluded."

"For now," Hunter threatened. He would, he decided, get back at Simms. He didn't know how, but he would think of something. He stalked out, fuming, and went catty-corner across the street toward the Mogollon Saloon. He would, he told himself angrily, build this sawmill—and stay in Tall Pine. He was tired of these people and their behavior. But the more they tried to bother him, the more stubborn he would become. He would not let them drive him out.

"Whoa, boy," Stone said jovially, slapping a mug of foamy beer on the bar. "You look like you just tangled with a cougar and got whupped good."

Hunter poured a goodly portion of the beer into his gullet in one shot. "Hell," he muttered.

"What in hell's eatin' at you, Jake?" The saloon was nearly empty, so he had plenty of time to chat. And even if he hadn't, he would've taken the time for a friend.

Reluctantly at first, but gathering steam, Hunter told

162

him about his idea for the sawmill. "That damned Simms won't lend me the money."

"I ain't surprised," Stone said. "He tell you why?"

"Said I had no collateral. But worse'n that, he gave me some booshwa about not having been here long enough, and because I lived with the Chinese for a spell."

"He said that?" Stone asked, eyebrows raised.

"Not in words. But there was no mistaking his meaning."

"You are a damn fool every now and again," Stone said, with friendliness.

"What's that supposed to mean?" Hunter asked sourly, finishing the mug of beer.

Stone got him another, and a shot of whiskey to go with it. "You should've come to me first off."

It was Hunter's turn to be surprised. He stopped with the shot glass halfway to his lips. "What?" he asked.

"Drink that shot before you spill the damn thing."

Hunter did as he was told, and Stone poured himself a shot and a beer. "Look, Jake, you helped me out of a tight spot last week with that mob. I don't reckon it would've gotten ugly enough for me to get really hurt, but at least a couple of them Chinese would've gotten strung up if those idiots outside had gotten past me. That's what I figure they were gonna do with Crane whacking me over the head. But you stopped that — at considerable risk."

He paused to chug down the shot and chase it with a mouthful of beer. "I think it's a hell of an idea. I reckon Simms does, too, knowin' that sneaky son of a bitch."

Hunter looked surprised again.

"Fortney Simms is a sly one," Stone said. "I reckon as soon as you mentioned a sawmill to him, he saw greenbacks flashin' before his eyes. If it didn't hit him then, it will have by now. A sawmill here will mean a lot to the town, and somebody as money-grubbin' as Simms can't fail to see it. I reckon he'll either give one of his cronies the money, and let them make it, or he'll lend himself the money and hire the job out."

"That son of a . . ." Hunter bit back his anger. It would do him no good. He needed clear thinking. "So what does all that mean for me?" he asked.

"I reckon I can risk some cash on such a venture," Stone said simply. "I reckon I'll get my investment, and then some, back soon enough."

Hunter thought for a few moments, sipping. Then he shook his head. "I'm obliged, Linc," he said sincerely, "but I can't be beholden to someone I consider a friend."

"Booshwa. You'll take the dimes, pledgin' me you'll pay me back, or you'll offend me to no end. And I ain't friends with folk who think so poorly of me as to do such a thing."

Hunter looked worried. "Supposing it don't make out?" he asked.

Stone shrugged giant shoulders. "Then I'll be out some *dinero*." He smiled. "But I'll still have a friend."

A grin spread slowly across Hunter's face. He stuck out his hand. "You got yourself a deal."

Chapter 19

It took only a month for Hunter to get his sawmill built and operating. He and Stone decided they should waste no time, not with the likelihood of Fortney Simms undercutting them as soon as he could.

Stone figured Simms would not do anything until spring, so he pushed Hunter into moving fast. Two days after they struck their bargain, Hunter said goodbye to Li-Sung—who was none too happy about Hunter going—and rode out on one of Stone's horses, a fine, sure-footed dun. Because of the mare's coloration, he called her Mudpie.

He left late in the day. By the time anyone realized he was gone, if anyone was interested, he would be halfway to Mazatzal.

No sooner had he hit the well-worn trail to Mazatzal, about fifty hard miles away, than it started snowing softly. He rode through the night, and by morning he was riding into the midst of a blizzard. The wind howled and tore at him and the horse, whipping the hard snow to lash at them.

Hunter stopped and tied a bandanna around the lower half of his face, and a piece of sacking around the horse's head, cutting eyeholes in the rough cloth. It was the best he could do. He thought of turning back, but decided he would be no better off that way than he would be continuing on.

He tried to follow the road, though that was difficult. He was so tired, and his strength so sapped from the weather, that he could barely keep himself in the saddle. He dozed fitfully now and again, jerking awake when he shivered, or when a strong gust smacked him.

Mudpie was wearing down, too, and Hunter was concerned for the horse. He finally pulled into a copse of thick pines. It seemed silent in the trees, compared with the open trail, since the trees cut the wind considerably. It also was a little warmer.

As he went searching for firewood—stumbling almost incoherently was more like it, he thought, in a moment of lucidity—the horse cropped at the sparse vegetation in the area. There were small pockets of brown grass protected from the snow by the thick boughs of the pines, and several types of bushes.

Hunter managed to get a fire made. He threw on bacon, a pot of beans and a pot of coffee. None of it was fully done, but he didn't care. He tore into the food like a starving grizzly, chomping down large baits of meat and beans, and sucking in long draughts of hot, not thoroughly brewed coffee.

He felt considerably better when he had finished. He unsaddled the horse, got out the feedbag, filled it with half the oats he had brought, and hung it over the horse's head. He probably should have done that when they first pulled in here, he thought, but he needed to get himself fed first, before he could take care of the horse.

He managed to stay awake long enough for the horse to munch all the oats in the feedbag. Then Hunter hobbled the horse so he could get around somewhat, and took the feedbag off so he could forage. He pulled out his bedroll, hoping it would be adequate, and spread it out near the fire. He built up the fire, rolled up in his blankets, and was asleep within minutes.

It was light when he awoke, and warmer. He lay in the blankets a few minutes, listening. It seemed the wind had died down. With renewed spirits, he rose and rekindled the fire. He made a proper breakfast of bacon and jonnycakes, ate, fed the horse more oats, and packed.

The blizzard had stopped, but the ground was covered with crystalline snow that glittered and sparkled in the sun. Hunter cut slits in the bandanna he had used on his face and put it on over his eyes to avoid snowblindness.

The deep, crusted snow made the going tough for Mudpie, but Hunter did not push him.

The rest of the trip was uneventful, if made at a crawl. In all, it took him five days to make the trip, instead of the two days it usually took.

The huge mercantile store had nearly everything he needed. What it didn't have, the owner vowed he would get in a day or two.

Hunter gave the man half the money he owed. "You'll get the rest when I get everything up in Tall Pine," he said sternly.

The store owner agreed.

"I expect everything to be delivered in four days. If it ain't there in a week, I'll be back." The merchant did not seem impressed. "And I'll bring my partner," he added. "Linc Stone."

The merchant's eyes grew big, and fear smoldered deep in them. "You'll have everything in four days," he promised.

Hunter spent the night in Mazatzal. As he was leaving town the next morning, he saw the store owner directing the loading of several wagons with the merchandise he had bought. He tipped his hat in the merchant's direction.

Four days later, the wagons rolled into Tall Pine, the merchant's son leading them. Hunter and Stone had picked their site—on Apache Street, behind Hunter's place and across from Stone's house. The mill would front on Apache Street, backed up almost against the mountain—the one which lifted Fool's Trail up toward the Mogollon Rim.

Hunter spent the next two weeks directing the building, fitting and gearing up of the sawmill. He hired several townsmen for construction but had trouble finding enough, so he went to Xiang and asked for help finding Chinese workers. He did, but because of it some whites quit. A few whites stayed, though, needing the money. They soon realized the Chinese were hard workers—harder than they, most times, embarrassing them. The burly Americans could no longer use the excuse that the Chinese were a burden to work with because of their size.

Many of the American workers were confused when they found it hard to hate these small, strong, industrious men after working shoulder-to-shoulder with them. How could they hate men, no matter what their color, who worked so hard for themselves and their families? They began to warm to their new co-workers somewhat, even if it did cost them some friends.

The sawmill took shape quickly, and soon the steam engine was running. It was fueled by the scraps of wood left over from construction. Barrels of water were brought up from the river in wagons and stored in a tin water tower behind the mill.

Hunter and Stone stood outside it the day after it was finished. The men from the store in Mazatzal had long before been paid and gone. The hiring had been done, and they were ready to open the mill. Soon the whine of the saw in the mill, and the rumbling of rough wagons loaded with logs heading to the mill or finished planking leaving the mill, were heard all over the town.

The hiring of millworkers had been the most interesting aspect of all this, Hunter thought. The earlier hiring for construction had assured that. He had set up at a table in back of the Mogollon Saloon. He had sent out word that he would be looking for people not only to work in the sawmill, but also up in the wooded mountains all around. He was surprised at the turnout. He figured to hire six men for the mill and six for logging, at least at first. Sixty-three men turned out, about one-third of them Chinese.

Hunter was overwhelmed by it. He sifted through some of them rather fast, knowing them unreliable for a myriad of reasons. Those he thought might have promise he asked to come back the next day. When they did, he talked to each, trying to find the man's skills, and he ended each interview by asking the whites if they minded working with Chinese, and asking the Chinese if they minded spending their workday with whites.

Eighteen answered no to the last question, and from them, Hunter picked his twelve. He told the other six that if business picked up and he needed more men to work, he would come to them first.

Over the next several weeks, Hunter began to notice some subtle changes in Tall Pine. Just little things at first, but progress nonetheless. There seemed a minute lessening of tension between the white and Chinese quarters. Tensions were still high, and in some cases even exacerbated, as loyalties and thinking shifted.

There were many, on both sides, who retained their bigotry, unwilling to give it up. But the workers in the sawmill ignored those people, for the most part. They got along well at work, though there was little socializing after hours. Even that began to change as more of the Chinese workers took to spending time in the Mogollon Saloon with their white co-workers.

The millworkers' ties grew closer. And several times, after the mill opened, they banded together and fought with bigoted townspeople in the streets after swallowing enough insults.

Hunter precipitated such a brawl as he was leaving the Mogollon Saloon one day. He had started taking his lunches there often, as did most of the millworkers. Seeing the interest, Stone had hired a cook. Hunter left there one afternoon and was strolling back toward his shop when he heard a man he knew only as Digger Mike insult Wei Pang, a friend of Li-Sung's. Wei Pang was about the same age as Li-Sung and quite attractive. But it did not matter to Hunter that she was comely. She could have been old and wrinkled, hunchbacked or otherwise deformed. Hunter would not have suffered those insults to any woman.

The woman had kept on walking, but Hunter could tell by her stiff back and flushed face that she was hurt and afraid. "I suppose," Hunter said quietly to Digger Mike, "that you think you're the height of humor, eh?"

"What the hell do you care, Hunter?" Mike snapped. "She ain't nothin' but one of them yellow fillies. All of 'em's whores. It's why the Chinamen bring 'em over here. Hell, ain't no Chinee man gonna want to marry one. That's why they're always tryin' to get white women."

Hunter was stunned by the man's overt stupidity. He knew it was no use arguing, so he did the next best thing. He punched Digger Mike in the face, knocking him against the wall of the saloon.

"What the hell was that for?" Mike muttered, rubbing his jaw. "Good Lord, Hunter, you gone *loco?*"

"I don't expect that at your age—and with your lack of sense—you can learn anything, Mike, but I'd advise you to watch your tongue around women."

"What women?" Digger Mike asked, bewildered. He looked up the street, surprised. "You mean that yellow bit . . ."

Hunter's fist in his mouth prevented Mike from finishing that sentence. Mike hit the wall and bounced off, straight into a right cross from Hunter. That knocked him sideways. He didn't fall, but he was wobbly. Hunter moved in to finish Mike off. Then he was grabbed from behind and flung off the sidewalk into the street. He landed hard, grunting.

The next thing he knew he was in the middle of a pack of howling men trying to whale the tar out of him. He fought like a crazy man, lashing out with feet and fists and knees and elbows. He bit one man, sending him yelping off, and jammed a thumb into another's eye. But he went down under a wave of bodies, and he knew he was done for.

That did not stop him, though, as he continued to fight, flat on his back. He managed to land several good punches, not even really seeing any of the faces of those attacking him. They were just a blur of drab coats, hard fists and dull faces.

It seemed after a few minutes that he was making some headway. Fewer bodies were crowding him, and he was able to land more punches. Then he heard a bellowing, somewhat akin to an enraged buffalo bull: "Get the hell off him, you . . . goddamn . . . no-good . . . mean-spirited, ill-bred . . ."

Stone seemed incapable at the moment of finishing a sentence, as he picked men up bodily and flung them away like used sacking.

Hunter almost laughed, but at the moment he was too interested in cracking an elbow against some rotted teeth he saw hanging over him. The man groaned and fell off to the side.

Suddenly Stone's huge face loomed into Hunter's vision, and with a great deal of relief Hunter realized there were no more fists or feet trying to thump him.

"Well, you gonna just lay there *all* the day?" Stone asked, grinning.

Hunter did just that for a moment. He was having

trouble catching up on his breathing. He liked the peace and quiet, too, although the frozen ground was letting a chill creep through his coat and into his back. "Reckon I just might, Linc. Why? You got something else in mind?"

"Well, I like keepin' the streets out in front of my saloon free of litter. It's what I was doin' here a moment ago. Thought I was done, but I reckon I can find the strength to remove one more piece of booshwa."

Hunter believed him. The bartender was standing there, not even breathing hard, in his shirtsleeves and apron. "Reckon I've had enough of a nap," Hunter said, standing and brushing off the snow. He touched his lip and came away with blood. He did the same with his nose. "Lord, Li-Sung ain't going to be happy with this at all," he said.

"She'll forgive you," Stone laughed.

"Reckon so. Thanks, Linc."

"None needed. You would've done the same for me. You did, in fact, if you can remember back a couple weeks. Though at your advanced age, that might be a chore."

Hunter made a rude noise in Stone's direction.

"Come on back in the saloon," Stone said. "I'll have Crooked-Eye fix you up. Unless you'd rather someone else did it. I can send somebody to get Li-Sung, if you'd like."

"Sal'll do, if she don't mind."

"She won't."

Hunter was sitting in a chair in the saloon, with Sal working over him with water and some kind of disinfectant that stung, when Sheriff Webster came in and pulled up a chair near him.

"I told you a while back, Hunter," he said, without preliminary, "that I wasn't gonna allow no brawlin' and such in the street. Especially not when it concerns them damn Celestials. I reckon I got no choice but to take

172

you in this time for precipitatin' that set-to out there."

"Rattle your hocks, Sheriff. I got no time for dealing with an oaf like you."

Webster looked as if he was going to bust a vein. "I'll use my persuader, if I have to." He tapped the Colt on his hip.

Stone stomped up behind the lawman and rested the muzzle of a scattergun on his right shoulder, edging far enough ahead so that Webster could see what it was. "You pull that Colt and I'll make sausage of your head."

"I'll have you arrested for this, Stone."

"I'm quakin' in my boots. Digger Mike started all this. You want to arrest somebody, arrest him. But you leave me'n Jake alone from now on. I don't even want to see your ugly puss around here. We'll take care of our own affairs from now on. Now git your butt out of my saloon."

Webster glared at Hunter, who grinned back ingratiatingly. Then the lawman got up stiffly and left.

Chapter 20

Hunter slept better now, knowing Li-Sung was truly his. He had even mentioned marriage. She was willing, but she told him to wait; she wanted things to settle down in Tall Pine before proceeding. And Hunter was, he had to admit, still quite tied up in the mill and getting it operating, as well as in his carpentry work.

So it was unusual that the muffled thump woke him in the middle of the night four days after the brawl with Digger Mike. It had not been that loud.

He got up, figuring he might as well use the time constructively and go make water. He stuffed his feet into boots and threw on his coat over his nightshirt.

It was March, and occasionally the days had a little warmth to them, but the nights were still well below freezing. He went out the door on the side away from Apache Street and headed toward the outhouse several yards away.

There was another roar, louder this time. The shock of the blast momentarily stunned him. Pieces of wood began to settle on him. By the time he recovered and realized it was a blast at the sawmill, the mill was in flames. "Lord, no," he gasped, seeing his future going up with the bright flames. He headed, running, across the street, slipping on the snow and ice.

But Stone was awake and had come out on his

porch. He assessed the situation in seconds. He reached back inside and grabbed a shotgun from next to the door. At the edge of the porch he fired off both barrels of the gun, aiming so he would hit neither his porch nor anyone's house. "Fire!" he roared, in a voice that would wake the occupants of Boot Hill.

Lanterns began to flick on at houses. "Fire!" Stone roared again, rattling the glass in his own windows.

Hunter swerved toward the mill. Stone caught up with him seconds later. By the time they reached the mill, people in various states of dress were streaming up Apache Street toward the mill. A few Chinese mingled with the Americans as lines formed.

Stone yanked the mill doors open and grabbed the tongue of a wagon. Hunter took a spot right behind him, and the two yanked and pulled. The heat inside was intense, and they thought they might choke on the clouds of smoke. There was a gaping hole in the back from one explosion, and another hole in the north side.

The wagon began to move. Once it was rolling, it was easy to haul it along. They got it outside and out of the way, and raced back for another, without respite.

A bucket brigade was operating smoothly. Several men stood with large double-bit axes and chopped at one of the great mounds of snow piled up near the back of Hunter's house. Others started the buckets going by scooping up the loosened snow. The buckets were passed until slush was tossed onto the flames.

It was impossible to save the building, but Hunter and Stone managed to get all the wagons out, as well as some of the other equipment and lumber. The bucket brigade had worked fairly well, with the people tossing their slushy ice water on or near the giant main saw and the two smaller saws. It would, they hoped, keep the wood framework of those vital pieces of equipment from burning down. It worked.

By dawn, dozens of weary men and women were

trudging back toward their homes. The sawmill building lay in smoldering piles. Hunter and Stone, both near exhaustion, stood and looked over it sadly.

"Well, don't you fret, Linc," Hunter said, with a sigh. "I'll still pay you back every penny. It might take a spell longer'n I figured, but you'll get all your money back." The depression sat heavy in him.

"I sure as hell will," Stone growled. "With a new sawmill." He grinned.

"This ain't the time for joshing, Linc," Hunter said irritably.

"I ain't joshin', Jake."

"We ain't got the dimes for a new mill."

"Hell, we got most of the big equipment. We need a few things we'll need to get from Mazatzal. And a new building. We got enough plankin' layin' around to almost get it done. We get a frame on there and then a roof, and we can use the big saw to get whatever other lumber we need for it."

"Still, it's a big investment we lost, and I can't ask you to put up more money for whatever replacement equipment we'll need."

"You ain't asked me," Stone growled. "Now go home and get some rest."

That was easier said than done, since he tossed and turned, worried. But eventually he drifted off, and his sleep was filled with dreams of fires in which dollar bills were burning by the hundreds. He awoke stiff and unrefreshed.

He went to the saloon for some food. Stone was there, as jovial as ever. Two well-dressed Chinese were sitting at a large table to one side and, only a little surprisingly these days, the rest of the place was filled with whites. There had been a little trouble when the Chinese workers from the mill first started coming to the saloon, but Stone had quickly put a stop to the name-calling and challenges by thumping the bejesus

176

out of four men at once. He lost a few of his white customers because of his new policy, but he did not mind.

The other whites had felt funny at first, coming into a saloon that allowed Chinese, but then they decided it was not the end of the world. Mainly, they just ignored the Chinese.

"Afternoon, partner," Stone said, with his usual good humor.

"Bah."

"Beer?"

"Coffee. And something to eat."

"Comin' up." His grin looked like the Grand Canyon.

"What'n hell are you so damn cheerful about?" Hunter groused.

"I told you this mornin' things'd work out, didn't I?"

"Yeah. So?" Hunter said, interested.

"Well, they have. Come on, let me introduce you to someone." As he came out from behind the bar, he whispered something to one of the Hawes brothers, who headed toward the kitchen. Stone took Hunter to the table where the two Chinese sat. Several other Chinese, who worked at the mill, sat at another table nearby. And next to them were some of the white millworkers.

"Gentlemen," Stone said, "this is my partner, Jake Hunter. He is the one responsible for the sawmill in Tall Pine. Jake, meet Mr. Tong and his associate, Mr. Ling."

Hunter nodded at them and sat, bewildered. Tong was very old, with wrinkled skin and thick epicanthic folds around his eyes. His hair was long, thin and white, as was his drooping mustache. He wore silk clothes in the Chinese style, and gold-rimmed spectacles.

Ling was about forty, short, almost entirely bald, portly, silent, and wore a bland expression. He was well

177

dressed in a black, American-cut suit with a sharp white shirt. A bowler hat sat on the table near his left hand.

"Mr. Hunter," Tong said, in a thick Chinese accent that Hunter found hard to decipher, "I wish to thank you for your efforts on our behalf."

"What efforts?"

"The sawmill. And others. But I need not list your accomplishments."

Hunter was aware that a number of whites—including those who had worked in the sawmill—had gathered behind the two Chinese.

"We wish to repay you," Tong said. "My people have not had much desire to use the First Union Bank of Tall Pine. We prefer to keep our own counsel concerning money. Mr. Ling sees to such matters for us." Ling bowed his head once, sharply, and Tong continued. "Thus, we have a considerable amount of cash available to invest. We propose to loan you and Mr. Stone the money to rebuild your sawmill."

"Why?" Hunter asked, shocked. But he looked more alert.

"You were willing to hire my people to work there. You were able to get some of your people to work with mine without conflict. You have taken the side of my people against many who wish to see us all dead." It was said simply, in a flat, if heavily accented, monotone. But still the words had weight.

"And what do you want in return?" Hunter asked, skeptical.

"An honest return on our investment. And continued use of Chinese workers."

"He on the up-and-up, Linc?" Hunter asked, turning to look at his friend.

"I would say. Mr. Tong is sort of the head Chinese in these parts. The Chinese go to him for guidance and such. And he wouldn't be sittin' here if he didn't think

178

this was important, Jake."

Hunter nodded, relieved. Then he began to worry again. "You know, don't you, Mr. Tong, that whoever blew up the sawmill last night probably'll try it again if we rebuild?" The elongated skull nodded once. "You also realize I'll have to ride back to Mazatzal for equipment, endangering myself, and that Mr. Stone will be vulnerable to attack?"

"I have thought of all these things, Mr. Hunter."

"The most important thing, Mr. Tong," he said, afraid he might be overstepping his bounds, but needing an answer, "is have you thought of something to do about 'em?"

"Yes," He smiled. "Some of the Han workers came to me with this problem. They introduced me to some of the American men they work with. We thought on this and have come up with solutions."

He seems mighty certain of himself, Hunter thought.

"What will happen," he said in that same self-assured tone, "is this. You will be accompanied on your trip to Mazatzal by several sawmill workers—some Chinese, some Americans. The others will watch over the remains of the mill, your equipment, your shop—and Mr. Stone."

"You boys agree to that?" he asked, looking beyond the two Chinese at the table to the men—white and yellow—behind. All nodded.

The cook slapped a plate of eggs and beefsteak in front of Hunter, along with a pot of coffee and a mug.

Hunter nodded thanks and looked at Stone. "That suit you, Linc?" he asked.

"Yep," Stone said, without hesitation.

"I accept your offer, Mr. Tong," Hunter said. He dug into his breakfast.

Tong nodded, looking pleased. He sipped some tea. "One other thing, Mr. Hunter?"

"Yeah?" Hunter asked, around a mouthful of half-

179

raw steak. It was too bad, he thought, that Stone hadn't thought to hire a *good* cook when he hired a cook.

"When I was approached by the Chinese workers in the mill, I agreed to help. Since then, other people have let it be known that they would like to help in this enterprise."

"Who? And how?"

"A number of people, both American and Chinese. A number have expressed interest in working at the mill later."

"You mean they help us now, and I hire 'em when the mill's open again?"

"Yes. But not right away. All understand the mill must make a profit before more money can be put out. They will wait."

"Good. How are they going to help now?"

"They will help the others in ensuring the safety of you and Mr. Stone."

Hunter shrugged. "Reckon I don't mind that."

"Done, then." Tong stood and left, with Ling following.

Hunter looked up at the men still there. "You boys might be getting in over your heads. But if you plan to go, I'm leaving at dawn. Can you get 'em horses if they need 'em, Linc?"

"Yep."

Chapter 21

It took only two weeks to get the sawmill operating again. Hunter had made his journey—in a large wagon, surrounded by hard-looking men—with a feeling of safety.

The mercantile store owner had almost choked when Hunter had come into his place with eight armed men—five white and three Chinese. He figured he had done something wrong, somehow, and Hunter was coming back for retribution. He was greatly relieved when Hunter explained what had happened and then bought several hundred dollars more in equipment.

When Hunter and his men got back to Tall Pine, he was delightfully surprised to see that the men left behind had made deep inroads into the rebuilding by clearing out the debris of the old mill and starting work on the new one.

"You find out anything on who might've done this, Linc?" Hunter asked right after getting back. Both suspected Quint Boyd and his men, but they could not prove it.

"Nothin' that'd put anybody away. But it was Boyd, sure as hell. He and his boys been runnin' around town, laughin' it up over our 'misfortune.' Seems they're gloatin' over what happened. I reckon Boyd thinks it's a real hoot."

"Webster been any help?"

"What do you think?"

"Just wanted to know for certain. I wasn't really counting on him for any help."

"Neither am I. But we got to do something, Jake."

"We will. But I reckon I need more proof that somebody's guilty. Just 'cause Boyd and his cronies have been pokin' fun at what happened, don't prove they did it."

Stone understood the reasoning, and mostly agreed with it.

The work on the sawmill went quickly and smoothly, and once the mill was operating again, Hunter hired half a dozen more men. He wasn't sure he could use them in the mill, or even to supply wood, but he wanted people on guard, in case someone got the notion to dynamite the place again.

Hunter gave them their orders separately by teams — one American and one Chinese. This way no one knew when anyone else was on duty, and it also allowed him to take a turn at it himself.

Hunter was prowling inside the mill alone on the fourth night after it reopened when he heard something toward a back corner, outside. He hurried to the back there, silent. With ear pressed against the inside of the back wall, then the side wall, he heard voices, but he could not distinguish what they were saying. Then he smelled coal oil.

He turned and ran for the front, quietly, his Springfield in hand, and let himself out a side door near the front. The night was frigid, and his breath frosted in the air. There was heavy cloud cover.

Hunter slipped along the wall to the back and moved silently along that wall. As he drew near the corner, he could hear three — at least he thought it was three — men talking quietly. He thought he recognized Oakley Skagg's voice, but he was not sure. He moved away from the building to the jagged line of boulders near the foot of the steeply rising hill behind the sawmill.

Just after he got to the rocks, three men came around the corner of the building to the back. One held several glass bottles, and another held what looked to be several sticks of dynamite. The third held one jar, the contents of which he was pouring onto the wood wall of the sawmill. He finished and tossed the bottle, laughing a little when it broke. He took another from the man holding the supply and went back to what he was doing.

The clouds broke a little, and in the light of the half-moon Hunter thought he recognized Oakley Skagg, Barney Crane and Dolph Connor. In the darkness he could not be sure; he thought it possible that he might want to see those three.

He slid the Springfield rifle up over the boulder, aimed at the one holding the jars, and fired. A moment later, when the powder smoke had cleared, Hunter saw that one of the three men was down. The other two were hightailing it toward Mogollon Street. Hunter sat patiently. He reloaded the Springfield and waited. He wanted to see if the man on the ground was faking. He also wanted to see if the others returned.

He heard some people come out of their houses and inquire among themselves about the gunshot. But no one came near the sawmill to investigate, and within minutes the town was quiet again. The silence was broken only by the barking of dogs and the dull groan of the occasional wind.

The hole in the clouds closed up again, and the night grew colder. A chill drizzle began, and Hunter hunched his shoulders against it.

After an hour, Hunter finally moved. He stood, his legs numb from all the squatting, and walked slowly toward the body, which was still lying on its face. He got a boot under the chest and shoved, rolling the body over, then Hunter knelt next to it and looked. Most of Dolph Connor's forehead was gone from where the ball had exploded out the front of the head.

Hunter nodded. He was not happy about this, but neither was he bothered. He grabbed the shoulder of Connor's coat and rolled the body back the way it had originally fallen. The smell of coal oil was thick in the air. Hunter hoped the rain and sleet that were falling would dilute the coal oil enough to make it nonflammable, or if the building did catch fire, he hoped the precipitation would stop it before it got out of hand. With an itch of worry, he left the sticks of dynamite where they were.

Hunter went back behind the boulder and crouched uncomfortably in the chilling drizzle, waiting to see if the other two men would be back. If they were Skagg and Crane, as he thought, he figured they would not be.

He was right. When dawn began breaking, Hunter hurried home. Inside, he got out of his wet clothes, dried by the fire, and dressed warmly. He cleaned, dried, and reloaded the Springfield and set it on its hooks over the door. He was drinking his second cup of hot coffee when he heard the commotion at the sawmill. He knew Connor's body had been found. He smiled. With only a small sense of guilt, he went to breakfast at the Mogollon Saloon and told Linc Stone what had happened.

"Maybe this'll make Boyd and his pals cool their heels," Stone said, without conviction.

"I hope so. But I'd not wager the food money on it."

As Hunter left the saloon, a nervous Sheriff Webster approached him. "Sheriff," Hunter said, stiffly polite, touching the brim of his hat.

"Can I have a word with you, Mr. Hunter?" Webster asked.

"Reckon so. Long's we stay under the roof so we're

184

out of the rain."

"We found a body near the sawmill this mornin'."

"Oh?" Hunter asked. "Tell me about it."

"Thought you might know."

"How would I?" Hunter asked flatly.

Webster shrugged. "Half his face was shot away."

"Know who it was?" Hunter asked, knowing that Webster figured he was involved and was hoping Hunter might trip himself up.

"Dolph Connor," Webster said, after a moment.

"Pity," Hunter said, without feeling. "You have any idea what he might've been doing by my sawmill?"

"Thought you might be able to tell me."

"If I was to guess," he said tartly, "I'd say he was up to no good. Like maybe trying to blow up my sawmill again."

"Why would you say that?" Webster probed.

"Sheriff, you know well's I do that Boyd and his cronies dynamited the sawmill. If you don't know it, you're dumber'n I ever thought you were. Now we're back in business, it don't seem unlikely they'd try again."

"Why?"

"You'd be a heap better off askin' that of Boyd. You got any more damnfool questions?"

"Reckon not." Webster did not look happy. In fact, he looked as though his stomach was terribly upset.

"Then I'll be going about my business. But I expect you, as sheriff," Hunter said harshly, "to try to find out who it was blasted the mill. And what Connor was doing at my sawmill that was bad enough to get himself killed."

"I'll do what I can," Webster said lamely.

"I bet," Hunter muttered as he headed up the street.

Hunter's sleep was troubled that night, and he awoke shortly before dawn. What sleep he had gotten did not seem to have helped much. It was very cold in the

185

room, and Hunter shivered as he built up the fire in the small Franklin stove. After it was going, Hunter threw on pants, boots, gloves and heavy coat.

He stepped outside into the predawn darkness. The wind whistled around the corner of the house, and he estimated the temperature at zero or lower. An odd creaking sound cut through the soughing of the wind. Hunter could not figure out what it was, and finally he put it down to the overworkings of a burdened mind.

He headed for the privy that stood under the large oak tree just where the Fool's Trail started its rise. And he almost walked into the body hanging from the tree.

"Lord," he muttered, looking up. The wind had twisted the body around, and its swinging had made the rope creak.

Hunter hurried to the outhouse, his need to go urgent. When he finished, a faint pinkish-gray was coloring the high country to the east. He walked to the body. In the fractional light, Hunter saw that the body was of a Chinese man he knew only slightly. His name was Fu Shun.

Fu's hands were tied behind his back. As the body twisted, Hunter noticed that both Fu's ears had been slicked off, as had his long pigtail. The pigtail was lying in the splotches of frozen blood on the ground. The body, too, was frozen in the frigid air, the head at an odd angle, where it had been snapped by the rope.

Hunter stood for a moment, listening to the sighing of the wind and the sad creaking of the hemp rope. A dog barked somewhere. With a cold rage lying in his belly like a rock, Hunter got a ladder from the shed.

Across the street, Linc Stone came out of his house. As he always did these days, he glanced toward Hunter's place to see that all was well. Dawn had broken, and despite the mist, Stone could see the oak tree. He was shocked when he saw the body dangling from it.

Stone hurried over and grabbed the legs as Hunter climbed the ladder and cut the rope.

"You know who did this?" Stone asked, as he gently set Fu's body on the ground.

"I can guess," Hunter said, in a voice as cold as the morning.

"We gonna do somethin' about it?"

"I am."

Stone didn't want to argue. He figured he'd see some action sooner or later. "What's your plan?"

"Ain't got one yet. But I will."

That afternoon, long after Fu's body had been taken to the mortuary, and after Hunter and Stone had talked, Hunter arrived at the Xiang house. He shook the rain from his hat and coat and hung them on the rack in the hall. He went into the living room with Li-Sung, nodding a greeting to Xiang.

"I got to be gone a few days, Li-Sung," he said, as they sat on a divan. She looked worried. "Shouldn't be more than two days. Three or four at most."

"What . . . ?"

"I can't tell you. But I'll be leaving as soon as I can. However," he added, clearing his throat, "there was something I wanted to ask of you and your father before I left."

Li-Sung's eyes gleamed brightly in the lantern light. Xiang looked as he always did, though he was sure the man tensed up.

"Xiang Li-Sung," Hunter said, with feeling, "I'd like you to become my wife. We've talked about it before, I know. But you never said yes or no directly. I'd like to make it official, if you're willing. And I'd like to have your father's blessing."

"I accept," Li-Sung said firmly, without hesitation. "Father?" She and her fiancé turned toward the older man.

"I cannot say no." He tried to smile, but managed

only a slight lifting of his upper lip.

Li-Sung smiled enough for the two of them, and when Hunter added his grin, it was positively brilliant in the room. Hunter stood. "Well, I've got to go, Li-Sung."

She nodded and walked out to the foyer with him. "You are leaving soon?" she asked.

"I was planning on it."

"You do not have perhaps an hour . . . ?"

"I reckon I can manage that."

An hour and twenty minutes later, Li-Sung slipped out of Hunter's house and headed home.

Hunter had to work at it, but he finally forced his mind away from the delights of Xiang Li-Sung and back to his plan. He packed saddlebags and a canvas pouch, and went down to the livery, where he saddled Mudpie. He rode south, out of town.

Two miles away, he pulled off the road and wound into the forest toward the mountainside. He found a cave, gathered firewood, made a fire, cooked and ate. He and the horse were warm, reasonably comfortable and secure in the cave.

Chapter 22

Just after dark, Hunter kicked out his fire and bundled up. He saddled the horse and headed toward town. Just before Verde Street, he cut into the pines and worked around until he was behind most of the buildings on the east side of Tall Pine. Again the night was covered with clouds, and drizzle spat down intermittently. But Hunter wore longjohns, thick wool shirt, heavy wool pants, two pairs of socks under his boots, a scarf wrapped around his head from top to bottom, covering his ears, and a hat, heavy coat, and thick leather gloves. He was warm enough.

He knew Boyd and his men always stayed at the Ponderosa Boardinghouse. Hunter stopped near the privy behind the rooming house, hoping the outlaws were there, and not in the Verde Saloon.

Two cold hours later, Barney Crane strode out of the boardinghouse, heading for the privy. Hunter slipped into the two-holer without being seen, and stood, knife in hand, in a corner.

The door opened and Crane entered, carrying a lantern, which he set between the two holes. He urinated with a great sigh, and then a loud breaking of wind. He refastened his trousers and turned, reaching for the lantern; he stopped when he saw Hunter.

"You've overstayed your welcome, Crane," Hunter said calmly.

"What do you want with me, Hunter?" Crane asked roughly.

"Just to pay back what I owe."

"Eh?"

"Didn't your mama ever tell you you shouldn't play with dynamite?"

Crane's right hand was on the lantern handle; the other started reaching for a Starr revolver.

Hunter grinned viciously. He took one step forward and jolted Crane with an uppercut from his left hand. The punch snapped Crane's head backward, exposing his throat. Hunter's right hand flashed up and across before Crane could draw his revolver. Suddenly a gaping slit appeared bloodily in Crane's neck.

Crane choked, still trying to draw the Starr with his left hand. His right hand dropped the lantern handle and flew to his bloody throat. He fell back against the side wall of the privy, then slid down it until he was sitting on the dirt floor.

Hunter knelt over Crane and wiped the blade of the knife on Crane's coat. Crane lived, but had no strength left, as his blood flowed out onto his chest.

Hunter slid the knife away. He cracked the door open, peered around and then stepped into the night.

Hunter was back in Tall Pine the next night, hiding in the shadows behind the Ponderosa Boardinghouse.

After dispatching Crane the night before, Hunter had ridden back to the cave. There he rekindled the fire, fed Mudpie and cooked a good meal of mutton and biscuits. He slept long, waking well after dawn. He stayed in the area during the day, hardly venturing out of the cave; he napped occasionally, wanting to be ready for his duties of that night.

Under cover of darkness again, he rode into Tall Pine. It was rather warmer than the night before, about freezing, and the drizzling had let up during the day. It was darn near pleasant, Hunter decided.

He decided that Boyd's men were still at the boardinghouse, and so he stationed himself near the privy again. More than an hour later, Oakley Skagg arrived. He scurried toward the outhouse, lantern in hand, like the rat he resembled. Hunter barely had time to get inside the privy and flatten back against the wall when Skagg burst in, almost breathless. He had to make water so badly that he was lucky to get his pants unfastened before the flow started.

Hunter waited until Skagg was done and buttoning his pants. Then he moved forward, silent as death. He grabbed Skagg's greasy long hair in his left hand and yanked backward, whipping the right hand—with the knife—around until the blade rested on Skagg's adam's apple.

"Goodbye, Rat," he whispered, just before slicing Skagg's throat.

A font of blood spurted out and splattered the back wall of the privy. Skagg shivered and shook in a dance of death while Hunter held him up. Then Hunter released the little rodent-faced man, shoving him as he did. The man's face smacked the wall and he slid down it, face hanging half into the hole of the privy.

In a few seconds, Hunter had cleaned his knife on Skagg's coat and was riding the dun horse toward the cave.

Two more nights he waited in the dark outside the boardinghouse, but to no avail. Neither Boyd nor O'Rourke showed themselves, and he finally reasoned that they had left town. Still, Hunter harbored no delusions: They would be back.

The next morning, tired after only a short nap in the cave, Hunter rode back into Tall Pine and turned Mudpie in at the livery. Taking his saddlebags, Springfield and pouch, he stopped by the Mogollon Saloon for breakfast, then went home.

He was just finishing his shave, specks of soap on his face, razor with a clump of hairy shaving soap on it, when there was a knock on the shop door. He looked out. Li-Sung stood there.

He grinned and opened the door. "Sorry about the way I look, Li-Sung," he apologized. He was in stocking feet and wore no shirt. He had a towel, full of drying shaving soap, tossed over his left shoulder.

"You look fine to me," Li-Sung said.

Hunter wiped off his face, and then the razor, with the towel as Li-Sung entered. In his room at back, he tossed the cloth aside and, facing away from her, began to put on his shirt.

"That isn't necessary," Li-Sung said, smiling. She came up to him and rested her cheek on his back as she wrapped her hands around his middle. "You're cold," she said.

"You can fix that," he muttered.

"Have you heard what's happened here?" Li-Sung asked.

She and Hunter were nude, resting in the bed, the covers pulled to their necks against the chill. Li-Sung lay in Hunter's embrace, her head against the top of his chest, where shoulder and neck met.

"No," he lied. "What?"

She told him how the bodies of Crane and Skagg had been found. "It seems odd it happened just after you left. And now that it's stopped, you're back." She traced circles on his chest with a slim index finger.

"You accusing me of something?" he asked, not sure if he should be angry.

"Did you do it?" she asked, twisting so she could look at him.

192

He hesitated only a moment. She would probably find out sooner or later, anyway. If it was going to make a difference in their relationship, better she should know now, from him. He hoped their love was strong enough to withstand this.

"Yes," he said quietly.

"I thought so."

"Does it make a difference?" he asked, suddenly gripped by worry.

"Not in how I feel about you." She relaxed. "I just had to know," she said, shrugging her slim shoulders. "I'm glad you didn't lie to me. That would've been worse than what you did."

He pulled her face around so that he could kiss her. "Still willing to marry me?" he asked.

"You aren't getting away that easy."

He grinned. The smile faded when another knock came. Hunter stood and pulled on pants, a shirt left unbuttoned, and boots. He went to the door and opened it, scowling.

"I'd like a few words with you, Mr. Hunter," Webster said.

"You're getting to be worse'n a cloud of skeeters, Sheriff. Can't this wait a spell?"

"Got company?" Webster asked, trying to peer around Hunter inside the shop.

"Yep."

"Well, this here's mighty important. . . ."

"It's all right," Li-Sung said from behind Hunter. She sounded defiant.

Hunter stepped back and let Webster in. The sheriff's eyes narrowed in hatred when he saw Li-Sung. Then he just stared. The woman wore only the cover from Hunter's bed, which she held around her. She looked, Hunter thought, half-embarrassed, half-laughing, like what she was: a very beautiful, just-made-love-to

193

woman. She turned, and with incredible dignity, sashayed back into the bedroom.

"It's going to be mighty hard for you to talk with your jaw on my floor, Sheriff," Hunter said. He was proud of Li-Sung, but he was rather annoyed at having the lawman gape at her like this. If he wasn't so angry, he might have been amused at how Webster's bigotry could not stop him from staring, the lust naked in his eyes.

"Ah . . . huh?" Webster said, gibbering.

"Say what you wanted to say, Sheriff," Hunter said, moving between Li-Sung and Webster's line of vision. He heard Li-Sung giggle.

"Oh, yeah," Webster mumbled, bringing his thoughts back to the matter at hand. He sat in a chair at one of Hunter's work tables. Hunter sat at his old desk, throwing his feet up on a low railing that separated a couple of workbenches.

"It seems," Webster said, after clearing his throat, "that Barney Crane and Oakley Skagg were killed in the last couple days."

"So I heard."

Webster let that pass. He appeared to pick up some courage, saying, "I have my suspicions as to who done it."

"I reckon," Hunter said archly, "that since you're sitting here telling me this, you figure I had something to do with all this."

"It seems mighty damn suspicious that you were out of town the couple days it happened."

Hunter shrugged but said nothing. He looked bored.

"Time will tell, Mr. Hunter. If you are guilty—and I'd wager a couple months' wages that you are—then I'm gonna prove it."

"Till you do, Sheriff," Hunter said, without hint of humor, "you better keep your butt out of my path."

194

Their eyes locked; there was no friendliness lost between the men.

"I ought to arrest you right now, damnit," Webster snapped.

"You ain't got the stones, Sheriff." Hunter dropped his hand to his crotch to make sure Webster got his meaning. "You're afraid of me. Or Linc. Either way, you're all wind."

Webster stood. "I'll be watching every move you make from now on, Hunter," he said, trying to sound harsh.

"Then you're going to be mighty bored, Sheriff. Except"—he glanced toward the bedroom and then looked back at the lawman—"in a few cases. I'd invite you in to give you some pointers, but I don't expect the lessons'd take with someone with your limited capacity."

Webster flushed and headed for the door. He stopped with his hand on the latch and looked back. "By the way, Mr. Hunter, Quint Boyd and Dell O'Rourke have left town."

"So?"

"Well, if you should get into another of your murderous binges," he said in an accusatory tone, "you'll not find them around to vent yourself on."

"Well," Hunter said laconically, "should I ever have such an urge, there are other targets." He stared hard at the lawman.

Webster paled and left, slamming the door behind him. Hunter went back to Li-Sung, who said, "That man's a fool. But he's a dangerous fool."

"Dangerous?" Hunter laughed.

"He has too much hate in him. People who hate as much as he does, especially when it's blind hate, are always dangerous."

"I ain't afraid of him," Hunter said, crawling back onto the bed.

"I didn't say you should fear him. Just be wary. You

can never tell what a man like him will do."

"I'll watch it," he said seriously. Then he grinned. "But I'd much rather watch you."

"Watch me what?" She giggled.

"Watch you do anything."

"Like this, maybe?" she asked, smiling. She reached a hand toward his groin.

Chapter 23

Quint Boyd showed up in Tall Pine again four days later. He apparently had gone recruiting, since he rode into town with three new men as well as Dell O'Rourke. It was a warm day, the warmest they had had in some time. It meant that spring might be arriving within the next month or so.

Because it was a warm day, there were more people outside than was usual at this time of year. Boyd and his four companions stopped in front of the Mogollon Saloon and dismounted. After tying off their horses, they moved onto the wood sidewalk. Boyd stood on the edge, overlooking the street. The other four stood behind him, their thumbs hooked in their gunbelts.

"Fellow citizens of Tall Pine," Boyd shouted, attracting some attention. "Come on now, gather round, folks. That's right," he roared, as a crowd began to gather. "I'm lookin' for some people willin' to stand up for what's theirs, to stand up and put a stop to this creepin' yellow poison that's spreadin' over our town."

The four gunmen behind him shouted and yelled, trying to drum up support.

"This ain't your town, Boyd," someone shouted from the street.

"Who said that?" Boyd demanded. But no one in the growing crowd gathering in the middle of the street would own up to it. Boyd smiled. "Well, there's always a fool in a crowd."

Now that he had a group gathered, he figured he could whip them into a frenzy of hate against the Chinese, and anyone who dealt with the Chinese. "There's been some bad things happenin' in this town," he charged. "Yellow men trying to act like real men, bringin' their heathen, Celestial ways into your homes and stores. And now they've gone and killed two of your fellow citizens. Those boys were friends of mine — and yours. They . . ."

"Go home, Boyd," someone yelled. "Wherever that is."

Boyd looked ready to panic. He scanned the crowd. There didn't seem to be one friendly face in it. Then he noticed there were several Chinese faces amid the sea of white ones. He was confused, worried, disgusted. He found Sheriff Webster's eyes in the crowd, but the lawman looked away nervously.

"Damn," he growled. "You people'll be sorry," he shouted. "You'll learn soon enough that goin' against the good Lord's ways like you're doin' here will bring nothin' but trouble."

But people were drifting off already, bored with Boyd and his shouting. Even those citizens who still believed that the mingling of the races went against God's law seemed to have decided that living in peace with the Chinese was preferable to constant turmoil and bloodshed.

Boyd scowled and headed for his horse. There was nothing else for him to do. He could either leave and try to regroup, talk some sense into these people another time, or he could stand here shouting till he was blue in the face — with no one listening.

He spurred his horse viciously and charged out of town, the four others following in his cloudy wake.

* * *

When Hunter pushed through the doors of the Mogollon Saloon that night, the place was roaring. The girls were busy, and the gambling tables were in full swing. Most of the rest of the tables were full. The noise was horrendous, and a pall of smoke hung overhead.

Hunter was halfway across the saloon, toward the bar that ran along the back, when he spotted Quint Boyd. Anger grew, and he hesitated a step, wondering if he should try to convince Boyd to leave. He decided against it, and continued to the bar. "What're they doing here, Linc?" Hunter asked angrily, jerking a thumb over his shoulder toward Boyd and his companions.

Stone set down a mug of beer. "They're paying customers, Jake," he said, unconcerned.

"But . . ."

"I let the Chinese in here, Jake. I'll let Boyd and his cronies in. Long's they pay their way and don't cause trouble."

"But they're the ones who blasted the mill," Hunter said angrily, "and most likely lynched Fu Shun from my oak tree. Not to mention killing Jimmy Wing."

Stone grinned. "How better to keep an eye on 'em than havin' 'em right underfoot? I'm watchin' em, and so are some of the boys from the mill. This way we know right where they are and what they're doin'." He moved down the bar to serve a customer.

Hunter was angry, but he could not stay that way. He let the joy of the evening in the friendly saloon spread over him. That and the mug of beer helped him considerably.

He was even beginning to enjoy himself when Boyd pulled up next to Hunter. "Well, as I live and breathe, if it ain't the white Chinaman," Boyd said, with a forced laugh.

Hunter tensed, then relaxed. He turned sideways to face Boyd. Behind Boyd were his four henchmen. "Lord, you are dumb as a fencepost, ain't you, Boyd?" Hunter remarked. He leaned his left elbow on the bar and reached around to lift the mug of beer with his right.

"What's that mean?" Boyd asked, irritable.

"Well, it seems you never learn anything. You tried drumming up support for your booshwa with the people in town this afternoon and didn't get anywhere with it. Now you come in here—of all places—and try'n prod me into something."

"I've done no such thing," Boyd said, sounding offended and deeply hurt.

"A remark like you made ain't a good way to make friends, Boyd," Hunter said reasonably.

"Didn't say I wanted to make friends with the likes of you, Hunter." Boyd's tone hardened.

Hunter was unconcerned. Over Boyd's shoulder, beyond Boyd's companions, he could see that Stone had strapped on the Colt in the shoulder holster, and was standing, listening. He had the scattergun in hand. That had gathered attention from those drinking at the bar, and those men were now watching the exchange between Hunter and Boyd with interest. Some of the millworkers had left their tables and moved in closer, too.

"You can't have it both ways, Boyd. If you ain't trying to be friendly, then you must be trying to prod me. When you make up your mind, you let me know." Hunter calmly sipped beer, his eyes twinkling with deadly light above the glass.

"Suppose I was tryin' to call you out," Boyd managed, after some seconds of silence as he tried to think of something to say.

"Then," Hunter said with a grin, "you need to be more direct. Something like 'Hey, Mr. Hunter, I'm calling you out' usually works pretty well. If it don't, at least it doesn't confuse people—they know what you're talking about. Instead of all this pussyfooting around."

Boyd seethed. "Then let's go on outside and finish this off," he said, with a growling rasp of frustration and anger.

Almost everyone in the place was gathered in a semicircle around Hunter and the five men facing him.

"I didn't say I'd take you up on it," Hunter said, grinning. There was a small burst of laughter. "I just said it'd be more direct and folks'd know what you were jawing about." He grinned and started to lift the mug of beer to his lips.

Boyd lashed out with his left hand, slapping the mug away. The beer sprayed out of the mug as it was sailing out of Hunter's hand. The mug landed on the bar and bounced off onto the floor behind the bar. The crowd gasped, and then fell silent.

Hunter was angry, but he controlled it well, keeping a neutral look on his face. "Now," he said blandly, wiping away flecks of beer from his shirt front, "that's no way to behave in a public establishment. It shows ill-breeding and a lack of proper bringing up. Besides," he added, with a boyish grin, "it wasted half a mug of good beer."

The crowd laughed. Even two of the men behind Boyd chuckled, though they tried to stifle it.

"Reckon you owe me another, Boyd,"

Boyd moved up two steps and grabbed the front of Hunter's shirt. He crumpled it in his right fist as he hissed, "Now, you listen to me, you Chinee-lovin' bastard. I've had enough of your lip. Now you either step outside so we can finish this, or by God I'll shoot you down right here." His left hand rested on the butt of his Colt revolver.

Hunter stared dead into Boyd's eyes. His expression was calm, but inside he was like a tornado. Without seeming to move, he suddenly had the large, wicked-looking knife in his hand. It rested lightly against the inside of Boyd's wrist, where the hand gripped Hunter's shirt.

"I reckon," Hunter said, tight-lipped, "that if you'd like to keep that hand, you had better move it."

Boyd stared at him, seeing his death, or perhaps maiming, in the carpenter's eyes. He let go of the shirt, and with exaggerated gestures, he straightened it out against Hunter's chest. "Whoa, there, pard," he said, trying to sound brave, "ain't no call for gettin' unruly." He wanted nothing more than to gun Hunter down.

"I agree. Buy me another beer and we'll be square."

"Reckon not, Hunter." Boyd tried to stare the carpenter down, to no avail. "Me'n you are gonna have it out one of these days, and . . ."

"We already did," Hunter said ruthlessly. "If you recall, you tried putting spurs to me in the street not so long ago. As I recall, I whupped the snot out of you. And," he attacked, "when one of your damnfool cronies tried drawing down on me, I planted his butt in the bone orchard."

Boyd's eyes bulged, and a vein throbbed in his temple. He was close to bursting.

"Seems like I heard you lost several other boys to violence, too. Such things ought to teach you to mind your manners, eh?"

Boyd was nearly beside himself with anger. He could not speak, and his face was mottled with rage.

"Of course," Hunter dug in deeper, "I reckon someone's got as little brains as you gets frazzled real easy trying to think." He grinned, and there was a twitter of amused excitement from the crowd.

One of Boyd's men shoved forward, until he was standing next to Boyd. "You can't talk to Mr. Boyd that way, you sniv'lin' coward," he said.

Hunter stared at him a minute, the tight grin never dropping. The man was of medium height, and well-built. He was only about twenty years old, but had a hard glint to his deep brown eyes. His forehead sloped back sharply into the Stetson he wore. Thin lips were closed tightly between a sweeping hook of a nose and a pointed chin.

"And who are you?" Hunter asked.

"Name's Arliss Pettibone. I hail from Carver's Creek, Texas." He sounded proud of the fact.

"Never heard of it," Hunter said, stifling another grin. "And it's too bad that down in Carver's Crack . . ."

"Creek," Pettibone interjected.

". . . they don't teach manners. Boys should keep their mouths shut around their betters."

"You ain't my better," Pettibone snapped. "And even if you was, you ain't Mr. Boyd's better."

"Well, now," Hunter said slowly, "I just reckon I am."

"How so?"

He shrugged. "It just goes to show how much of a fool Boyd is that he hired an oaf like you to ride with him. I'd never do such a damnfool thing. Now step back, boy," Hunter snapped, voice and face suddenly growing hard with menace, "or I'll pound your butt into the floor."

"I ain't afraid of you," Pettibone sneered. He moved back a step, and loosened the small strap from the hammer of his Colt Navy revolver. His hand rested near the butt.

"Didn't say you were afraid, boy," Hunter said harshly. "Just said you were an idiot. You maybe got more stones than your boss there, but you sure ain't got no more brains."

203

"I've killed men for lesser insults," Pettibone said, trying to sound tougher than he was.

Hunter shrugged. "You're still a fool." He pointed with the knife over the young man's shoulder. Then he put the knife away.

Pettibone looked uncertain, figuring Hunter was trying to trick him. But he finally gave in and looked. Eight feet away, Linc Stone was standing, pointing the muzzles of a scattergun at him. Stone waved a beefy hand at Pettibone, who gulped and faced Hunter again.

"Now keep that flap of yours buttoned, eh?" Hunter said. He turned his attention back to Boyd. "I reckon you ought to take this riffraff and get out of here, Boyd. Me and the others appreciate your show. But I think we've had about all the humorous entertainment we can stand for one night. You might want to check, though, to see if Linc wants you to come back to do another show tomorrow. But next time, bring some dancing girls instead of these oafs."

"You're lucky," Boyd managed to sputter, "that you got that big ape back there with that scattergun. People in Tall Pine ain't gonna let Chinee-consortin' folks like you and him get away with such nonsense much longer."

"They might," Hunter said simply. "The days of living in two separate towns here in Tall Pine are over, Boyd. Folks like you can't accept that will have to move on. Most people here are decent folks and ain't about to let the likes of you go on telling 'em what to do."

"You might have 'em swayed now, Hunter," Boyd growled, angry. He itched to gun this man down, but he knew he could do nothing with Stone and his shotgun behind him. "But the tide'll turn. Soon's folks remember what those yellow heathens are really like, they'll ride you out of town."

"Until they do, I reckon you and your cronies ought

204

to make yourself scarce. Go back to robbing stage-coaches or whatever it is you do when you disappear."

Boyd was jolted. He had thought no one knew. "I ain't done no such thing," he snapped. "I ought to clout you for even sayin' such a thing."

"Have at me," Hunter sneered. "You won't have no better outcome than you did the last time. 'Course, I got no objection to exercising my fists against your face regular." He grinned insultingly.

Boyd fumed, rage making him stand there silent, stiff. The crowd began to chuckle, then started to laugh a little. Finally there were guffaws of laughter ringing Boyd and his men.

"Kick up dust, Boyd," someone shouted. It was echoed by a chorus.

Boyd's face was as red as a dusty sunset. With an animal-like growl of frustration and hurt, he shoved through the hooting, jeering crowd of men. His companions followed, embarrassed, as they headed for the door.

"You might not have to fight that punk," Stone said, moving up. He had already taken off the pistol and stowed it and the shotgun away. "You and him have a few more confrontations and he'll burst somethin' inside that'll kill him for you."

"Save me some grief if it happened that way," Hunter said, with a grin. He strolled home feeling good. With the exception of his troubles with Boyd, life was almost pleasant in Tall Pine these days. He went to sleep with thoughts of his impending marriage to Li-Sung in his mind. They had, just that afternoon, set the date—July Fourth.

He awoke to a clamor. It was still dark. Slowly the call of "Fire!" filtered its way into his consciousness. He stumbled up, fear gripping him, and managed to pull on a pair of pants. He stuffed his nightshirt in hurriedly buttoned the pants, then stuffed his feet into boots, without socks, grabbed his coat, and ran for the side door.

Outside, he was surprised when he saw no activity around the sawmill. He turned slowly, and saw an orangish glow in the sky from Chinatown. His stomach lurched and his heart crept toward his throat. *It couldn't be,* he thought. Then he ran.

Hunter's dread increased with each step, until his worst fears were realized. Xiang Li-Sung's house was burning, the flames snapping and crackling.

A bucket brigade was pouring water from melted snow and a horse trough onto the fire.

Hunter spotted Stone — easy because of the bar owner's size — and he hurried there. "You seen Li-Sung?" he asked loudly, desperately.

Stone was at the front of the house, tossing buckets of water and slush at the fire. The flames gave an eerie coloration to his face. The roaring of the fire was loud and sounded like doom to Hunter.

"No," Stone bellowed. "Her father, neither."

"Good Lord," Hunter said. He ran for the inferno.

Chapter 24

A huge hand clamped on Hunter's shoulder, slowing and, moments later, stopping him. He was barely six feet from the flaming front of the Xiang house.

"Far enough, Jake," Stone said, his voice loud enough even at normal volume to be heard over the thundering, sucking hiss of the flames.

"No!" Hunter screamed. "I got to find Li-Sung!"

"If she's in there," Stone said, trying to sound consoling even with his volume, "she ain't alive no more. Nothin' could live in there. Come away now."

He hauled Hunter away from the fire. Though Hunter fought against it, he was no match for Stone's size and strength. When they were some distance away, Hunter finally shouted, "That's far enough, Linc."

Stone stopped. "You sure?" he asked, looking and sounding skeptical.

"Yeah."

Stone released Hunter, who stood looking back toward the Xiang house. He felt a sadness so deep he didn't think he could bear it. "Maybe," he said, hope blossoming a bit, "they got out before the fire."

"Maybe," Stone said, wanting to humor his friend. He did not want to mention that if that had been the case, Xiang Sen would have almost certainly joined in fighting the fire. But Sen had not been seen.

"I got to find out," Hunter said. "I'll check with Mr. Tong and some of the others."

"You ain't gonna do nothin' stupid, are you, Jake?" Stone asked, ready to hogtie Hunter to make sure, if necessary.

"No," Hunter said. The house collapsed in on itself, sending up a spectacular eruption of sparks and flame-lit smoke. The sadness settled deep into his stomach, nesting there.

Hunter walked off, seemingly in a dream. Stone watched for a few moments before he headed back to help fight the fire. Saving the house was hopeless, but they could try to keep the flames from spreading to nearby homes.

Hunter plodded along, unaware even of the number of Americans that had come to help the Chinese. Nor would he have cared even if he had known. He found Tong and asked the old Chinese if he had seen either Sen or Li-Sung.

"No," Tong answered gravely.

Hunter nodded and moved on. He held no hope. If either Li-Sung or Sen were alive, they would have visited Tong, or someone else would have reported to him. Hunter asked several other people, knowing in advance what their answer would be.

Finally he stopped near Stone and—with the silent crowd of Americans and Chinese—watched the ruins burn down. He heard a familiar voice behind him say, "It's a pity such a thing has happened. But I warned you that bad events would be brought on by the mingling of the races."

Hunter turned. "You going to find out who did this, Sheriff?" he demanded.

"I got no idea who'd do such a thing," Webster said. "It must've been an accident. Besides, even if it was done on purpose, I wouldn't know where to start looking for the culprit."

"I reckon that's true," Hunter hissed. "You couldn't find your butt with both hands."

Despite the gravity of the situation, several people laughed low.

"Instead of standing there making stupid remarks, you ought to get off your butt and find the bastards who did this."

"I'm tellin' you, Hunter," Webster smirked, "there ain't nothin' I can do."

"Will do is more like it, you yellow-bellied coward," Hunter raved.

"Goddamnit, I'm tired of your troublemaking, boy. And of your insults, both to me, and to some of the other respectable folk of Tall Pine. I'm of a good mind to lock you up till you get some sense."

Hunter stared hard at the sheriff. Webster suddenly felt a chill of fear that sank deep into him. "I reckon I'll just do that," he mumbled hastily. "You been nothin' but trouble, and I know you're gonna start somethin'."

Webster reached for his Colt.

"Like hell!" Hunter roared. He reached out with both hands, his left heading for the Colt that Webster was hauling out, the right grabbing the sheriff by the throat. "You're the troublemaker here, Webster," Hunter shouted. "Always trying to pit the Chinese against the whites, stirring up hatred and such, throwing in with people like Boyd."

Hunter shoved the sheriff away with his right hand. His left got a grip on Webster's pistol and kept it in hand as the sheriff toppled backward.

"Get up," Hunter snarled, waving the gun at the sheriff.

The fire still burned in the background, giving a dull, ocher-colored cast to everything. The people watched

Hunter and Webster silently.

Webster was wary. "You're gonna be in big trouble here, Hunter," he said, his quavering voice betraying his fear. "I might be willin' to overlook this, if you give me back that Colt and come along peaceable."

Hunter let go a short, clipped laugh. "An earthworm's got more backbone than you got, Webster," he snarled. "I should've taken care of this a long time ago, but I didn't want to cause trouble." He seemed to be almost musing now, talking to himself. "I always tried to do right, trusting in the law to sort things out. But that ain't the case here in Tall Pine, is it, Webster?"

The sheriff, who thought he might be able to back away enough to flee while Hunter was distracted talking to himself, froze.

Hunter shook his head, as if trying to rein in his thoughts. "You let a beautiful, loving woman die just to serve your own twisted hatred," Hunter growled, the anger crushing the depression inside him and then mixing with the result.

"What're you gonna do?" Webster asked, terror covering his face as he stared deep into Hunter's flat, hard eyes.

"Set things to rights, Sheriff." Hunter lifted the Colt, looking at it for a moment. He smiled ruthlessly. Then he lashed out with the gun, bringing it in his right hand from his left side, so that the iron front sight of the barrel tore a chunk of flesh from Webster's cheek.

The sheriff howled and brought his hand up to the cheek. But Hunter had not stopped with the one blow. He brought the gun zipping back the other way, cracking Webster's left cheekbone with the side of the barrel. Webster screamed and weaved.

As people, both white and Chinese, watched silently, unprotesting, Hunter pistol-whipped the sheriff. He smashed the Colt against Webster's face and head again and again, ripping out chunks of flesh and scattering bones and teeth.

No one moved to stop him, until Stone stepped up and grabbed Hunter's right arm. "That's enough," Stone said, as quietly as he could in his deep rumble. Hunter stopped struggling against the giant after a few moments. He regained his senses. "Bastard," he muttered, dropping the Colt onto the nearly dead sheriff. He spat on Webster's face, which was no longer recognizable but a mass of bleeding, torn flesh.

Hunter turned to leave.

"We're comin' with you," someone said. Hunter turned back to see the speaker and three other men shove forward. All were men who worked in the sawmill.

"Thanks, boys. I'm obliged for the offer." Hunter felt dead inside, as if someone had snuffed out all the light of his being. "But I reckon I'll do this one alone."

"But, boss," the same one started to argue.

"No, Clem. I ain't putting no more of you at risk over something I've caused. You and the others got wives, young 'uns to think about. Stick to your jobs. Linc'll see you're all paid on time."

Clem Mossridge thought to argue some more, but decided against it when he saw Hunter's set jaw and flinty eyes.

"Yessir, boss." He paused, then added, "But you need help of any kind to set this right, you send for us." There was a growled chorus of assents from at least a dozen men.

Hunter nodded, grateful, but wanting to be away from here.

"You need anything?" Stone asked.

"A horse. Some ammunition."

"Take the dun mare. She's yours. By the time you're set, I'll have your ammunition. You need anything else,

211

come see me."

Hunter nodded. He walked swiftly to his house. In his room, he opened a locked box. Solemnly he pulled out the old Army Remington he'd thought he would no longer have any use for. For a moment, he held the .44-caliber, cap-and-ball Remington, before loading it. He did not like being forced into using it, but there was no choice now. Boyd and his men had made their play.

He strapped the flap holster around his waist, with the pistol on his left hip, butt pointing forward.

Then he got the Springfield and made sure it was charged. He looked around, seeing if there was anything else he needed. He stared for a moment at the rumpled, unmade bed, and the thoughts of what had occurred there between him and Li-Sung made him hurt inside. He felt as if he had been gutshot.

He saw nothing else he needed, so he headed through the shop toward the street.

When Hunter stepped outside, Stone was waiting with Mudpie, saddled and ready, including bedroll and saddlebags. "There's some jerky, bacon, beans and other grub in the saddlebags," Stone said. "And some paper cartridges, powder and lead. I put a mess of oats in a sack, too."

"Thanks, Linc," Hunter mumbled.

"It's nothin'."

Hunter pulled himself into the saddle. Dawn was breaking over the ridge of pine-covered mountains. It was cold, but it would be a nice day—weatherwise.

"You gonna be all right?" Stone asked, worried.

"Yep."

"Sure you don't want some company? I can be ready to ride in fifteen minutes."

"I'm sure."

Stone nodded. He was not happy with it, but he

212

would not argue, either. Not now. "You know which way you're goin'?"

"No." It was the one thing that perplexed him. He had no idea of where to look.

"Try there," Stone said, pointing toward Fool's Trail. Hunter's eyebrows shot up. "Why?"

"One of the Chinese told me he saw a half-dozen or so men riding hellbent-for-leather that way just before the fire started. And it starts right there near Chinatown."

Hunter nodded as he slipped the Springfield into the saddle scabbard.

"Watch your back, Jake," Stone growled, not liking to display his emotion.

"I'll do so, Linc." He touched his heels to the dun's sides. The horse snorted, eager to be on its way. Hunter rode out, following Fool's Trail. He began to feel better, now that the prospect of action was near.

He did not like the idea of traveling Fools' Trail again. But it did seem fitting, he thought, as he headed toward the rocky, narrow trail that meandered sharply upward to the north and east. It was Fool's Trail that had brought him here, and given him Li-Sung. It was apropros that he leave Tall Pine—maybe permanently—on the same route.

Chapter 25

Linc Stone stepped out onto his porch. It was very cold, and the darkness was lowering over Tall Pine. As he did every time he left his house now, Stone looked over toward Jake Hunter's place.

He wondered how his friend was faring. Hunter had been gone since dawn and couldn't reasonably be expected back for a while. Still, Stone wished he had gone with Jake.

"I'll be damned," he muttered. A man had hurriedly mounted a chestnut horse tied to the oak tree in Hunter's back yard, the same tree on which Fu Shun had been hanged. The man, mounted, crossed Mogollon Street hurriedly and galloped west.

In the last of the day's light, Stone saw the man disappear into the pine trees.

Stone opened his door and called in, "Polly."

His small, pretty, red-haired wife was at the door in a moment, wiping her hands on her apron.

Stone was reluctant to take his eyes off Hunter's place, just in case, so he said over his shoulder to his wife, "Fetch me my old sidearm, darlin'."

"Trouble?" Polly Stone asked, not really concerned. She had absolute faith in her husband and in his ability to handle any adversity.

"Ain't sure."

Polly left and returned in a few minutes with a heavy Colt Dragoon in a leather holster. She handed it to her husband and he buckled the belt on. He checked to make sure the pistol was loaded, and checked the small cartridge cases on the gunbelt. They were full, and he had plenty of caps made of fulminate of mercury. Even while he worked his eyes flickered between Hunter's house, and the spot—now invisible in the darkness—where the man had entered the forest.

"I might be gone a spell, darlin'," he said softly. "Go on down to the saloon and tell Will. Tell him to watch over things till I get back." He moved down the steps and across the street.

He found a note tacked to Hunter's back door, stuck there with a thorn hammered into a crack in the wood. Stone pulled the thorn out with two fingers. He scratched a match along the wall of the house and used the flickering flame to read the sprawling, almost childish writing.

Stone could not make out the signature, nor many of the words, but he got enough to know that someone was offering a challenge to Hunter. He chuckled, and muttered, "Goddamn, Jake, you sure got a heap of enemies for a quiet, easy-goin' fellah." He crumpled the paper and shoved it in a shirt pocket.

Feeling a sense of urgency, he hurried to the livery stable down near Verde Street on the south end of town. He saddled his favorite horse—a large, chocolate-brown gelding he called Puddin'. Then he rode, as swiftly as the darkness would allow, for where the man had entered the forest.

If it was dark out in town, it was Stygian in the depths of the heavy pine forest. A narrow, barely discernible trail meandered into the forest, and Stone let the horse pick its way slowly along. Periodically, Stone would stop and listen. Finally he was rewarded with the

215

sound of another horse ahead of him.

Stone grinned, but if the man he was following had seen it, he would not have been cheered by it.

The sounds came more frequently and were easier to hear after a while, so Stone held back a little. He had no idea of who was ahead. For all he knew, there could be a half-dozen outlaws in a camp up ahead. He had no intention of riding into such a place, if he could help it.

Eventually he heard the man stop and mutter, as if talking with someone who was not interested in answering. Stone found a small clearing just left off the trail. Without the curtain of pine boughs overhead, the sun could poke through. It gave Stone enough light to see by. He tied off the horse, unsaddled it and hung a feedbag full of oats on the animal.

Stone was a big man, with a big appetite, but he could not risk a fire. So he contented himself with two cans of peaches, a strip of jerky and a weeks-old biscuit he found in his saddlebags. It did little to improve his humor.

He was ill-prepared for such an expedition in other ways, too. He had only one thin blanket with him. It only made him more irritable, as he sat huddled in his blanket, waiting for the dawn, so many hours away. He fell asleep, finally. The cold woke him several times, but he finally settled it in his mind that he was here, had few supplies, and had to stick it out. He was not a man much given to musing about things that could not be or that he could not change. So eventually his anger was tempered, and he even managed to get a few hours of real sleep.

But another poor meal of canned peaches and leathery jerky tended to sour him again in the morning. Especially when he could smell Arbuckle's coffee and some bacon sizzling on a fire.

"Well," he grumbled softly to himself, "if them boys out there hope to keep their food, there better be a couple dozen of 'em to hold me off." He grinned at his own foolishness.

Stone stretched and yawned, trying to loosen muscles tightened by uncomfortable positions and deep cold. Then he strutted off where he had heard the other man stop last night, and toward where those enticing smells were coming from.

He slipped from tree to tree with surprising grace and stealth for a man of his size, especially one who was long out of the practice of sneaking around in the woods like this. He found the camp, not a very difficult task.

He stood behind a large tree and looked the camp over. The cave carved into the side of the base of the mountain's northern wall dominated the scene. There was only a small clearing in front of it. A fire was burning almost in the center of the mouth of the cave. A single horse—the one Stone had seen the night before at Hunter's—was tied to a blackberry bush. A spring bubbled a few yards to the east of the cave entrance.

Stone had gotten only a glimpse of the man at Hunter's last night, and that was in rapidly fading light. But when the young man came to the cave mouth and squatted at the fire, Stone knew it was the same man.

Stone's mouth watered from the smells of the cooking bacon and the brewed coffee, and his stomach grumbled. The man twisted on his boots and said something back into the cave. He looked a little angry, as if he did not get the reply he wanted.

As far as Stone could tell, the two—if there was only one other person in the cave—were the only people here. Maybe they were a young married couple, Stone thought. Still, why did he want to call Hunter out? The

217

man scooped some bacon and eggs onto a tin plate and disappeared into the cave. He returned a moment later and loaded another plate. He sat sitting at the fire, eating by himself. He looked decidedly unhappy.

He was young, fairly tall, and rugged-looking. Stone snorted, thinking, *Looks like a damn farm boy.* He was dressed in homespun pants and shirt, a ragged felt hat, and tall black boots. The Colt pistol at his hip looked incongruous.

Stone made his decision. He went back to the brown gelding and saddled it, then rode back along the trail a way. He grinned, hoping this would work. He took off the gunbelt and stuffed it into a saddlebag, then stuck the pistol into his belt at the small of his back. He turned around, heading toward the cave. He sang— loudly and well off-key—"When I Saw Sweet Nellie Home." As he rode into the little clearing before the cave, he saw the young man watching him intently.

"Howdy, fellow traveler," he shouted cordially, his smile positively radiant.

The young man looked worried. He cast nervous glances at the cave. "How do," he said warily.

"Do I smell coffee?" Stone said jovially. "And bacon?" He made exaggerated sniffing noises. "I must admit to a certain degree of hunger this fine morning. Alas, but if a black bear didn't get my grub two days ago."

"Sit to the fire," the young man said, still wary.

"Obliged." Stone stopped the horse and dismounted.

He scanned the area as best he could while being unobtrusive about it. He saw no one else. He marched to the fire and stood a moment, warming his hands, before squatting down across from the young man. It gave him a slight view of the cave's interior, but since the cave was dark and apparently curved to the left just past the mouth, he couldn't see much.

"You alone?" he asked, as he accepted with a nod the cup of coffee the young man held out.

The young man muttered something unintelligible. He was very nervous.

"Only way to travel, to my thinkin'," Stone said blandly. "Unless, of course, you have the company of a young lady." He laughed. The young man did not join in. Stone sipped a bit, then said, "My name's Linc Stone. Yours?"

The young man hemmed and hawed, stuttering and stammering. Then he blurted, "Bart." His nervousness grew.

"No last name?" Stone asked, eyebrows raised.

"Well . . ."

"I understand." Stone nodded. "Lots of folks don't want to be known. Well, Bart," Stone said easily, in friendly tones, "I don't suppose you got any more of that bacon left for a starvin' pilgrim, do you?"

"Reckon I could rustle some up," Bart said grudgingly. "Be right back." He looked as if he did not want to move, but he got up and entered the cave. There was a low mumble, and then Bart reappeared with some bacon rolled in slick paper. He tossed some in a frying pan. "Ain't got no more eggs, though," he said. "But there's a few biscuits left."

Stone nodded, looking around nonchalantly, hoping to put the young man at his ease. He didn't think Bart was part of a gang. Perhaps he was just a traveler. Stone thought maybe Bart had a wife in the cave and was afraid of another man finding them.

Stone finished his coffee and poured some more. His humor had improved considerably, but he was still filled with questions. Within minutes his bacon was done, and he gobbled up the chunks of fatty meat and sopped up the grease with biscuits. Finished, he set the tin plate down and wiped his hands on his pants.

"Well, that hit the spot, Bart," he said with a smile. "Again, I'm obliged."

Bart had not relaxed any, and Stone figured he would have to make a play soon or Bart was going to ask him to leave. "Would you have some extra bacon or beans or such you might sell?" he asked.

"We got just enough for us," Bart said, without thinking.

"Us?" Stone queried, almost innocently. "I thought you were traveling alone."

"I never said that directly," Bart said, embers snapping in his eyes.

"Well, no matter," Stone said easily. "I don't mean to impose. If you ain't got enough, I understand. Reckon I'll make out." He stood and stretched. "Damn, sittin' in a saddle's startin' to wear on my old bones." He placed both hands on his lower back and bent backward at the waist.

When he straightened up, he had the Colt Dragoon in a meaty hand. "All right, Bart, or whoever the hell you really are," he growled, "what were you doin' at Jake Hunter's place?"

Bart started to go for his pistol, but a bullet from Stone's gun that came close to parting the young man's hair made Bart rethink that notion.

"Ease the pistol out, boy. Once you do, lay it down, and shove it easily toward me with your foot. You try'n get slick and I'll blow your brains all over the mountain."

Bart did as he was told.

Stone moved closer and bent to pick up the gun.

As he did, Bart tossed a handful of dirt at Stone, who caught some of it in his face. Bart leaped up and charged.

Stone surged upright and snapped his huge right arm out. His forearm caught Bart just under the chin, and the young man went down like an opened sack of beans.

"That was a damnfool thing to do, boy," Stone rumbled, as he blinked furiously to get the dirt out of his eyes. But Bart was too shaken to understand.

Stone pulled the caps off Bart's pistol, dropped them into his own pouch, and shoved the weapon into his saddlebag. Then he got a rope and tied Bart securely. The young man, still dazed, offered no resistance.

Done, Stone said, "Well, I reckon it's time to go see just what you've got hidin' in this here cave."

Warily, with his Dragoon pistol ready, Stone slipped into the cave. He hit the curve right away, and stopped out of the sunlight to let his eyes adjust to the gloom. He heard a noise and saw a flickering light from farther into the tunnel, and knew it to be a torch of some kind.

Unafraid, but cautious, Stone headed toward that light. As he got nearer the back of the cave, the noise grew more frequent, if not more intense. To Stone, it sounded as if there were someone tied up back there.

Suddenly there was light. "Oh, my Lord," he whispered. He jammed the Dragoon into the holster and rushed forward.

Chapter 26

Hunter found Ames Blythe first, just past noon. Blythe was alone, straggling behind his companions.

The outlaw heard Hunter's horse's hooves clunking on the talus that covered the steeply climbing Fool's Trail. He looked back and saw Hunter closing in; with a look of fear, he lashed his horse with the reins.

The animal squealed and lurched forward, finding it difficult to gain its footing on the thick coating of broken rock. It strained and surged, slipping and almost bucking, as Blythe clung desperately to the saddlehorn and whipped the horse. Blythe cast fearful glances back over his shoulders.

Hunter grinned grimly and plodded along, not pressing the dun more. Mudpie was one of the best horses Hunter had ever ridden, and he enjoyed the experience. Mudpie was sure-footed, responsive and stout of heart.

Blythe pulled out of Hunter's vision around the curve of the trail, but the carpenter could hear Blythe yelling at the horse, trying to speed it up the steep hill.

Hunter passed the spot where he had fallen off the edge of the world in his wagon. He stopped for a moment, looking down at the little remaining wreckage, and thinking back on all that had happened. He was saddened by it, and he felt the weight of his life heavily. The odd feeling that he was a threat to anyone who liked him came back with renewed fervor. Miriam, back in Pennsylvania, dead of diphtheria; his dour wife, Lucille, left behind in Iowa; Sarah Rogers, casting her love to the naive Burl Baker; faithful old Reb, who had come all this way; Jimmy Wing and Fu Shun; and now Li-Sung and Sen both dead.

"Come on, Mudpie," he said quietly, patting the animal's neck. The horse responded eargerly.

Two miles up the rocky trail, Hunter spotted Blythe again. The outlaw's horse was down, exhausted and its wind broke. The beast struggled to rise, but had nothing left inside. Hunter hated to see any animal treated in such a way. He shook his head. He eased Mudpie up alongside the downed horse. It was tricky, since there was barely room to manage it. Hunter drew his Remington and shot the horse in the side of the head, just under the ear.

The animal bucked as the bullet tore through its brain, slumping back, kicking in its death throes.

Hunter looked up the trail. Blythe was scrambling and sliding on the rocks, trying to run up the wicked trail about a quarter-mile away. "You're next, Blythe," Hunter shouted.

He moved on slowly, knowing Blythe could not get away from him. He was wary, however. There were numerous places where someone desperate enough could climb up the steep wall on the right and hide behind a boulder or in a crevice to ambush him.

But he reasoned that Blythe was not that bright — or brave. And despite the twists and turns of the trail, Hunter soon caught up with the fleeing outlaw. Blythe was walking slowly now, holding his side as if it hurt. He looked back, and Hunter thought that, under the fear, Blythe looked done in.

Hunter was unfeeling. He pushed the horse just a

little bit, closing the gap with Blythe. Blythe turned and pulled his pistol. He fired three times, but he was shaking so much from exhaustion and fear that his aim was nonexistent. All three bullets whined off rocks somewhere far above Hunter's head. Blythe turned and tried to run again.

Hunter touched his heels to Mudpie's sides, and the mare responded with a burst of speed, leaping forward, hooves managing to find footing. Blythe fired another shot over his shoulder without stopping.

Hunter got within ten feet of Blythe before stopping the dun. He pulled the Remington, thumbed back the hammer and aimed carefully. He fired twice, hitting the scrambling Blythe in the back. One lead ball thumped into the lower side of the Blythe's back, puncturing a kidney. The other smashed into the top of the spine, just under the neck. The impacts slammed Blythe forward onto his face, skidding on the loose stones.

Hunter moved up, stopping again a few feet away from the still form that had been Ames Blythe. He dismounted, pistol ready, and edged closer. He looked down at the bloody body without feelings or remorse. He put his pistol away. With the same lack of sympathy, he grabbed Blythe's hair and dragged the body to the precipice, dropped it and then kicked it over the edge.

He watched as the body bounced off rocks near the bottom of the canyon and then tumbled down the last part of the slope. "Let the wolves have at you, damnit," Hunter muttered.

Hunter climbed on the mare and rode on. As dusk began to fall, he stopped. There was a not-so-steep slope to the left, covered with brush, some old grass, and pines. He managed to gather enough wood for a fire, and forage for the horse. He built the fire right on

224

the trail and cooked a mess of beans and the beefsteak Linc Stone had stowed in his pack.

He filled the mare's feedbag with oats and tied the animal to a boulder. Then he cleaned the Remington and reloaded it. Finally he spread out his blankets, shivering a bit in the cold. He was asleep almost instantly.

Hunter found Dell O'Rourke and Red Rockingham late the next day. They were camping near a spring atop the Mogollon Rim. It was a mostly flat area, populated with thick stands of ponderosa pines, and scattered, stunted oaks. Hunter recognized the spot—it was less than half a mile from the main road to Cartersville. He had passed it on his way toward Fool's Trail.

Hunter smelled their campfire long before he saw the men, so he pulled off into the forest and let the mare pick her way slowly between the trees. When he could hear men talking, he dismounted and tied the horse off. Then he proceeded on foot.

He stopped behind a huge ponderosa and peered around. O'Rourke and Rockingham sat at a small fire of fragrant pine wood. A jackrabbit dangled over the fire on a stick, sizzling, and a pot of coffee was brewing. It reminded Hunter that he had not eaten in a while.

There was no reason to delay, he decided. He pulled the Remington and walked out from the trees. He was almost atop the men before they realized someone was coming.

"Evening, boys," Hunter said sardonically. He cocked the pistol and shot Rockingham twice in the side of the head, splattering a tree just beyond him with blood and brains.

He turned the gun toward O'Rourke. The tall, cadaverous outlaw had his hands up high. His face was etched with terror. "Holy Mother of God!" O'Rourke squeaked. "Don't kill me, Mr. Hunter."

"Why not?" Hunter asked, voice croaking from the hatred that flowed through his veins as if he had been born with it.

"I didn't have nothin' to do with it," O'Rourke warbled.

"With what?" Hunter asked, voice as cold as the temperature in Tall Pine in January.

"With anythin'." He looked about ready to make water in his pants, but Hunter had no sympathy for him, not with the great, dark, festering dead spot in his heart. "Anythin' Quint did. And the others. I was just along for the ride."

"You lyin' pile of buffalo droppings," Hunter hissed.

"No. I swear. It's true." He seemed on the verge of tears.

Hunter was unmoved. "Take out your pistol and toss it out into the trees," he said curtly. "Slowly, if you don't mind."

O'Rourke nodded his skeletal head. Very slowly he pulled out the revolver and heaved it into the growing shadows.

Hunter relaxed. He doubted O'Rourke was sly enough to carry a hidden gun. Or shrewd enough for lying to save his skin. Hunter knew O'Rourke was lying about his participation in the gang's atrocities, but he figured lying was second nature to O'Rourke. It meant little to O'Rourke, and less to Hunter. Hunter put the Remington in the holster and snapped the flap shut.

O'Rourke's eyes grew very wide, looking strangely white in the pallid face. "You're lettin' me go?" he asked.

"Not quite. But I'm going to give you a chance to fight for your miserable hide. It's more'n you did for Li-Sung. . . ."

"Who?"

"The woman who lived in the house you burned down the other night. We were going to get married, you know," Hunter said matter-of-factly. He was surprised at his own detachment.

"Oh." O'Rourke stood. He was close to seven feet tall, Hunter estimated, with long arms and legs. But Hunter would have wagered that the man did not even weigh as much as his own one hundred eighty pounds. "We gonna fight with fists?" O'Rourke asked, sounding eager. He could beat almost any man with his fists, if only because of his incredible reach.

"Do I look as stupid as you?" Hunter asked.

Fear replaced the eagerness in O'Rourke's eyes. Hunter grinned, a not very comforting sight to O'Rourke. Then Hunter unstrapped his pistol belt, never taking his eyes off O'Rourke. He wrapped the belt around the holster and set in on the ground, then removed his heavy coat and dropped it atop the holster. Last, he tossed his hat down after it.

"You can do the same, if you're of a mind to."

The tall, gangly man took off his coat and set it down. "What happens now?" he asked, licking his lips nervously.

"You use your fists. And I use this." Hunter slid out the heavy knife he always carried.

O'Rourke blanched. "That ain't fair," he gasped.

"Life ain't fair, you stinkin' backshooter."

O'Rourke's eyes got even wider, if that was possible. "You're the one who . . ." His lips flapped shut. "You," he tried again, "you're . . . who done in Oakley and Barney, ain't you?"

"Effective, wasn't it?" Hunter said, with a cutting edge to his voice. "And a particularly apt place, don't you think?" He paused. "Now, I'm givin' you a chance. Maybe it ain't much of one, but it's more than you ever gave. So come on at me, damn you, or I'll cut your ears off for you. Just like you and the others did to Fu Shun, you miserable son of a . . ."

O'Rourke leaped across the fire and covered the ground between himself and Hunter with gigantic bounds. He was on Hunter almost before the carpenter knew it.

Then Hunter was not there anymore. He was several yards to the side, and O'Rourke swished past the spot where Hunter had been, arms squeezing air. O'Rourke stopped and turned, bewildered. "Ain't nice," he whined.

O'Rourke charged again, long arms waving out toward the sides, hoping to engulf Hunter. If he could wrap the carpenter up in his long arms, keep him from using the knife, he could smother the knife-wielding man against his bony chest. He was a lot stronger than he looked. Folks usually didn't realize that—until it was too late for them.

But Hunter again easily slid out of the way of those long, grasping appendages. And several more times. O'Rourke was getting winded by all this chasing after nothing. "You oughtta stand still," O'Rourke grumbled.

"I might," Hunter said, almost amiably, "if you quit coming at me like a *loco* stork."

O'Rourke caught his breath and moved toward Hunter warily, ever conscious of that large, deadly-looking knife. He knew, from having been the one to find both Skagg's and Crane's bodies, that Hunter knew how to use the weapon with deadly efficiency, and apparently grim favor.

228

Hunter crouched, knowing he was taking a big chance with this stretched-out, skeletal outlaw. But he was beyond worrying about such things anymore.

O'Rourke moved in, closer and closer, weaving back and forth, trying to lull Hunter. It seemed to be working, so he flicked out a fist. Hunter sloughed it off to the side, but O'Rourke was encouraged. Hunter had seemed a little sluggish. He flicked the other fist out at the end of the far-reaching arm. It brushed against Hunter's nose before being shoved away.

Suddenly O'Rourke began windmilling his arms and moving in fast. The onslaught seemed to catch Hunter by surprise, and the carpenter caught several punches on his sides and shoulders. He blocked off his face, then crouched, hunching over, and spun, turning his back to his attacker.

O'Rourke was elated. This was his chance, he figured. He whipped out his arms and swept them back in, gathering Hunter in. "Got you," he muttered, as he straightened, bringing Hunter up against his chest.

Then he realized, with a sudden sinking dread, that he had managed to capture only Hunter's left hand. The right—the one with the knife—was still loose. He realized, too, that he had been trapped. But it was too late.

Hunter wasted no time. He held the knife as he always had—for slicing upward, rather than for chopping downward. It was but a moment's work to snap his right hand back over his shoulder.

O'Rourke screamed as the knife punctured his right eye. He continued screaming as he dropped Hunter and slapped both hands up to his eye. The animal-like sounds floated into the trees, silencing the coyotes and owls.

O'Rourke stumbled backward and sank to his knees.

One hand still covered the eye while the other scrabbled around, trying to gather snow. He thought in his pain-ravaged mind that if he could get snow on his eye, freeze it, he would be all right.

He never did see Hunter walk up calmly. He did see Hunter's grim face when Hunter pulled his head back by the thinning hair. It was the last thing he ever saw, as Hunter slashed O'Rourke's throat. Blood squirted out, all over Hunter's shirt and pants, but he paid it no mind.

Without remorse, he dragged the body by the hair until it was well back into the woods. No reason to attract hungry critters around the camp during the night, Hunter thought. Hunter returned and dragged Rockingham's body into the trees, dropping it next to O'Rourke's.

Then he got Mudpie. He led the horse to the camp and hobbled it, letting it find some of its own forage. Hunter sat and, without much enjoyment, tore into the rabbit. He hadn't realized how hungry he was. By the time he had finished off half the hare, he felt a little better. Three cups of hot, incredibly strong coffee also did its part in improving his disposition.

He awoke several times during the night as wolves or coyotes tore at the flesh of the two dead men. Hunter would roll over each time, after assuring himself he was in no danger, and go back to sleep.

"Only Boyd and that new one, Pettibone, to see to before our work's done," Hunter said to Mudpie as he saddled the horse in the morning. He had eaten the rest of the jackrabbit with some corncakes, and had more coffee. He felt almost as though he wanted to live.

He set off, following the path through the trees, but by noon, he had lost Boyd's trail. He circled and circled, eyes searching the ground, but he could not pick up the trail again on the rocky, frozen, snow-covered ground. He was angry and frustrated. He made camp and slept fitfully, rage burning inside him, eating at him. More than once he snapped upright, sitting, as thoughts of Li-Sung burned into his very being.

He missed Li-Sung something terrible. That would never change—or even dim. But he had to go on living, at least until he was through with what he had to do. He did have the memories of her, and those he could—would—keep forever.

Hunter decided, as the cold sun began rising above the Rim, that he would head back to Tall Pine and pack his belongings. He would sell the sawmill to Stone, if the bar owner wanted it. If not, he could probably sell it to Fortney Simms, the banker. He almost chuckled, thinking back on how Simms had been enraged when Hunter rode into town with all the equipment for the mill.

He would pay off his few small debts, sell or store his tools and few other belongings, and head off. He would find Quint Boyd and Arliss Pettibone—and kill them—if it took the rest of his life. He would have no other purpose in life than to hunt those two men down and make them pay full price for what they had done.

When that was done, maybe, just maybe, he could go on living again.

Chapter 27

Hunter was a hate-filled and angry man when he rode back into Tall Pine. He was tired and hungry, unshaved for nearly a week, broken-hearted, and mean as a disturbed rattler.

He wanted nothing to do with anyone. All he wanted was a hot meal, a bath, shave and haircut, and one good night's sleep. Then he would gather his things and get out of Tall Pine.

As he made his way down the final stretches of the trail, he saw the steam from the sawmill and heard the annoying buzz of the saws. He stopped just over the last hump of the trail, on the rocky ledge overlooking the town just before the final sharp descent. The town hadn't changed in the past four days, though he had not expected it to. Still, it seemed odd that nothing had changed, since it seemed he had been gone for months rather than days.

He wondered about Webster. If the lawman had died, the town might be ready to string him up. He decided he didn't care, but the cost for lynching him would come dear. He rode slowly, thankful he had only yards to go from the foot of the trail to the back of his house. He did not want to be seen, at least for a while.

He tied the horse to the hitching post near the northeast corner of the house. Some grass was popping up amid the dirty snow, and Mudpie started cropping it right away. Hunter pulled off the saddle, bridle, and bit and tossed them into his storage shed. From a barrel inside the shed, Hunter scooped out two buckets of oats and set them down in front of Mudpie. The horse could eat right from the wood buckets.

With his Springfield in one hand, and his mostly empty saddlebags over his left shoulder, Hunter went through the door that opened into his living quarters.

As soon as the door opened, he smelled Li-Sung's perfume. "Damn," he muttered, the ache of loneliness and loss cramping his gut. He was not prepared for having her presence still so strong in his room after all this time. It was almost as if she had been there but a moment ago. He shook his head.

He stepped into the room and dropped the saddlebags on the floor. He was about to set the rifle against the wall when he heard a noise from the shop area. He snapped alert, but before he could bring the Springfield up and move, Li-Sung stood in the doorway between the two rooms.

The shock staggered Hunter, and his vision blurred. He leaned back against the wall, staring blankly. Not even during the horror of the war had he experienced such a shock. If it was a shock, he wondered. He closed his eyes. The vision might go away. He opened them again, but still she stood there, smiling. Perhaps he had gone crazy. He had heard of such things happening to men; he had even seen it in others during the war. When someone's grief or loss or horror had gotten the better of him, his mind had gone awry.

But he had never thought it could happen to him.

233

He had seen too much, suffered too much, survived too much.

He cracked his eyes open again, but the vision persisted. Worse! It was moving toward him. Well, by God, he would not face whatever demon he had conjured up with his eyes closed and leaning back against the wall. He straightened and opened his eyes. *But, good Lord,* he thought, *did you have to make her so real looking?*

The vision had been smiling brightly when he had first seen it. Now a look of concern spread over the vision's beautiful face. And it spoke!

"Jake?" Li-Sung asked. "Are you all right?" She was worried. She came up to him and laid a soft hand on his forehead to see if he was feverish.

Hunter gasped at the touch, before stiffening his resolve. *She's so real!* he thought. Her fresh, special smell, her finely crafted features, her touch, and her voice. Voice? What was she saying? He tried to concentrate.

"I'm fine," he heard himself answering. His eyes grew as big as saucers. "Lord, you're alive!" he roared. "God." He dropped the rifle and scooped Li-Sung up in his arms and squeezed her.

Li-Sung laughed, happy. She feared he might break her ribs, but she really didn't care. Not now. It could not compare with the fear she had felt with each passing day when Hunter had not come back. But he was here, and alive, and crushing her with his joy.

He finally set her down, embarrassed at his recent display—first of shock, and then his happiness when he realized she was alive.

She smiled up at him, and to Hunter she had never looked more beautiful. Or desirable. He felt a welcome warmth growing in his middle. He grabbed her again, and planted a kiss on her mouth, hungrily trying to devour her.

She finally pulled away somewhat, breathless. "Not now," she whispered.

"Why?" he asked, disappointed. Then he brought himself under control. "Sorry, Li-Sung," he mumbled.

"There is nothing to be sorry about, Jake," she said, joy mingled with sadness dancing around her words. "But you must be tired, and hungry."

"And filthy as a hog, too, ain't I?" he said, with a lopsided grin. "You mind washing my back?" he asked lecherously.

"I would be happy to, kind sir," she said, smiling. She put her palms together against her chest, just under her chin, and bowed. "But you must eat first. I brought some things from . . ." she stumbled to a halt, a stab of sadness overcoming her. It clouded her face for a moment.

In his happiness to see Li-Sung alive, he had forgotten about Xiang Sen. "Your father?" he asked softly, remembering.

She had a faraway look in her eyes. She shook her head and began to sob.

"I understand," he said consolingly, feeling hopelessly inadequate.

"I grieve for my father," she said softly, around her tears. "But we have learned, my people, to deal with such things. I will miss him, but now he is with our venerable ancestors, and so much happier."

He nodded and said nothing. He just held Li-Sung close to him, feeling the shaking of her slim shoulders. She sniffed and sobbed a little while, before collecting herself. She wiped her eyes and blew her nose, and within minutes looked normal again. Only her red-flecked eyes gave away her grief.

"You get some things cooking," Hunter said softly. "While you do that, I'll fetch that old tub from outside. We can heat water while we eat."

Soon they were eating chicken and peas and potatoes. There was hot coffee for him and tea for her to wash it down.

"How?" Hunter asked. "Why? I thought you were dead. I . . ."

"Everyone else thought I was dead, too. I had been with Lin Fuang. Her husband died about four months ago. She was pregnant, and her time due. My father sent me down there late. She has a place in the ravine beyond Fool's Trail, an out-of-the-way place. She had the child—a boy—without complications. When that was done, it was late, and I was heading home. Suddenly a man—a stranger—confronted me."

"What?" Hunter asked, a sickening feeling in his intestines souring his food.

She nodded. "A white man. He said little. Just threw some sacking over my head, put me on a horse. We rode a while, and then he tied me up inside a cave.

Hunter was beginning to feel like an idiot. Too many shocks had hit him all at once, and he was slow in responding, or even processing the information. "How? Who? Why?" he blathered.

"I don't know," Li-Sung said quietly, afraid she would lose his love. "He never said who he was. I think he wanted to kill you."

"Why?" Hunter asked, stunned. His food was forgotten.

"Something about a woman. He didn't say much." Li-Sung raised one arched eyebrow at him. "Is there something I don't know about?"

"Not that I know of," he answered truthfully.

236

"How'd you get free?" he asked, still amazed that she was alive at all.

"Mr. Stone rescued me a day after you left." She explained what little she knew about the rescue.

"Linc didn't kill him?" Hunter asked in surprise.

"No. He thought you might want to talk with the man. He's in the jail."

Hunter nodded, then asked, "Sheriff Webster?"

"Mr. Stone said the sheriff died later that day. I didn't know anything about what happened after I was taken, until Mr. Stone brought me back. He told me about my father. The fire must have started not long after I was taken." She paused. "Mr. Stone also told me what you did to Sheriff Webster." She touched his cheek softly, her eyes clouded with the pain they had both experienced too much of lately.

Hunter almost wanted to grin. "Linc can't keep his mouth shut," he muttered. Then, "The law looking for me because of that?" He thought he should be worried about it, but he wasn't.

"No." She cast her eyes down, then looked up at him and grinned. "It was difficult getting enough people to make a funeral for the sheriff. He wasn't well liked. Though it has only been a few days, things have changed in Tall Pine. There is less animosity between our two peoples. Most people recognize Sheriff Webster now for what he always was."

Hunter nodded again. Worry—or perhaps it was fear, and he did not want to admit to that—burrowed into his bowels. "Are you all right?" he asked quietly.

She stared at him, trying to figure out exactly what he meant, but she could not.

Hunter's mouth was dry. "The man who kidnapped you," he croaked. "Did he . . . do . . . anything . . . Did he . . . ?"

237

"No!" Li-Sung said, as she understood. "No! He took me to a cave and kept me tied up there until Mr. Stone rescued me. But other than to loosen the ropes so I could eat, he never touched me. He only wanted to use me to get to you."

The relief that flooded over Hunter was almost as great as the relief he had felt when he realized Li-Sung was alive.

They fell into silence for some moments. Then, "What you must have gone through," Li-Sung said solemnly.

"Me?" he asked, surprised. She had lost her father, thought she might lose her man, too, and had been kidnapped. Yet she was more concerned about him.

They hugged. "Well, I'll not go away again," he whispered.

"Promise?"

"Promise." He sat back and said huskily, "I reckon that water's plenty heated up."

She grinned. "Yes."

Soon, Hunter was stripped down and sitting in a tub of steaming water. He lay back with his head on one edge of the copper tub and his feet hanging over the other end.

"I can't wash your back that way," Li-Sung chided playfully.

"There's time," Hunter said. He was comfortable here in the warm water, the steam curling up around his face.

Eventually—"in order to do the best job," she told him—Li-Sung joined Hunter in the small tub. It was cramped, but neither minded. And soon they repaired to the wide, warm bed.

* * *

Hunter felt funny strapping on the Remington in Li-Sung's presence. He didn't like wearing it, but he had told her about his journey, including losing Boyd's trail. As he buckled the belt on, he said, "Until I get Boyd—or until I know he's gone for good—I ain't taking any more chances. Especially not with you."

It was early morning, and cold out, so they bundled up—Li-Sung in a thick wool shawl, Hunter in his short, heavy wool coat. With Hunter leading Mudpie, he and Li-Sung headed toward the livery. He felt proud to have Xiang Li-Sung walking by his side.

Linc Stone, opening up the saloon, saw him and called a cheery greeting. He had seen Mudpie behind Hunter's house and knew his friend was back. Hunter grinned and waved, but he felt a touch of concern. Stone was wearing the shoulder holster with the heavy Colt .44. Hunter figured the big bar owner must be expecting trouble.

Hunter was conscious of the people—almost all of them friendly—watching as he and Li-Sung walked slowly down Mogollon Street. A few called out in welcome, which Hunter happily acknowledged.

They left Mudpie at the livery and started their stroll up the street. At the door of the Mogollon Saloon, Li-Sung demurred. "It is no place for a woman," she said.

"Do you mind?"

"Of course not," she said, with a smile. "Mr. Stone is a good friend. We owe him everything. And you will want to talk with that man." She wanted to kiss him, but did not think it proper to do so here in public. She settled for touching his freshly shaved cheek. "But don't be too long. I will miss you."

"I won't." Hunter watched a moment as Li-Sung stepped off the sidewalk and walked across the street,

239

heading for the shop—now their home.

He turned and entered the saloon, where he was greeted with bluff good humor and much shouting by Stone and some of the sawmill workers, and even a reserved Crooked-Eye Sal. Will and Carter Hawes worked behind the bar, and Joy Fung sat at a table in a corner. She looked bored.

After the initial exuberance, Hunter and Stone sat at a table near the bar, food and coffee in front of them. Hunter quickly explained what had happened on his trek, and his frustration at not having caught Boyd. Then he ordered, "Tell me about this kidnapping, Linc."

Stone went over it quickly, filling in the bits Li-Sung had not known.

"And you say his name's Bart?" Hunter asked. "I don't know any Barts."

"That's the name he gave me. Reckon it could be an alias. You want to talk to him?"

"Might as well."

Stone called Will Hawes over and said, "Go and fetch our prisoner."

As Hawes left, Hunter asked, "You the new law in town now, Linc?"

Stone laughed. "Naw. Just usin' the jail a bit. I been considerin' runnin' for sheriff come election day, though."

"Hell, I'll have to move out of town, you get elected," Hunter said, laughing.

He quieted and said, "You told me this dude tacked a note to my door. You got it?"

Stone looked embarrassed. "Well, no. I tried to read it when I pulled it loose, but I couldn't make out much of it. So I stuck it in my shirt pocket and lit out after the guy. After I got Li-Sung back here safe and sound, I went to sleep. Polly went and took my shirt over to Soo Ling's Laundry." He shrugged, looking sheepish.

"Good thing I never trusted you with anything valuable," Hunter joked.

They finished their breakfast, and heard a commotion at the door. "Must be Will comin' back with that dude," Stone said. He and Hunter turned to watch the door.

Chapter 28

"I'll be darned," Hunter muttered in amazement, as Will Hawes walked up to the table, prodding the prisoner before him.

"You know him, Jake?" Stone asked.

"Linc, meet Burl Baker," Hunter said, recovering from his surprise. He looked up at Baker. "What in hell are you doing here, Burl?"

Baker stood mute.

"Take off them cuffs, Will," Stone said. When Baker's hands were free, and he was rubbing them, Stone said to him. "Have a seat, boy."

Baker made no move other than to rub his hands.

"I said sit, boy," Stone growled. "I'm nearabout out of patience with you, and I'd as soon knock you down as ask you again."

Baker sat. Hawes headed back to the bar.

"What's his beef with you, Jake?" Stone asked.

"Ain't sure. He was put out at me 'cause we were courting the same woman for a spell. But he won her over. That was back in Las Vegas, over in New Mexico Territory. I ain't heard—or thought—of him since. That's all I know about it." He looked at Baker. "What brought you here, Burl?" he asked.

"I come lookin' to kill you," Baker snarled.

"Why?" Hunter asked, surprised.

"Because of Sarah." Rage coated the words like jam on bread.

"But why?" Hunter asked, stunned. "You won her over. She told me so back there in Las Vegas."

"Sarah would've been my wife by now if you hadn't poisoned her mind against me that day. I aim to see you in hell for that."

"You gone *loco?*" Hunter asked, bewildered.

"No," Baker said. But there was the fervor of true belief in his eyes, and Hunter began to wonder about Burl Baker's sanity.

"How'd I poison her mind against you, boy?" Hunter asked harshly, a kernel of anger settling in his stomach. Too many people had been trying to kill him—or his loved ones—lately, and he was not at all happy with that.

"Tellin' her them stories about how you had nothin' to do with Chas's death and such. It turned her against me. Soon after that, she started havin' doubts. A wife can't have those kind of doubts about her man's honor and courage. She began harpin' on it, and bringin' up your name. Kept tellin' me what you'd done was brave and that more people would've died if it wasn't for you."

His eyes gleamed with an almost religious zeal. "You were so brave, she kept tellin' me," he said with a sneer. "Big goddamn hero. Hell." He spat on the floor, earning an angry glance from Stone. "Along about Christmas, just before we was goin' to be married, she called it off."

Baker looked as if he wanted to cry—or explode. "I been lookin' for you ever since. I finally tracked you here. I kept out of sight a few days, watchin' you, trying to think up a plan. That's how I learned about that yellow whore of yours." He was breathing heavily with the pent-up anger. He wished he had his gun. Even if he died in the doing, he would die happy if he could kill Jake Hunter.

"I'd watch what you said, boy," Stone said quietly, as Hunter sat fighting down the rage that engulfed him. "Far better men than you have come to a bad end at Jake's hands from such talk."

Hunter sat in thought, knowing Stone's eyes were on him. This was more serious than he had thought. As Baker had done when Chas was killed, he again had a fixed scenario in his mind about Sarah Rogers that more easily accommodated his grief, pain and needs. The one lie, to make himself look bigger—and Hunter smaller—in Sarah's eyes had backfired, and brought on another lie. This one to himself. Hunter knew that Baker could not accept the truth.

"Why'd you take Li-Sung?" Hunter asked sharply.

Hunter's fists resting on the table were white-knuckled, and his eyes bored holes in Baker. The young man gulped. With voice cracking, he said, "I thought I could use her to get to you."

"Why didn't you just call me out?" Hunter said tightly.

"After seein' how you connived Sarah, I didn't reckon you'd be willin' to meet me face-to-face," Baker said. He was sweating now. Facing Hunter, who looked like a hungry wolf, and the huge Stone, was nerve-wracking. "I wanted to make sure you came alone."

Hunter's eyes still burned angrily, but he said nothing for a while. He sat thinking. He could almost understand Baker's thinking. The young man had almost lost the woman he loved to Hunter, a man with more experience and more to offer that a simple farm boy could. Then the woman had started throwing Hunter up in his face again. Baker could easily delude himself into thinking that he was alone against the world. Hunter almost felt sorry for the young man.

"Look, Burl," Hunter finally said quietly, having let the anger simmer down, "I didn't poison Miss Rogers's mind against you. If she thinks that, she's mistaken. And if she's made you believe that, she's wrong." He paused and looked at Stone, who gazed back levelly, wearing a small grin. "As far's I'm concerned, it's all over and done with."

"What's gonna happen to me?" Baker asked, hope leaping unbidden into his eyes.

"You can go," Hunter said simply, hoping he was doing the right thing. *"If* you leave Tall Pine and don't come looking for me. You give me your word on those two things, and I'll not have you tried on kidnapping charges."

"No yellow whore could say anything against me in court, anyway," Baker sneered defiantly. He got cocky, since Hunter was, as Baker had thought all along, proving to be a coward.

Hunter was on Baker like a cat on a mouse. He practically leaped over the table to get at Baker, beating Stone to the young man by a fraction of a second. Baker's chair crashed over backward, and Hunter landed on the farmer's chest.

Hunter smashed his fists into Baker's face more times than he could count. He finally stopped and stood, hauling Baker up by the shirt as he did. He shook Baker, his eyes crackling with rage, and shoved him away. Baker staggered backward. Hunter pursued him, punching him steadily, each blow knocking Baker a few more steps back.

Baker slammed into the bar and hung his cocked elbows over it, hanging on, holding himself up. Hunter turned and walked away. Suddenly he spun, whipping out the Remington. "You miserable bastard!" he hissed. He fired. Baker flinched as the bullet plowed into the bar inches from his side. And again. And twice more.

Hunter carried only five cartridges in his pistol most times. As he thumbed back the hammer, the cylinder clicked the last one into place. He aimed at a spot between Baker's eyes.

Baker wet his pants and almost cried from fear—and embarrassment. He screwed his eyelids shut to hold back the tears and to block the sight of the muzzle of Hunter's pistol.

"Open your eyes, boy." Hunter seethed.

Baker did, sweat coating his face.

Hunter sneered, moved the pistol to the side a couple of inches, and fired. Baker could feel the bullet's rush past his ear, and he almost fainted.

"Leave Tall Pine, boy, and don't ever come looking for me again," Hunter snarled. There was death in his voice.

The Hawes brothers, Crooked-Eye Sal, Joy Fung, and several customers laughed as Baker tried to walk on his rubbery legs—and with urine-soaked pants—toward the door. Still laughing, Hawes grabbed Baker's hat from the table where he had been sitting and hurried after him.

"Don't forget your hat, boy," Hawes called, chuckling. He caught up with Baker and held the hat out.

Baker turned slowly and reached out tentatively. Suddenly he lunged, grabbing the outstretched arm. He yanked Hawes forward, and swung a still-wobbly knee up. It slammed into Hawes's pelvic bone, and Hawes grunted. At the same time, his left hand snaked out and snatched Hawes's Colt from the holster.

As he shoved Hawes away with his right hand, Baker's left moved up and smoothly transferred the pistol to the other hand. He threw his arm up and fired.

Hunter was not laughing, though Stone was, as the two men sat back at the table. Hunter stared down at his tightly clenched fists on the table. Rage still raced through his veins, and he found it hard to think straight.

Stone, chuckles still percolating up from his massive belly and chest, watched off-handedly as Will Hawes chased after Burl Baker with the young man's hat. Then Hawes was falling and Baker had Hawes's gun in his hand.

"Jake!" Stone roared. He leaped up, swiping across the table with a huge arm. The limb caught Hunter in the chest and knocked him backward in the chair.

There was a shot, and a bullet cut a swath across the floor just behind where Hunter's chair had been. By the time the sound of the second shot had come, Stone had yanked his Colt out of the shoulder holster. His first shot and Baker's third came almost as one.

Stone felt a stinging as Baker's bullet skirted the top of his shoulder. Stone did not even flinch, but he grinned with satisfaction as the bullet ripped into Baker's midsection. He fired again, but missed, since Baker had fallen.

Hunter stumbled up, shaken—both by the blow and by the suddenness of it all. He recovered quickly as he and Stone walked to where Baker lay. Hawes had gotten up, and while he still had trouble breathing, he had managed to retrieve his pistol.

"Sorry, boss," he muttered.

"No harm done," Stone said agreeably. "Nobody could've known he'd pull such a damnfool stunt."

The three looked down at Baker.

"Want me to get the doc?" Hawes asked.

"No," Stone said harshly. "You and your brother can

haul him down to Murphy's."

"The mortuary?" Hawes questioned. "But he ain't dead yet, boss."

"Then take your time gettin' there," Stone said, unconcerned. He turned and walked away.

"I reckon," Hunter said, "that Linc don't take kindly to folks aiming to kill him—or his friends."

"Yessir," Hawes said.

Baker moaned.

"I'll tell you something else, Will," Hunter said quietly. "I saw a heap of gutshot men during the war. Ain't a one of 'em lived when they were hit like this. He's a dead man sure as you're standing here. There's nothing any doctor could do for him."

"Yessir," Hawes said quietly.

Hunter nodded back toward Stone, who saluted him with a mug of beer. Hunter headed for his house.

Chapter 29

Hunter had a beer, but sipped it slowly while chatting with Stone. It was early afternoon. After Stone had killed Baker, Hunter had gone home to tell Li-Sung what had happened with her kidnapper. They had made love again. And before Hunter went back to the saloon, he carefully cleaned the Remington and reloaded it.

It had been nearly noon then, and many of the men from the mill had stopped by for lunch, and to welcome Hunter back to town. Finally it had calmed enough so that Stone and Hunter could talk peacefully. Suddenly there was an enraged shout of "Hunter!"

Hunter turned slowly. With the light streaming through the doorway, all he could see was a silhouette. "Who are you?" Hunter asked, setting down the beer. "And what do you want?" He moved a hand down to unsnap the holster flap.

"You might remember me, Hunter," the silhouette said. "Arliss Pettibone from Carver Creek, Texas."

"Yeah, I remember you," Hunter said. He wondered why Texans—or at least this one—seemed so inordinately proud of whatever little backwater town they hailed from. And yet they never stayed in those places. "I always remember fools and pretty women. It's real obvious which one you are. What do you want with me?"

"Me and Mr. Boyd are invitin' you outside to settle our differences. Like men. Unless you're afraid." The sneer could not be seen, but it could be heard.

"Afraid of a knobhead like you?" Hunter laughed. "I'll be a dozen years dead before such a thing." His blood raced. The thought of the action—and knowing that it would finally be over—excited him.

"Then let's head outside, and kick the lid off things," Pettibone snapped.

"At your pleasure, boy," Hunter said contemptuously. He had a suspicion that Pettibone was a lot more frightened than he tried to let on. "But you can tell your master he better be out in the street where I can see him before I walk out that door."

The silhouette's head bobbed. Pettibone walked out, leaving the doors swinging.

"I'm ready, Jake," Stone said. He was cradling a shotgun.

"This one's mine to handle, Linc. Stay out of it."

"I'll do no such thing," Stone said, offended.

"You did your part this morning, when you saved my butt from Baker. I'll see to this one."

"This mornin' was just practice. Baker was just a farm boy still wet behind the ears. These boys know what they're doin'."

"Baker might've been just a farm boy, but he got you," Hunter said with a tight smile.

"What, this?" Stone said, brushing a hand across the bits of dried blood on the shirt at the top part of his left shoulder. "I've drawn more blood blowin' my nose." It was, indeed, little more than a scratch, and Stone hardly noticed it.

Hunter thought a minute. "No, you've done too much for me," he finally said. "Saving Li-Sung—and then me this morning. I reckon I ought to start holding up my end of things."

"Well, I ain't gonna just sit here and watch you get your butt shot off. I'd sooner get killed myself." He grinned. "See, if I let you get killed, Li-Sung's gonna have my hide nailed to the saloon wall."

Hunter nodded, unable to manage a grin. "All right, go on out the back way and keep me covered, just in case Boyd's thinking of bushwacking me."

Stone nodded unhappily. He liked a good fight as much as anyone, and was angry at the prospect of missing this one. He considered arguing, but decided that would only cause ill will. He could be more effective by coming up behind the outlaws and offering whatever help was called for—even if Hunter didn't know it.

Stone grunted and walked toward the rear of the saloon. Hunter headed for the door, stuffing the flap of the holster behind it so it would be out of the way. He stopped at the side of the door and peered out. Boyd and Pettibone stood in the middle of the street, guns holstered, watching the saloon door. Hunter craned his neck, but could see no one who might be a threat to him.

He shoved outside and hopped off the sidewalk. Boyd and Pettibone followed him with their eyes, and turned slowly to follow him as he moved toward the middle of the street twenty yards away from the two. It was strangely quiet in the town, with only the zing of the sawmill ringing out regularly.

Hunter waited, hands crossed, relaxed, just below the butt of the pistol. "Well?" he asked. "You boys wanted this party. I reckon you ought to be the ones to commence shooting."

Both Pettibone and Boyd yanked out their Colts and fired at the same time.

Hunter was much slower clearing leather, and he winced as two slugs hit him—one banging into the lower left side of his abdomen, the other creasing his right thigh.

As the two gunmen fired, Hunter raised the Remington quickly, but not recklessly, and aimed. He squeezed off four shots as quickly as he could, trying to aim for Boyd first and Pettibone second.

As he spun and ran to his right several feet, he thought he heard a shotgun roar twice, and that worried him. He stopped and crouched, Remington held at arm's length. Out of the cloud of powder smoke, he saw both foes down. Boyd was still, but Pettibone was still moving about, trying to sit up.

Pettibone managed to get up to his knees. Trying to focus, he sought out a target. His Colt wavered in his hand. He spotted Hunter. "You son of a bitch!" he shouted, trying to steady the revolver on Hunter.

Hunter's leg felt as if it was on fire. But it was the side that really hurt. Pain radiated in circles from the wound, and Hunter could feel blood running down into his pants. He was afraid to look at the wound. He also was determined to finish off Pettibone before the Texan got off another shot.

He raised the Remington and drew a bead. He was sweating despite the chill temperature, and it obscured his vision a little. He squeezed the trigger. He carried only five loads in the pistol, and this was his last. If he missed, he might be dead.

The ball punched a bloody hole through Pettibone's sloping forehead, just above the left eyebrow. Pettibone was snapped back, bent over with his back making a rough arch.

With the pain almost overwhelming him, Hunter limped slowly toward the two downed gunmen. Pettibone was dead now, too. His open eyes were glazed, staring at nothing. Boyd was lying on his stomach, his back ripped to shreds by a shotgun blast, maybe two. Stone's handiwork, Hunter figured. He wasn't even sure he had hit Boyd, but he no longer cared.

With his peripheral vision, Hunter saw Li-Sung racing toward him from the house. And from the other side, Stone was running—shotgun in hand—from around the corner of the saloon.

Stone got there first. He dropped the shotgun and grabbed Hunter as he began to topple. "I'm scared, Linc," Hunter whispered. "I don't want to die." He had felt that way many times, but Stone was the only one to whom he had ever voiced it.

"You ain't gonna die," Stone growled. Hunter was not really gutshot. And while he knew it must hurt like the devil, he didn't think Hunter's wound was all that bad. He held Hunter as easily as he would a baby. With Stone holding Hunter on his feet, they headed toward the doctor's.

"Li-Sung?" Hunter asked.

"I'm here, Jake," she said breathlessly, after her run. She slipped an arm around his back so that he could lean on her, too, and grinned at him. "And I'm not letting you go."

J.J. MARRIC MYSTERIES

time passes quickly . . . As *DAY* blends with *NIGHT* and *WEEK* flies into *MONTH*, Gideon must fit together the pieces of death and destruction before time runs out!

GIDEON'S DAY (2721, $3.95)
They mysterious death of a young police detective is only the beginning of a bizarre series of events which end in the fatal knifing of a seven-year-old girl. But for commander George gideon of New Scotland Yard, it is all in a day's work!

GIDEON'S MONTH (2766, $3.95)
A smudged page on his calendar, Gideon's month is blackened by brazen and bizarre offenses ranging from mischief to murder. Gideon must put a halt to the sinister events which involve the corruption of children and a homicidal housekeeper, before the city drowns in blood!

GIDEON'S NIGHT (2734, $3.50)
When an unusually virulent pair of psychopaths leaves behind a trail of pain, grief, and blood, Gideon once again is on the move. This time the terror all at once comes to a head and he must stop the deadly duel that is victimizing young women and children — in only one night!

GIDEON'S WEEK (2722, $3.95)
When battered wife Ruby Benson set up her killer husband for capture by the cops, she never considered the possibility of his escape. Now Commander George Gideon of Scotland Yard must save Ruby from the vengeance of her sadistic spouse . . . or die trying!

MYSTERIES TO KEEP YOU GUESSING
by John Dickson Carr

CASTLE SKULL   (1974, $3.50)
The hand may be quicker than the eye, but ghost stories
didn't hoodwink Henri Bencolin. A very real murderer was
afoot in Castle Skull—a murderer who must be found before he strikes again.

IT WALKS BY NIGHT   (1931, $3.50)
The police burst in and found the Duc's severed head staring at them from the center of the room. Both the doors
had been guarded, yet the murderer had gone in and out
without having been seen!

THE EIGHT OF SWORDS   (1881, $3.50)
The evidence showed that while waiting to kill Mr. Dep-
ping, the murderer had calmly eaten his victim's dinner.
But before famed crime-solver Dr. Gideon Fell could serve
up the killer to Scotland Yard, there would be another
course of murder.

THE MAN WHO COULD NOT SHUDDER (1703, $3.50)
Three guests at Martin Clarke's weekend party swore they
saw the pistol lifted from the wall, levelled, and shot. *Yet
no hand held it*. It couldn't have happened—but there was
a dead body on the floor to prove that it had.

THE PROBLEM OF THE WIRE CAGE   (1702, $3.50)
There was only one set of footsteps in the soft clay surface—and those footsteps belonged to the victim. It
seemed impossible to prove that anyone had killed Frank
Dorrance.

*Available wherever paperbacks are sold, or order direct from the
Publisher. Send cover price plus 50¢ per copy for mailing and
handling to Zebra Books, Dept. 3047, 475 Park Avenue South,
New York, N.Y. 10016. Residents of New York, New Jersey and
Pennsylvania must include sales tax. DO NOT SEND CASH.*